PERFECT TIMING

Praise for Dena Blake

Just One Moment

"One of the things I liked is that the story is set after the glorious days of falling in love, after the time when everything is exciting. It shows how sometimes, trying to make life better really makes it more complicated…It's also, and mainly, a reminder of how important communication is between partners, and that as solid as trust seems between two lovers, misunderstandings happen very easily."—*Jude in the Stars*

"Blake does angst particularly well and she's wrung every possible ounce out of this one…I found myself getting sucked right into the story—I do love a good bit of angst and enjoy the copious amounts of drama on occasion."—*C-Spot Reviews*

Friends Without Benefits

"This is the book when the Friends to Lovers trope doesn't work out. When you tell your best friend you are in love with her and she doesn't return your feelings. This book is real life and I think I loved it more for that."—*Les Rêveur*

A Country Girl's Heart

"Dena Blake just goes from strength to strength."—*Les Reveur*

Unchained Memories

"There is a lot of angst and the book covers some difficult topics but it does that well. The writing is gripping and the plot flows."—*Melina Bickard, Librarian, Waterloo Library (UK)*

"This story had me cycling between lovely romantic scenes to white-knuckle gripping, on the edge of the seat (or in my case, the bed) scenarios. This story had me rooting for a sequel and I can certainly place my stamp of approval on this novel as a must read book."—*The Lesbian Review*

"The pace and character development was perfect for such an involved story line, I couldn't help but turn each page. This book has so many wonderful plot twists that you will be in suspense with every chapter that follows."—*Les Reveur*

Where the Light Glows

"From first time author Dena Blake, *Where the Light Glows* is a sure winner."—*A Bookworm's Loft*

"[T]he vivid descriptions of the Pacific Northwest will make readers hungry for food and travel. The chemistry between Mel and Izzy is palpable."—*RT Book Reviews*

"I'm still shocked this was Dena Blake's first novel…It was fantastic…It was written extremely well and more than once I wondered if this was a true account of someone close to the author because it was really raw and realistic. It seemed to flow very naturally and I am truly surprised that this is the author's first novel as it reads like a seasoned writer."—*Les Reveur*

By the Author

Where the Light Glows

Unchained Memories

A Country Girl's Heart

Racing Hearts

Friends Without Benefits

Just One Moment

Perfect Timing

Visit us at www.boldstrokesbooks.com

PERFECT TIMING

by

Dena Blake

2020

Credits
Editor: Shelley Thrasher
Production Design: Stacia Seaman
Cover Design by Tammy Seidick

Acknowledgments

Thanks to Radclyffe, Sandy Lowe, and the rest of the Bold Strokes Books team. You let me do what I love, and I am forever thankful for that.

Shelley Thrasher, you are my grammar guru aka my editor extraordinaire. You tirelessly correct my grammar and make my words come to life in the best way possible.

My writing family, I am truly grateful for your friendship and love. The support you all provide is something of which I am still in awe.

Kate, Wes, Haley, and my family, you are my rocks. I love you so much and don't know what I would do without you.

Thanks to all you readers who have taken time out of your lives to join me in my adventures. Your notes and comments always make my days brighter.

To those who have dared to step into the unknown and start over.
There is strength in solidarity.

CHAPTER ONE

Five a.m. felt like four a.m. this morning. Maggie had been up well past midnight and hadn't slept easily once she'd actually made it into bed. Fumbling in the dark, she was surprised she could find her way around the bedroom, let alone locate her socks and shoes. After throwing on her clothes, she grabbed a travel mug of coffee and a granola bar to eat on the five-minute walk to the hospital.

The sun was just beginning to show some light when she got outside. It was going to be a glorious day—one she wouldn't get to experience, but glorious all the same. She stood just outside the main entrance staring at the massive structure in front of her. All her dreams had come true. She was a doctor. Well, technically, an intern, but still a doctor. Only a few more hurdles to jump until she was well seated in the career she'd known she'd wanted to be in since she was a child. She walked through the main entrance and breathed in the familiar antiseptic hospital scent she adored. The rush that came over her made her almost giddy. During the next few years she'd spend more time here than at her actual apartment. This would be her home.

Once she'd swiped in for the day, she went to the locker room, changed into a pair of scrubs, and put on her coat. Then she headed to the pediatrics-floor nurses' station to report for rounds. Maggie and three other interns, two guys and another girl, were assigned to a third-year resident, Phillip Baird, M.D., to manage his workload. Dr. Baird would manage four first-year interns, each of whom might carry a caseload of up to twelve patients, and two Johns Hopkins University Medical School students. He in turn would be supervised by Ben Cozzi, M.D., an attending physician, whom they would meet later in the day. Dr. Baird had two prime directives. First, he wanted to reduce the caseload of the interns. Twelve patients were far too many to handle. Half would be better. Second, he would like to expose both the interns and medical students to as many different experiences as possible as they followed him throughout his day. As expected, he was all business.

Maggie was prepared to fight for every case that came in. She was at the top of her game and wasn't about to drop in the standings. Her confidence was bolstered even further when Dr. Baird said, "Just remember. You are the ones who keep the hospital and the doctors who train you on the cutting edge of medicine, and you will remind every physician why they got into this business in the first place." Apparently, he expected to learn from them as well, and she respected him for that attitude, impressed that he'd actually told them directly. He ended his speech by saying, "Make sure you rest when you can. You are the doctors who lend energy and enthusiasm to a profession overflowing with long hours and endless paperwork. Don't ever lose sight of that fact."

Maggie first had to check in with the doctors on the night shift and receive sign-out on the patients. She hoped they'd had a decent number of admissions overnight, or she'd have to spend her first day trying to outpace the other interns.

"Okay, folks. It's been a busy night," Dr. Baird said. "Apparently a stomach bug's going around." He motioned to the stack of tablets on the counter. "So grab a tablet and start reviewing."

Ugh. This wasn't how Maggie had envisioned her first day, but at least she'd stay busy. The first patient they saw had been brought in about an hour ago and didn't seem in distress. It was Maggie's turn to do the exam and look for potential causes for the patient's symptoms, and wouldn't you know, the patient took that opportunity to spew her breakfast all over her. "Oh my God" came out of her own mouth, and she instinctively backed up, grabbed an emesis bag from the container on the wall, and held it in front of the patient. The girl heaved another time or two, but she'd already emptied most of her stomach contents onto Maggie. Not until then did the smell get to her. She had to force herself to breathe through her mouth and ignore it, or else she'd do the same thing all over the patient.

"Henderson, take the bag from Randall," Dr. Baird said to the medical student and then pointed to Maggie. "You go clean up and get back here ASAP."

Maggie rushed to the locker room, grabbed a new set of scrubs, and found her spare coat in her locker, the place that would house everything from clothes to toothpaste for the next four years. Thank God she'd brought the coat with her this morning. She quickly changed, put the dirty one in a plastic bag, and stuffed it into her locker. She'd have to take care of it later.

After catching up with the group and finishing the rest of morning rounds without further event, they ended up at Balducci's, an Italian deli in the hospital, for lunch. The distraction this morning had unsettled her, and the whole morning had been a blur.

"This is where I'll leave you for lunch. Be in the auditorium in an hour," Dr. Baird said before he went to the stand-up cooler and picked out a sandwich, an apple, and a few other items to take with him. At Balducci's you could order something from the deli or grab something from the cooler to take with you. The menu included a variety of tasty sandwiches and huge salads. This little nugget would be Maggie's savior on days when she was swamped and forgot to eat.

They all stood for a moment before they went various ways to get what they wanted to eat. After she'd picked out a chef salad and water, she went to the cashier and reached for her badge, which wasn't hanging on her collar. *Shit.* She'd left it on her other coat when she'd switched out earlier.

"Change your mind?" A voice came from behind her in line. She turned to see a woman with dark hair and vibrant blue eyes, dressed in scrubs, staring at her.

"I don't have my badge." Maggie picked up her food and started toward the cooler to put it back.

"Hang on. I'll get it," the woman said.

"Thanks, but that isn't necessary."

"I know that." She glanced at the name on Maggie's coat and grinned like she knew just how hellacious her day had been so far. "Maggie." She handed her badge to the cashier to scan. "First day?"

Maggie's cheeks warmed as she nodded. "A patient vomited on me this morning, and I had to change." *Smooth line, Maggie.*

The woman leaned in and whispered, "I was wondering what scent you're wearing. Sounds like you got the full welcome, then." The woman took her badge from the cashier. "Good luck." She winked and headed across the room and out of the eating area.

Maggie sighed as she watched her walk away. *Way to impress the first beautiful woman you meet, Randall.* She took a seat at one of the long high-top tables centering the room, soon surrounded by not only the three people she'd come in with but several others who she assumed were also interns and medical students.

She tried to read their names on their coats but didn't want to end up looking like a weirdo-stalker. So she finished chewing the forkful of lettuce in her mouth, then said, "My name's Maggie. I'm from Boston University."

The guy sitting across from her set down the first half of his twelve-inch sub sandwich and wiped his hands before he spoke. "Russell, from Stanford." He reached across the table and shook her hand.

The woman to her right did the same. "Stacy, from Baylor."

The guy on her left didn't look up, just said, "Jonathan, from Columbia."

The rest of the people at the table went in sequence announcing their names and where they were from. She'd never remember them all. They were from all over, including NYU, Duke, and Vanderbilt. Suddenly, she didn't feel so alone anymore.

After a few solid minutes of eating, Stacy, to her right, said, "Anyone living close by and need a roommate? I have limited funds and don't have a car."

"I'm in a studio but always have room in my bed." Jonathan bounced his eyebrows.

Ugh. Maggie rolled her eyes. Was this really how this discussion would go down?

NYU girl spoke up and said, "Sorry. I need my space."

Russell answered next. "I'm in a one-bedroom, but I have a couch you can use until you find a place." It seemed Russell was the sweet one of the bunch, and considering his chiseled chin and sculpted, model-like looks, that comment was unexpected, but nice. Maggie would remember that fact about him.

Stacy looked directly at Maggie, the last one to make eye contact.

The small apartment Maggie had found located at Jefferson Square at Washington Hill on Wolfe Street was only a short distance from the hospital. Far enough to get away from the hospital and close enough to get here quickly when necessary. She'd wanted a studio because she wouldn't be spending much time there, but none were available. She'd been able to find only a thousand-square-feet two-bedroom, two-bathroom, with an open kitchen and living room, plus a balcony that overlooked the pool. Not that she'd use the pool much, but it was nice to know she could sit outside or swim if she wanted. She'd specifically not wanted a two-bedroom apartment to avoid any possibility of having a roommate, but the waiting list was ridiculously long.

The rent was more than she'd wanted to spend, but the place was nice and convenient, and would do for the time being. It wasn't the smallest and was, by far, not the largest. The complex contained many nice amenities, including a parking garage, gym, and bar area with a pool table, as well as community space downstairs to study and hang out with other people if she felt the need to socialize. However, when she got home she usually wasn't up for socializing. She'd spent her first Saturday night in her apartment completely alone, binge-watching something on Netflix.

Maggie had hoped to at least get to know a few people before she opened the roommate door, but it seemed the door was being kicked open for her. At least the refrigerator would be fuller.

"Where are you living now?" she asked.

"Anywhere I can find a soft surface to crash."

"So, you've been essentially homeless since you arrived?"

"Pretty much."

"Jesus." She sighed. She couldn't turn Stacy away now. "Where's your stuff?"

"Storage locker," Stacy said between bites of her sandwich.

"I have a spare bedroom." She shoveled a bite of salad into her mouth, avoiding the huge smile breaking on Stacy's face. "We can talk about it after lunch."

She really didn't want to give everyone at the table the details about her apartment, especially not Jonathan, who seemed to be looking for a different kind of roommate. Even after knowing him a short time, she could tell he thought he was the most beautiful man in the world, and he might be to any heterosexual woman. But any woman with brains would walk away as soon as he opened his mouth.

Stacy was right behind her when she turned around after dropping her empty container in the trash. They headed down the hallway and took the stairs back up. "I'm at Jefferson Square, two blocks south. Second floor, apartment nineteen. Meet me in the locker room after shift, and we can walk over together. Then we can figure out how to get your stuff moved." That was the extent of the conversation. She wouldn't share her private life with Stacy. She wasn't up to doing that with anyone yet. Who knew if it would even work out? The only good aspect of having a roommate was that money wouldn't be so tight anymore.

"Thanks for being so awesome." Stacy giggled and clapped. She seemed to already be planning to be her bestie for life.

She nodded and pushed open the door to the floor where the auditorium was located, where Grand Rounds would be held. Thankfully, she'd paid attention at orientation and found the entrance easily. Grand Rounds was a weekly ritual where interns and residents presented medical problems and treatment of a particular patient to an audience consisting of doctors, residents, medical students, and nurses. Usually an attending physician was in charge who would quiz the audience on diagnosis and give actual results. A number of interns and residents were already seated, and the two of them took seats midway up and in the middle. Most of the seats around them remained empty, no doubt due to her ripe aroma of vomit, but soon Russell inched down the row and squeezed into a chair next to her. Another point for him.

CHAPTER TWO

Maggie flipped the deadbolt on her apartment door, immediately went to the laundry room, and held her breath as she let the soiled doctor's coat drop from the bag into the washing machine. She plucked her badge from the collar before tossing a soap pod in along with it and then shut the lid and took a breath. The coat reminded her of the subtle stench that had accompanied her on her first day. Even though she wasn't sure others noticed it, she hadn't had time to worry about it if they had, and she'd become immune to the odor quickly.

When she reached her apartment, after stripping off her clothes, she wanted to shower and crawl into bed. The dozen or so boxes staring at her from the middle of the living room made that luxury impossible. She'd made a deal with herself to unpack at least one box a night before she showered and slept. If she had to endure chaos daily at work, she needed her house in order. Now that Stacy was becoming part of her household, she needed to be even more organized. Who knew what kind of roommate Stacy would be—sloppy, clean, noisy, quiet. If first impressions were any indication, Stacy would be ideal, but she'd been wrong before, and she wasn't taking any chances with her belongings.

She dropped her bag onto the chair and headed into the bedroom. Considering how miserably her day had started, she would shower first. After her shift, she'd met Stacy briefly and given her the directions and apartment number. Thankfully, Stacy had opted to stay later and familiarize herself with her cases. Maggie knew that would put Stacy ahead of her with the attending physician, but her first day had been exhausting, and she couldn't stand the smell of puke one minute longer. She just didn't care.

As the hot water rained over her head and across her sore limbs, she warmed. It seemed like she'd spent more time on her feet today than she had in her four years of medical school. She needed a new pair of sneakers but would take care of that on her next day off, whenever that was. As she thought about her day, vivid blue eyes popped into her head—the woman who'd bought her lunch. She didn't know if she was a doctor, nurse, or someone else who worked at the hospital, but Maggie would find her and repay her somehow. She appeared sweet, snarky, and beautiful, the perfect combination. *Stop.* She shook her head and smiled. She'd didn't have room for romance in her life right now. And that was only one of the reasons she'd made it so easy for her girlfriend, Brenda, to stay behind in Boston. The others concerned the foundation on which their relationship was based, which wasn't much.

After showering, she towel-dried her hair before she pulled on a pair of sweatpants and a Boston University T-shirt and walked to the kitchen to forage for food. She'd been to the grocery store a few times in the past several weeks, so she had milk, juice, cheese, and bread. A cheese sandwich it would be for tonight's dinner.

The knock on the door wasn't loud. In fact, if she hadn't been in the kitchen, she probably wouldn't have heard it. She figured it was Stacy but looked through the peephole just to make sure. She wasn't in the mood for anyone selling anything. Even a Girl Scout *giving* away cookies would get the worst of her tonight.

"Hey," Stacy said as she bent her arm at the elbow and waved. Getting to know this one on a personal level was either going to be fun or miserable, with no in-between.

Maggie moved to the side and swept her arm in the air like she was displaying a prize. "Welcome home."

"Again, I'm so thankful for this." Stacy had already thanked her about a hundred times since she'd offered her the room at lunch.

"You can stop that now. You're in." She grinned. "You'll have to take the couch until we can get your bed and the rest of your stuff moved in." She led Stacy to the empty bedroom to the left of the living room. "This one's yours." Maggie's flanked the other side of the living room.

Stacy smiled widely. "I don't have a ton of stuff—just a bed, nightstand, and dresser. I'll search the internet tonight and find someone to move it on my next day off."

"Maybe we can tap some of the guys on our service."

"That's an idea. Russell looks pretty strong." Stacy's voice perked up as she spoke, which made Maggie wonder if Stacy was interested in him.

"Jonathan looks pretty sturdy too."

"Yeah, but he's kind of an ass. I doubt he'll help." Stacy's voice was firm.

"You already know that?" She'd been leaning that way but thought she'd give him a few days before she cemented her thoughts.

Stacy shrugged. "Just a feeling."

"Well then, Russell will be our muscle," she said, then grinned at the cheesy pun.

Stacy laughed, then sighed. "Definitely."

Now Maggie knew something was going on in Stacy's head about Russell. Only time would tell whether Stacy would get into his head as well.

After getting Stacy settled and offering what was in the kitchen to eat, Maggie took her cheese sandwich and went to her room. She wasn't up for much more interaction today. She'd just crawled into bed when her phone buzzed on the nightstand. She looked at the screen, hoping she could ignore it, but it was Brenda, and if she didn't answer, she'd just keep calling.

"Hey. I didn't expect to hear from you today." She took a bite of her sandwich and dropped it to the plate, deciding she really didn't want it after all.

"It's your first day. I wanted to see how it went," Brenda said, her voice light and cheery, a nice change from her usual pessimistic tone.

Maggie got in a few words about her day, and then, as usual, the conversation turned to Brenda's day and how shitty it was. Her eyes were closed as she half listened to Brenda ramble on about all the problems she'd encountered. It didn't sound like a terrible day to Maggie. It was a blip on the radar compared to her own, but Brenda was a glass-half-empty kind of girl. If anything positive ever happened to her, something negative always overshadowed the good. Somehow Maggie had learned to block out her negativity in the past, but tonight it irritated the fuck out of her.

When she heard the blip of another call, she immediately rolled to her side and checked out who it was. *Carrie.* Her best friend since college, who was having her own first day at Boston Children's Hospital. She immediately perked up. "Brenda. Brenda. Brenda!" Finally, Brenda stopped talking long enough to listen. "I have a call from the hospital that I need to take, so I'll have to call you back tomorrow." She was lying about both, but she didn't care. Brenda was a definite downer to cap off her day, and Carrie would change that and make her feel better about everything. Carrie and her aunt Lynn were so much alike in that way it was ridiculous, and it was one main reason they were still friends.

She switched to the FaceTime call before Brenda could protest. "Hey. I thought you'd be dead to the world by now," she said to Carrie.

"Same. The dark circles haven't totally filled in under my eyes, but they'll get there soon."

Maggie could see from the screen that Carrie was in bed too. "I don't even see them. You look great." It had been only a few weeks, but Maggie really missed their late-night talks and study sessions.

"I knew you were my best friend for a reason." Carrie tucked a pillow under her head and looked into the phone. "So, how was your first day?"

Maggie did the same with her pillow and filled her in on the puke incident. Carrie couldn't stop laughing and made a number of puns so ridiculously corny that soon they were both convulsing so hard they could hardly breathe. Talking to Carrie always reminded her to not take things so seriously. It was definitely a memorable first day, but it certainly wasn't the end of the world.

"So what about the beautiful blue-eyed brunette? Are you going to track her down, stalk her until you know everything about her?" Carrie asked, her voice rising.

"Like I have time for that."

"True. Well, maybe you'll run into her again soon." Carrie winked. "Accidentally on purpose."

"She was just being nice. Besides, she's way out of my league." She seemed to be very familiar with the hospital, so she was probably a resident. Not necessarily someone she'd tag for stress-relief sex.

"Stop that. You're at the top of your game. No woman with any sense would pass up a chance to date you. You just suck at picking the right women."

"Right. The boobs always distract me." In recent years, Maggie hadn't been good at looking past the outer shell, the aesthetics of a woman, probably because her heart wasn't up for grabs. It had been shattered before, and she refused to let that happen again. She also didn't have the time to dedicate to a *real* relationship.

Carrie let out a huge laugh. "I can't say I'm not attracted to a well-built chest myself." That was totally true. In Boston, Carrie worked out at the hospital facility frequently but mainly to meet guys involved in medicine in some way. People in that field understood the long hours, weird schedules, and crazy lifestyle that accompanied the profession. Keeping in shape was just an added perk.

"Any new prospects at the gym?"

"As a matter of fact…"

"What the hell?" She propped herself up against the headboard to stay awake. "You should've led with that. Spill, right now."

"His name's Scott. I've only talked to him a few times, but…" Carrie sighed, silent for a moment. "We just click. You know what I mean?"

"I do." And Maggie did. That feeling hadn't occurred recently, but she remember vividly what it was like.

"He's super smart and *gorgeous*."

Maggie started humming "Here Comes the Bride."

"He really is dreamy, Mags." Carrie's voice grew soft. "He may be the one."

Maggie had never heard this emotional lilt in Carrie's voice in relation to any of her boyfriends before. She seemed serious. "Wow. I was only kidding, but that's awesome. I can't wait to approve—I mean meet him," she said with a chuckle.

"I can't either. You'll have to come visit. Or maybe when we get a little further down the line, we'll come visit you. He's actually from Baltimore too."

"Definitely. If I ever get more than one day off, I'm in."

"I'm absolutely positive you'll like him."

"Okay, then I'll give him the benefit of all my doubts." If Carrie said he was the one, then most likely he was. She'd never heard those words from Carrie's lips before, and as long as he treated Carrie well, Maggie would do her best to like him even if she couldn't stand him. She hoped that wasn't the case, but that's what friendship was all about.

"I haven't told Auntie Lynn or Beth about him yet, so pinkie-swear you'll keep it to yourself if you run into either of them."

"Sure." She held up her finger and wiggled it in the air in front of the screen so Carrie could see it. Not that she had any contact with Lynn at this point anyway. "Jeez. I didn't realize how late it was. I need to sleep. Talk to you soon, okay?" She didn't want to discuss Lynn with Carrie or whether she'd been in contact with her. That would prompt a conversation she wasn't up to having tonight.

"Sounds good." Carrie ended the call.

If Carrie's romance went in the right direction and became serious, which it sounded like it might, Maggie would be pulled into situations where she'd be confronted with her own feelings soon enough. Until now, she'd blocked any thoughts of Lynn Monroe out of her mind. If she hadn't, she would've needed serious therapy or developed a monumental drinking problem.

On occasion, Carrie had volunteered information about her aunts, but Maggie hadn't asked about Lynn's life over the past few years. As it was, when she did mention Lynn and Beth, depression set in for days until she could again convince herself that leaving Baltimore for medical school in Boston was the best scenario for all of them. She couldn't have handled being on the outside of Lynn's life looking in and wanting to be fully involved in it.

Recently, Carrie had casually let the information about Lynn and Beth's divorce slip, a small bit of knowledge Carrie would never have given her willingly. Maggie's heart had pounded at the thought of a second chance, but then Carrie had apparently realized her slip of the tongue and mentioned that the divorce had happened almost three years ago. That fact had nearly killed her. All this time and Lynn hadn't made a single phone call to let her know she was free. The feelings they'd shared were definitely not one-sided. Why hadn't Lynn contacted her and told her about the divorce herself?

The next time she saw Lynn she could very well come away with her heart shattered again, but she would have to take that risk if the opportunity presented itself. It wouldn't happen today or tomorrow, but in the upcoming months, she'd make it a point to see Lynn. Otherwise Maggie would never get her out of her system. And even then, she might not succeed.

When Carrie had taken Maggie to her home in Baltimore for the first time, Maggie had been ridiculously nervous. She didn't have much family of her own—only her mother since her father had died a few years before—and from what Carrie had told her, Maggie's relationship with her mother wasn't near as close as the one Carrie had with her aunts. It had taken Maggie quite a while to even tell Carrie about what she'd dealt with since she'd lost her father. Thoughts of how welcoming Lynn had been filled her head as she closed her eyes, too sleepy to keep them open any longer.

"Hi, Aunt Lynn. I brought someone home with me this weekend." Carrie and Maggie wandered through the house.

"I'm out here in the garden," someone shouted from the backyard.

Carrie pulled the sliding screen door open and stepped outside, and Maggie followed her.

"Well, don't just stand there. Come on out and help me carry some of these tomatoes inside." Carrie's aunt glanced up, and Maggie's stomach catapulted into a full three-hundred-and-sixty-degree somersault. The woman was absolutely beautiful. "Bring your friend too. I've got enough to fill both your shirts."

Carrie pulled the bottom of her T-shirt out, making a fabric bucket for the tomatoes, and the gorgeous woman loaded them in. "You're full."

"You're next." Carrie turned and walked back to the house, while Maggie just stood and stared. Carrie's aunt had curly, dark hair pulled back and twisted up into a clip, and her vibrant green eyes twinkled in the sunlight when she looked up.

"Well, come here, honey."

Maggie moved closer and pulled her blue, cap-sleeve cotton shirt out for her to place the tomatoes in.

"You don't have to use your shirt." She handed her a few tomatoes. "But you can help me carry in the rest."

Maggie smiled but couldn't speak. She'd never been so tongue-tied.

"As you heard, my name's Lynn. What's yours?"

"Maggie," she finally choked out.

"You go to school with Carrie?"

"Yes."

"Are you from out of town?"

"No." Another one-word answer. Jesus, Maggie! Form a sentence, will you! *"I'm from Baltimore, just across town."*

"When Carrie decided to go to college at Johns Hopkins, we were thrilled she'd be able to come home when she wants to." Lynn gathered up the rest of the tomatoes and started to go inside.

"She loves coming here, and I can see why." Maggie stopped talking, and then decided she'd better finish the sentence. *"You're so...I mean, it's so beautiful here."* So beautiful.

"Well, thank you." Lynn pulled open the screen door and stepped inside. *"Carrie, you should bring Maggie home with you more often."* She put the tomatoes on the counter next to the fresh cucumbers and squash.

Maggie followed and did the same. Over the next few hours, Lynn kept the conversation going, making her feel so at ease that, when it was time, Maggie didn't want to leave. The woman seemed genuinely interested in her life. She wasn't only beautiful, but she was also warm and compassionate.

The alarm jolted Maggie out of her dream, and she bolted up in bed, trying to figure out where she was. The back of her neck heated as her anxiety kicked in full force. The dream had been so real she'd been catapulted back in time. Living in the same town as Lynn, the only woman she'd never been able to get out of her heart, was going to be difficult. Since she'd arrived, the medical career in which she'd driven herself to succeed no longer filled her dreams. A past she'd never regretted now governed them, but she was determined to keep it exactly where it had been while she was in Boston, far away from her thoughts.

CHAPTER THREE

L ynn looked around the floor and smiled. She loved being a nurse. It was now, more than anything else, her reason for living. The children she saw daily brought joy into her life, especially when they were able to go home with their parents feeling better than when they'd arrived. At one point in her life she hadn't thought she'd get this far. It had come to a complete stop when her older sister, Alice, couldn't handle the pressure of being a parent and went missing in action.

Carrie had been a regular visitor at Lynn and her wife Beth's home, frequently staying with them on weekends while Alice proceeded to live her own life. Alice was only sixteen when she'd had Carrie, which had been a life-altering event, considering she'd only just finished her sophomore year in high school. Their parents had begged her to keep the child, told her she could live with them as long as she wanted, and swore they'd help with her upbringing. But Lynn and her sister had both been born to aging parents, and raising a child had been too much for all of them.

Carrie had been ten years old when Lynn received the text from Alice, who'd dropped Carrie off for the weekend, only for good that time. Alice didn't intend to come back. Lynn had put her full-time education schedule on hold, and Carrie had become her number-one priority. Even though Beth was older and had already finished her residency, none of it had been easy. Lynn had worked part-time at a pediatrics practice, handling immunizations and well-baby visits while she finished the bulk of classes for her graduate degree by taking weekend and night classes. She'd grown close to a few of the doctors in the practice and formed several friendships during that time.

Once she'd freed herself from Beth, her life had taken on new meaning. Beth had been so preoccupied with her career of becoming a surgeon and Lynn had devoted so much of hers to raising Carrie, they hadn't taken time to nourish their relationship. Soon after Carrie left for medical school, Lynn realized she and Beth had nothing in common any longer. Since the divorce, she'd been able to explore what she really wanted in life. She'd finally reached a place in her life where she could do exactly that—experience new things and see new places without any strings attached.

It was about seven o'clock in the evening, and Lynn was just about to take her dinner break from her shift at Johns Hopkins Hospital when she remembered this was Carrie's first actual day as an intern at Boston Children's Hospital. Lynn usually worked the day shift on the pediatrics floor but had volunteered to trade with a coworker who had family in town this week. Knowing that the new interns would be starting this week, she'd actually jumped at the opportunity to avoid them as much as possible. She found an empty exam room, took her phone from her pocket, and hit Carrie's number in her favorites.

Carrie answered after the second ring. "Hey, Auntie. What's up?"

"What do you mean, what's up? How was your first day?"

"Exhausting." Carrie blew a sigh into the phone. "I thought med school was hard, but this is so much worse."

"I warned you. From what Pam told me, you're going to still get some of the scut work until you earn your place. She actually had to buy some poor intern's lunch today because someone threw up on her and she forgot to grab her badge from her coat when she changed."

"Oh my God. I've already heard this story."

"What? Did that happen there too?"

Carrie chuckled. "No. The intern was Maggie."

A rush of heat ripped through Lynn. "Maggie's here? In Baltimore?" Lynn hadn't seen her since Maggie left for Boston.

"Yeah. I just got off the phone with her. Haven't you seen her yet?"

"No. Why didn't you tell me?" If she'd known, she would've been on alert, and her stress level would already be topping out.

"I've been so busy I forgot. I thought for sure she would've contacted you by now, but she's probably been busier than me. I mean, with moving and all."

"Probably so." Lynn was silent. She knew why Maggie hadn't

contacted her and was torn between being relieved and sad about the whole situation. Admittedly, Lynn still had feelings for Maggie. She didn't know if their lack of contact meant Maggie still had feelings as well, or if she'd gotten over hers and just didn't care anymore. That would be clear soon enough. It was only a matter of time before they crossed paths at the hospital, and she had no way to prepare herself for that. Or did she? "She may have tried to contact me." Lynn tried to cover. "I've been pretty busy lately. When did she get here?"

"A couple of weeks ago."

"Do you know where she's staying?"

"I think she got a one-bedroom pretty close to the hospital. I forgot to ask the name of the place. I figured you'd get all the details when you see her."

That could be anywhere. A half dozen or more apartment complexes were located close to the hospital that housed many of the staff members.

"Hang on," Carrie said, and after a short minute, Lynn's phone buzzed in her hand. "I sent you her cell number, but considering how shitty her first day went, she's probably already asleep by now."

"Thanks. I'll get in touch with her," Lynn said as she contemplated what *getting in touch* would mean.

"I'm sure she'll be happy to hear from you." Carrie blew out a breath. "Well, I'm beat, Auntie, and am going to hit the sack."

"Okay. Get some rest, and I'll talk to you tomorrow. I love you, honey."

"I love you too," Carrie said, and the phone went silent.

Lynn let the phone slide from her ear and saw the text Carrie had sent. As she let her finger glide over Maggie's name, just the sight of it brought all sorts of conflicted emotions back to life. Those feelings should have been dead long ago. What was she going to do about this? She sighed. *Absolutely nothing right now, at least until I find a way to straighten myself out.* She slid her phone into her pocket, went to the nurses' station computer, and started scrolling through patient cases.

❖

By the time Lynn got home, she'd been on her feet for hours. She liked working second shift sometimes because it seemed to be the busiest. More work kept her mind off life, love, and the lack of sex she was having, among other things. Not tonight, though. Since she'd talked to Carrie, thoughts of Maggie had filled her every spare moment, which wasn't many, but enough to distract her. She crawled into bed and closed her eyes, her stomach clenching as she thought about her last encounter with Maggie.

It had been almost a week since Lynn had seen Maggie, and she lay in bed alone, wide-awake, wondering if she'd made the right decision. She and Beth had discussed their next steps. She'd thought divorce was inevitable, but, somehow, they'd both agreed to try again and to work harder on their marriage. Beth had gone with Carrie for another girls' weekend in Boston, but she'd planned to move back into the house when they got home. Lynn welcomed the time alone to begin focusing on working things out with Beth, but all she could think about was Maggie. She could still see the hurt look on Maggie's face clearly and knew exactly why she hadn't heard from her all week long. She couldn't say she wasn't relieved. The kiss they'd shared had been a mistake, a wonderful mistake, but a mistake just the same. Even though nothing else happened that night, letting her stay after the kiss had turned her feelings into a huge pile of regret.

The silence in the house was broken as a soft knock on the front door broke through her thoughts. It was so subtle that if the TV or any other device had been running, she wouldn't have even heard it. She threw back the covers and slid out of bed. After pulling her sweatpants on, she hurried down the hallway and peeked through the peephole in the door—no one there. She turned to go into the kitchen to get a glass of water and jumped when she heard a thud on the door.

"What the hell?" She unlocked the door and pulled it open.

Maggie was sitting on the porch, propped up against the wall. She looked up and said, "Hey."

"Hey," Lynn said, stepping outside. She could see by the glassy look in Maggie's eyes, she was drunk. "You want to come in?"

"You know I want to." Maggie's words slurred slightly as she tried to get up but ended up sliding back down against the wall. "It was perfect." She looked up into Lynn's eyes. "Wasn't it?"

"Yes, it was." Lynn sat down beside her and wrapped her arm around Maggie's shoulder. "But the situation hasn't changed."

"*I know. I shouldn't have come.*" Maggie rested her head on Lynn's chest. "*But I can't stop thinking about you.*"

"*Nor I, you.*"

Maggie lifted her head and stared into Lynn's eyes. The incredible look of need within them was suddenly laced with confusion. "*I should go.*" She pulled out of her arms and stumbled to her feet.

"*You're absolutely not driving tonight.*" Lynn stood up, steadied her, and looked for her car. "*How did you get here?*"

"*Uber. I think I'm gonna—*" She ran to the grass, dropped to her knees, and threw up.

Lynn followed her, taking Maggie's long blond hair in her hand behind her head as she heaved again. Her gut twisted knowing that Maggie was in this shape because of her. When it looked like she was finished, Lynn helped her to her feet and led her inside.

"*I'm sorry. I shouldn't have come here like this.*" She grabbed hold of the doorway as she weaved through it.

"*Let's get you cleaned up.*" Lynn led her through the bedroom into the master bath and flipped on the shower.

Before settling her into the vanity chair, Lynn undid Maggie's jeans and pulled them to the floor. She took the flip-flops and jeans from around her feet, then pulled the shirt over her head.

"*What on earth did you drink?*"

"*Jack Daniel's—shots—lots of them.*"

Lynn maneuvered her into the shower. Maggie let the water run across her face and then slid down the wall in the corner. She swiped the water from her face and looked up at Lynn. "*Make love to me.*"

"*Absolutely not.*" She shook her head. Mixed feelings swirled through her mind, and she shook them from her thoughts.

"*You hate me, Carrie hates me. I don't want to feel like this anymore.*" Still glassy-eyed, she stared up at Lynn. "*I love you.*"

"*I know.*" She turned the water off. "*Come on. Let's get you dried off and into bed.*"

She slipped one of her T-shirts over her head. With one hand she yanked the covers back and dropped Maggie onto the mattress, letting her head flop back onto the pillow.

"*You're putting me in bed with you?*"

"*I need to keep an eye on you. It's not like you're in any shape to do anything.*"

"But it would be nice, wouldn't it?"

"Do you know how long it takes a woman to come when she's drunk?"

Maggie smiled mischievously. "A long fucking time."

Lynn slid in on the other side of the bed, and Maggie rolled onto her side to face her. Lynn let out a heavy breath. "I should've turned and run the first time I saw you."

Maggie reached over and brushed her thumb across Lynn's lips. "Why does this have to be so complicated? Why did I have to fall in love with you?"

Love? Did Maggie really think she was in love? Lynn had known for quite some time now that she was attracted to Maggie and wished each and every night that she was free to take everything this woman was offering. But those damn vows kept creeping into her thoughts, and she knew she couldn't.

"Go to sleep." Lynn pressed her lips to Maggie's forehead. "We'll talk in the morning."

She was gone in the morning, and Lynn had never expected to see her again, maybe once or twice in her lifetime at most, but even then Carrie was supposed to be there when that happened. Working in the same hospital was a million-to-one shot, and it had happened. What did that mean? Was the universe telling her something? The whole thing was too much for her to fathom at the moment.

CHAPTER FOUR

As Maggie got out of her car and walked to the ball field, she wiped the moisture from the back of her neck. How had she gotten pulled into this? It had to be ninety-five degrees already, and the mug factor was growing thicker by the minute. She'd planned to sleep in this morning, since it was her first full day with nothing to do, but she didn't want to start off on the wrong foot with her colleagues. Yesterday, she'd overheard some of the nurses talking about the recreation softball league they participated in and had made the mistake of mentioning that she'd played competitive softball in college. Everything had spiraled from there. Soon she was handed a schedule and told where to be this afternoon. She'd also been told to keep it to herself, so no one else would try to recruit her.

She had no idea how this softball game would pan out. She hadn't played in years. The women on the field, all dressed in cleats, baseball pants, and jerseys with their team logos, seemed pretty competitive. All she could find to wear on such short notice were her black yoga pants, which weren't ideal, but they covered her legs in case she had to slide. She'd tossed her softball pants out long ago, but she did still have her cleats. They felt a little odd on her feet after all this while, but they'd do the trick until she had time to buy a new pair.

A couple of girls from the team were playing catch outside the fence before the softball game, and as Maggie started to walk behind them, the ball totally overshot one of them. Maggie caught it barehanded, then shook her hand, trying to relieve the sting. Thankfully, she'd been watching, or it would've hit her square in the head. Besides knocking her out, that might have put her on leave for a few days until the risk of possible concussion passed.

The girl who'd missed the catch spun around and ran to her. "Oh my God. I'm so sorry. Are you okay?"

"Yep. Just a little tingle in my fingers."

The girl who'd thrown the fireball came running over, dropped her glove, and took her hand, examining it. "Nothing broken," she said, holding it a little longer than Maggie expected. "I'm Andi, by the way," she said, not losing eye contact.

She continued to stare with her large, round, emerald-green eyes, and Maggie realized that was her cue to introduce herself. "I'm Maggie," she said, slipping her hand away.

"I haven't seen you out here before. Are you playing today?" Andi's dark ponytail swung as she looked at the field and then back at Maggie.

"Yep. My first game."

Andi's eyes grew brighter. "Oh yeah? Which team?"

"The Heavy Hitters."

Andi's smile lessened. "Not my side. I'm part of the competition."

"Which team?"

"Bat Intentions," Andi said and gave her a wink.

"What position do you play?"

Andi pointed to the infield. "Second base."

That wasn't a surprise. The woman had a rocket of an arm and dressed like she took her game very seriously in black Mizuno cleats, belted pants that she'd scrunched up just below the knee, and a jersey that fit just loose enough to give her good movement. Maggie was sure the body underneath was all muscle.

"Cool. I'll try to keep the ball away from you."

"Maybe I can buy you a beer after?" Andi asked.

Maggie hesitated, the quick move catching her a little off guard. Apparently, she'd been out of the dating game way too long.

"To make up for crushing your hand." Andi's cheeks reddened. "We all usually go out for pizza after the game."

"Yeah, sure." She shrugged. "Why not?" She really didn't have any interest in seeing anyone right now, but Andi seemed nice enough, and she didn't want to hurt her feelings. Andi's interest was actually kind of flattering.

Andi's smile grew even bigger. "Okay. Then I'll see you after the game." She grabbed her glove from the ground and ran across the field.

Somehow Maggie found herself as number one in the lineup. It was either a test or the team captain had read way too much into her college softball experience. Her heart hammered as the first pitch flew by. She always forced herself to let the first one go.

The umpire raised his fist and shouted, "Strike one."

The team chattered in the dugout as she prepared for the next pitch. She'd take it whether it was good or not. There it came, right across the middle of the plate, and she swung hard. As soon as she heard the ball hit the bat she dropped it and rushed to first base. Glancing toward the field as she ran, she saw the ball sail into left field just shy of the fielder. She rounded first and headed to second, making it without having to slide. The left fielder threw the ball infield to Andi.

Andi swiped Maggie lightly on the thigh with her glove. "Nice one."

"Thanks," Maggie said as she adjusted her sleeves on her shoulders. "I'm a little out of practice, but that was a perfect pitch."

"Yeah, well, she's the relief pitcher. You might not have gotten a hit off The Heater."

She glanced over to see a new catcher moving behind the plate. "What's that about?"

"Shift probably ended late. We kind of have set positions." Andi scrunched her face.

She watched as the new catcher stretched one leg and then the other. "Sounds like you take this game pretty seriously."

"Me, not so much. Others on the team do." Andi tipped her head to the catcher.

Maggie wondered how seriously as she watched her catch a few warm-up pitches and fire the ball back to the pitcher.

The next batter came to the plate, and Maggie took a small lead off the base. The batter hit the first pitch, and the ball sailed into the hole between center and right field. On her way to home plate, Maggie rounded third base and increased her speed down the baseline. But she hadn't expected the brick wall the catcher put up when she tried to cross the plate. Her chest stung as she hit, and she found herself propelled backward through the air. Pain shot through her leg as her ass hit the dirt, and she wasn't sure she could stand, but she had to

. The impact had landed the catcher on her ass as well, ːrambled to her feet and rushed to the plate. Jesus, Andi wasn't kidding about her team.

She spun around to the catcher. "What the hell are you doing? No one blocks a runner in rec ball." She immediately froze when the catcher pulled off her mask. She'd know that face anywhere. She should've recognized her ass. Maggie had spent the better part of her senior year in college memorizing them both. Sometimes she seemed like such a dude, letting her hormones control her, but much more than hormones were involved when it came to Lynn. The woman had found a place in her heart and never completely left.

Lynn didn't speak, just stared like she'd seen a ghost, which was entirely accurate. Once Maggie had left Baltimore for medical school in Boston, all communication between them had stopped.

Everything blurred as bodies separated them with hands reaching for high fives as they pulled her into the dugout. She'd only glimpsed Lynn staring before her new teammates hauled her off the field, but her confusion was clear.

❖

After the game, Maggie heard Lynn before she saw her. She would never forget the sound of her voice. Even when she was politely rejecting her, the low, sweet melody was the most incredibly sexy sound she'd ever heard. She couldn't help the smile that spread across her face when Lynn came into view. With her cheeks flushed from the game and her hair flying in the wind, she was more gorgeous now than she'd been four years ago.

Maggie's legs turned to jelly when their eyes met and Lynn tilted her head, smiled, and made a beeline for her. By the time Lynn reached her, Maggie was struggling to hold herself steady. She'd convinced herself that what she'd felt for Lynn had faded. After all, she'd seen other women, had great sex, lived her life as though she had no ghosts in her past. Yet it was perfectly clear now that her heart was still holding out for Lynn after all these years.

Lynn hauled her into her arms. "I thought that was you."

Maggie closed her eyes and enjoyed the sensations circling through her. "I'm sorry about knocking you down, but—"

"I shouldn't have been blocking the plate." Lynn reached for Maggie's shoulder and squeezed it. "A game-saving double. That's awesome."

"I guess it was my day," she said with a soft smile. "I had no idea you were playing softball again."

"It's new. I started a few weeks ago. This is actually my first season."

"Your team seems pretty competitive." She looked over at the dugout, where the rest of the team was gathering their belongings.

"They are, me included. It's a problem, I know. The best part is they *want* me to play." Lynn clenched her hands together in front of her chest and giggled.

Maggie smiled broadly. *No. Seeing you right here in front of me is the best part.* "What are you doing now?" She looked down at her hands. "I mean, do you have time for a drink or maybe a cup of coffee?"

"Well, I..." Lynn said, and then her attention focused over Maggie's shoulder. When Maggie turned she saw a woman hurrying toward Lynn. The same woman who'd paid for Maggie's lunch her first day.

"Awesome game!" She picked Lynn up and twirled her around.

"And I'm still in one piece." Lynn smiled widely at the woman, and Maggie suddenly felt like an intruder. When Lynn looked back to her, something was in her eyes, apprehension maybe, but it quickly vanished when she reached over and put her hand on Maggie's shoulder. "This is Maggie, a good friend of Carrie. She spent almost every waking moment at our house when they were in college."

"I think we've met." The woman offered her hand. "Hi. I'm Pam. It's nice to meet you, Maggie."

Maggie shook her hand as she tried to disperse the swirl of thoughts in her head. *Who is this woman, and how is she connected to Lynn?* "It's nice to meet you as well."

"Having better days at work than your first one, I hope."

Lynn's brows came together. "What happened your first day?"

Maggie chuckled and rolled her eyes. "What didn't happen would be a shorter list."

"I think she started in the middle of the stomach-bug week," Pam said.

"Oh, right. That was you. Carrie told me about that." Lynn said with a chuckle. "Well, at least you're getting seasoned."

"Are you ready to go? I bet you're hungry," Pam asked.

"That's what we were just discussing." Lynn looked over at Maggie. "The teams usually go for pizza at the place down the street after the game. Want to go with us?"

"Sure." Before she knew it, the words were out of her mouth. She wasn't hungry and definitely didn't want to have pizza with the two of them, plus she'd already committed to Andi. She would have to ask Andi for a rain check because she needed to know who this woman was to Lynn.

Lynn's heart had thundered when the flash of blond hair rounded third base. As she stood in front of the plate frozen, she'd barely glimpsed Maggie's face. It was only Lynn's third game in the recreational hospital softball league, and she never in a million years had expected to see Maggie on the opposing team. Maggie hadn't seen her behind the catcher's mask, and Lynn had almost taken her out when she tried to cross home plate. How Maggie could still have such an impact on her mystified Lynn. It had been years since she'd seen her.

She remembered how it had started all too well. The first time she felt their connection was during a purely innocent hug. Carrie had brought Maggie home for dinner again. She'd been doing that a lot lately, and sometimes Maggie even showed up alone. At that point, Lynn had no idea whether Carrie was interested in boys or girls and thought she and Maggie might have actually had a thing going, until that one afternoon when Maggie let Lynn know exactly how she felt about her and everything changed between them.

At that time, she'd chosen to make her marriage with Beth work, probably the biggest mistake of her life, and when Maggie had left for Boston she'd thought the only other person in the world she'd ever loved was long gone. Now Maggie had been dropped right back into her life again.

Reconciling with Beth had been the right decision at the time.

She'd still loved her wife back then, and she also had Carrie to consider, but something always seemed to be missing in her life. Many days she regretted pushing Maggie away, but she couldn't carry on two relationships and not feel guilty. Just the sight of Maggie made it clear that what was missing in her life had just come back.

CHAPTER FIVE

Maggie sat in her car for a few minutes, trying to get up her nerve to go inside. Seeing Lynn again was going to be more difficult than she thought, especially if she was involved with someone else. Someone like Pam, who was smart, beautiful, and seemingly the nicest person on the planet. She was well into a ridiculous panic attack when she heard a tap on the window and looked up to see Andi, staring down at her. She motioned for her to roll down the window.

She hit the button and the window whirred into the door. "Hi."

"You coming in?" Andi asked.

"Yep. Just cooling down a little." She hit the button to roll up the window, then killed the engine, and before she could open the door, Andi had pulled it open for her.

"That's what the beer's for," Andi said as she waited for her to get out of the car and then closed the door. "Looks like you know Lynn and Pam, huh?"

"I've known Lynn for a long time."

"Well, I wish we'd gotten hold of you first. That was a helluva hit." Andi grinned. "You've played softball before."

"Yeah, but I'm a little rusty."

Andi opened the restaurant door for her. "Not from what I saw."

The delicious aroma of pizza immediately hit her, and her stomach growled. Someone at the end of the table threw up a hand and waved. It looked like one of the other girls on Andi's team.

The door closed behind them, and Andi stopped before continuing to the far end of the long table filled with players. "We're down there."

She seemed to notice Maggie's hesitance. "I understand if you want a rain check."

She scrunched her nose. "Are you okay with that?" She glanced at the other end of the table and caught a glimpse of Lynn seated next to Pam. "It's kind of complicated, and we need to catch up."

Andi tilted her head as though waiting for more information and then, after a minute, said, "Next time, then." Andi smiled widely.

"Count on it." She glanced at the rest of the team, who were now watching them intently. Her palms were already sweaty, and the back of her neck began to tingle. At this point, she didn't know which end of the table was more terrifying.

Maggie found a spot across from where Lynn and Pam were sitting, and Pam popped up from her chair. "I'm going to get a pitcher and order the pizza—pepperoni and black olives okay?" She glanced from Lynn to Maggie.

"That's good with me," she said, reaching for the twenty she'd stashed in her pocket and holding it out to Pam.

Pam waved her off. "I got it." She didn't look back as she headed to the bar.

"So you're a doctor now." Lynn kept eye contact. "At Johns Hopkins, no less."

"Yep. I thought for sure I'd stay in Boston, but it just wasn't in the cards."

Lynn reached across the table and touched her hand. "It's so good to see you."

Her cheeks warmed. She hadn't expected those words or the way her body was responding to them.

They sat in silence for a minute just staring into each other's eyes, until Pam came back with a pitcher of beer and three icy mugs.

"Twenty minutes," Pam said as she filled each one. "How's your first week been?"

"Extremely busy."

Pam chuckled. "It'll be better after you get used to the hospital."

"I sure hope so. It's hard to believe that, after twelve years of school, four years of college, and four years of medical school, I still have *so much* to learn."

"That never changes for any of us." Pam sipped her beer. "Especially in trauma."

"Pam is chief of trauma," Lynn said, and Maggie couldn't help but notice her reach over and clasp her hand. A clear sign they were involved. She took in a deep breath and tried to calm her stomach.

"So, another doctor for you, huh?"

"I guess it's in my blood."

Pam tilted her head and looked at Lynn before she smiled. "Lynn takes good care of me."

"I'm sure she does." She tipped her lips up slightly but couldn't suppress the sadness in her voice. It wasn't like she had time for a relationship, but the hope always lingered. Now that was gone too.

"How about you, Maggie? Do you have anyone special in your life?" Pam asked.

"No. Not right now. Life's a little too hectic." She didn't want to mention Brenda because that would only prompt more questions she wasn't ready to answer in front of Lynn. But then again, maybe she should. Lynn certainly didn't have a problem flaunting her romance.

The pizza arrived just in time. Maggie choked down as much as her stomach would handle right now and said she needed to get home to research a case. A total lie, but she couldn't sit there with Lynn and her new love just acting like everything was all peachy, when it totally wasn't. She gave Lynn her number and left it at that. She probably wouldn't call, which was fine with Maggie.

Pam parked the car, popped the trunk, and got out. She handed Lynn her softball bag and waited as she slung it over her shoulder. She'd thought she might get away without having to explain, but no such luck. "Are you going to tell me what that was about?" Pam asked as she followed Lynn into the apartment building.

"You want to come up for a minute?" Several people were sitting in the common area, and voices echoed throughout it like an underground cave. Lynn didn't want to broadcast the personal details of her life.

"Sure," Pam said as they stepped into the elevator. "Not that I mind people thinking I'm your girlfriend, but Heather might have an issue with it."

"I know. I'm sorry. Maggie and I have history I'm not sure I want to revisit." Lynn sighed and fell back against the elevator wall as they rode to the third floor. Most days, Lynn took the stairs, but it had been a long day, and running into Maggie at the game had zapped what little energy she had left.

After they entered Lynn's apartment, she tugged open the refrigerator, took out two bottles of water, and handed one to Pam.

"And you're not ready to share it yet?" Pam pulled out a chair and sat at the kitchen table, then raised her eyebrows as she took a swig of water. Lynn accepted Pam's familiar gesture as a nudge for her to continue.

For reasons unknown to Lynn, the words just weren't flowing. Even though she'd thought she was prepared to see Maggie again, she clearly wasn't. She'd thought Maggie was buried deep in her past, but that didn't seem to be the case. She took a deep breath, trying to still the emotions swirling inside her. "Something happened long ago." It seemed like another lifetime.

"Did she have anything to do with your divorce?" Pam's voice was soft and without judgment. They'd been friends since Lynn started at the hospital, and Pam had always been good to her.

"Not directly, but she was the catalyst that made me reassess my happiness in life."

"Okay, then. I like her."

"She's so young, Pam. She has her whole life ahead of her, and I'm not part of that."

"Young, but mature. From what I saw tonight, she seems very interested in revisiting whatever happened, or didn't happen, between you two in your past." Pam chugged down the rest of her water.

The details were messier than Lynn wanted to explain right now, so she didn't give Pam all of them. She told her only about the connection she and Maggie had felt when she'd spent time with them during college and how she'd chosen to give her marriage another chance.

Pam's expression was unreadable. Pam had advised her many times before at work, but they didn't touch on her love life often.

Pam bit her bottom lip and then blew out a breath. "You should use that number she gave you." With that, Pam got up, tossed her empty bottle into the trash, and strode to the door. "Second chances don't happen often, and when they do, it's for a reason," she said as she opened the door and stepped out into the hallway. Lynn followed her out and watched her walk to the elevator and wait for the doors to open. Pam glanced back and gave her a thumbs-up as she stepped into it.

After she showered and changed her clothes, Lynn flopped onto her bed. She couldn't get Maggie's sparkling blue eyes out of her head. Whether it was today or years ago, they'd never left her thoughts for long. Lynn felt guilty for letting Maggie believe she was involved with Pam, but she honestly didn't know how to handle Maggie's reappearance in her life. She hadn't admitted it for a long time after the divorce, but Maggie *had* been the catalyst for the split with Beth. The memory of the first time Lynn felt the attraction came in strong, like it had just happened yesterday.

Lynn stood at the window watching her niece, Carrie, scramble for the ball as her best friend, Maggie, fired pitches at her. They'd been at it for over an hour, and Maggie was nowhere close to finding the sweet spot. Something was interrupting Maggie's concentration—school, her mother, or possibly the heat. It had been unbearably hot this summer and didn't seem to be getting any cooler. Lynn didn't know what was bothering Maggie, but she'd seen her pitch hundreds of times, and Maggie wasn't usually this inconsistent.

She'd been so glad when Carrie had finally brought a friend home with her during her freshman year of college. It was hard to believe she was twenty-two already and graduating from college in the spring. Then they'd both be off to medical school in Boston. That would leave her alone with Beth, and her life would be empty. She'd have to go back to work full-time to remedy that situation.

"Hey, Lynn. Can I help with anything?" Maggie asked, following Carrie in from the backyard.

"Looks like someone's got a little control problem out there."

"I was just trying to help her with her fast pitch." Carrie slapped the softball into the glove and tossed it onto the counter. "But someone doesn't take advice very well."

"You're not releasing soon enough."

Maggie's brows pulled together.

"I was watching from the window." She stood behind Maggie, took her hand, and held it up in front of her waist. "This is where you're releasing." She let go of her hand and patted Maggie's thigh. "As soon as the inside of your forearm brushes your thigh, you should let go."

Maggie looked at Lynn's hand, which she'd moved to her hip.

Lynn backed up and cleared her throat. "If you release too soon the pitch goes low. Release too late and the ball goes high."

"I don't have enough speed."

"Then you're not getting enough momentum on the downswing." Lynn stood back and rotated her arm. "You have to snap it down quickly and then release."

"I told her you could show her."

Lynn picked up the catcher's glove from the counter. "Come on. I'll give you a few pointers. Then I have to finish up dinner. Beth will be here soon."

Within fifteen minutes, Lynn had Maggie shooting her pitches exactly where she wanted them to go, and they were back in the kitchen.

"Wow, thanks, Lynn. That really helped a lot," Maggie said as she slid onto a barstool.

"Good. Now you can help me with dinner." She grinned. "You'll find some cucumbers in the fridge that need to be peeled and sliced."

Maggie opened the refrigerator and rummaged through the drawer until she found them. After dropping them onto the counter next to the sink, she pulled open a few other drawers, looking for the peeler.

"It should be in the last one on the left," she said.

Maggie pulled it open. "Got it." She peeled all four cucumbers, cut them up, and put them in a bowl, and then, with Lynn's direction, she added a mixture of vinegar, water, and salt.

"Now what?"

"Honey, you really don't have to do any of this." She turned to Maggie and smiled. "You should just go on in there with Carrie."

"You think I come over here to hang out with her?"

She smiled softly, wondering what was coming next. She had an idea but didn't want to encourage Maggie. "That would be the natural assumption."

"Hell, no. I see enough of her at school. I come here to see you," Maggie said as she popped a slice of cucumber into her mouth. "And for your softball coaching. Your cooking isn't bad either."

She was taken by Maggie's beautiful smile as Maggie held eye contact for a moment. Lynn didn't want or need this development in her life right now. Especially with all the issues she'd been having with Beth. "How's your mom doing?" Maggie's mom was doing better, but she'd had a complete breakdown after Maggie's dad died. From what Carrie had told Lynn, Maggie had spent her senior year of high school caring for her.

"She's good. She's having dinner with her church group tonight."

"I'm glad to hear she's made some friends." And taken the burden off Maggie. "Now, I know I'm a lot of fun." She chuckled and turned back to the stove. "But wouldn't you rather be hanging out with Carrie?" She tried to steer Maggie back to where she belonged.

"What, and play PS2 all night?" She blew out a short breath. "No, thanks."

"Is that all Carrie does?"

"That's pretty much it, outside of softball and school."

"Well, then I need to have a talk with that girl. Pretty girls like you should be out having fun." She cringed. She should have kept that observation to herself.

"You think I'm pretty?"

Just how was she going to get out of this one? She took in a deep breath. "Of course I do. You're both beautiful girls." She dropped the pasta into the water. "Carrie just hasn't moved out of that tomboy stage. When this finishes cooking, I'm going to tell her to stop playing that game." She didn't dare turn around.

"No, don't." Lynn startled when she felt Maggie's hands on her sides creeping down to her hips. "This is right where I want to be."

She could feel Maggie's breath against her neck, and heat shot through her as she reacted in ways she shouldn't. Alarm bells went off in her head. She hadn't seen this coming. Well, maybe she had, but she hadn't encouraged Maggie, had she? She spun around and they stood face-to-face, staring into each other's eyes. Lynn was frozen, unable to look away. Maggie moved closer. She was going to kiss her.

She immediately put a hand on Maggie's chest and said, "Absolutely not."

The hurt in her eyes was clear.

"Is dinner ready yet?" Carrie's voice vibrated from the living room.

"Almost," Lynn said, panic coursing through her as she whipped back around to the stove. "You should—"

"I know. I'll go." Maggie's voice deflated as she walked into the living room. Lynn heard her tell Carrie she had to go home to check on

her mother and couldn't stay for dinner, and then the door opened and shut as she left.

Not that they'd ever done anything wrong, but she'd wanted to, and the unexpected sizzle she'd felt for Maggie had made Lynn realize she wanted more from life than being Beth's housekeeper. She wanted to be happy, which she wasn't then, but she was happy now, at least that's what she thought. She hadn't questioned her state of being until today. Seeing Maggie again made her painfully aware of the difference between being content and being genuinely happy with your life and who you allowed into it.

CHAPTER SIX

"I'm so glad you decided to come out tonight," Stacy said. "I thought you might bail on me again."

Maggie laughed. "Are you trying to say I'm not fun?"

"No. That's not what I meant at all." Stacy looked totally embarrassed as she vaulted off the bar stool. "You're a blast at work, but you never let loose."

She swayed slightly, so Maggie put her hand on Stacy's shoulder and settled her onto the barstool as she slipped into the space beside her. "Settle down, Stacy. I'm only kidding." She glanced around the bar. "How long have you been here?"

"About an hour. I came over right after my shift."

"Alone?" It seemed Stacy liked to party. She'd asked her to go out multiple times during the less than two weeks she'd known her.

"Nah. Russell's here. He's in the bathroom."

"So, you and Russell, huh?"

"He's gorgeous, right?"

They both spotted him coming across the bar.

"You could do worse."

Stacy hesitated, and her face went blank for a moment before she clutched Maggie's arm. "You're not into him, are you?"

"No. I'm not into that muscled, masculine type at all." She hadn't known Stacy all that long and wondered if she should keep her preference to herself. But if they were going to be friends, which it seemed they were, she needed to clue her in. "I'm more into the feminine, curvy type."

"Oh, thank God. Competing with you would be hell."

"Hey, Mags," Russell said as he took the stool on the other side of Stacy. "You want a drink?"

"Just a beer, thanks." She had a shift in the morning, but one beer wouldn't hurt.

He waved the bartender down and ordered drinks for the three of them before he focused on Stacy. It was clear Russell only had eyes for her, and Maggie suddenly felt like a third wheel. She twisted around to peruse the crowd, her stomach jumping when she noticed Lynn and Pam huddled together at a table in the corner. *Of course she's involved with the beautiful blonde with the dazzling blue eyes.* Maggie shouldn't have expected anything else. Lynn was gorgeous and wouldn't stay single for long. If only she'd been single four years ago when Maggie had graduated from college in Baltimore. She remembered the day vividly.

She glanced at Lynn as she drove, looking completely gorgeous in a flower-patterned dress that accentuated every curve. Eyes straight on the road, Lynn weaved through traffic heading back home. Somehow, Lynn and Maggie had been left to ride to the house together. Maggie had only one other thing to worry about today: how was she going to get this wonderful woman out of her system? Lynn's generosity and good nature had pierced her heart, and the more time she spent with .*her, the more Maggie wanted to be with her.*

Lynn pulled into the driveway, killed the engine, got out of the car, and then waited for her at the walkway while she retrieved her graduation gown from the back seat of the car. "I'm so proud of you. You've overcome a mountain of obstacles to get this far," she said, pulling her into a hug.

"Thank you." Tears welled in her eyes. "I wouldn't have been able to do it without you." The only good thing about life after graduation was knowing that Lynn was proud of her.

Lynn sighed. "I was hoping your mom would show up," she said, putting the key in the lock and opening the front door, letting Maggie enter before her.

"Guess your call didn't help." She pulled her lips into a sad smile. "Thanks for trying." She draped her black gown, yellow hood, and honors regalia over the couch and then followed Lynn into the kitchen.

Lynn dropped her purse into one of the maple chairs surrounding the table. "Sure. I don't know if she'll come around or not, but I'm here whenever you need me."

The glimmer in Lynn's eye was different today, sensual somehow, as they stood only a few inches apart in the kitchen. A bolt of electricity shot through her, and she moved closer. "Lynn, I need to tell you—"

"You girls ready to go?" Beth's voice echoed from the living room, and Lynn immediately backed up before Beth stepped into the kitchen. She'd met them at the graduation, coming straight from the hospital, dressed in heather-gray pants accented with a blazer of the same color and a charcoal button-down shirt underneath. Hanging from her hand were a pair of dark khaki pants and a royal-blue Ralph Lauren polo shirt. Apparently she planned to go out with them to celebrate. Carrie followed Beth into the kitchen and stared at them both peculiarly.

"I'm going to pass on dinner, Carrie. I have a bit of a headache." Lynn took the bottle of ibuprofen from the cabinet, popped the top, and shook a few pills into her palm. "Your Aunt Beth will have to do tonight. Then after dinner, you and Maggie can go celebrate."

"You do look a little flushed." Carrie definitely looked disappointed. "If you're not feeling well, maybe I should stay home."

"Tell you what." Maggie glanced at Carrie. "Why don't you and Beth go? I'll stay and make sure Lynn's okay." She slid onto a barstool at the counter. "Then you can take Beth to the party afterward."

"No. You should go, Maggie. It's your graduation too," Lynn said. "I'll be fine."

"It wouldn't be the same without you there." Her gaze met Lynn's and then flittered back to Carrie. "I mean they'll just talk about sports all night." She yawned. "I'm kind of tired, anyway. It's been a long day."

"I'd be happy to stay." Beth glanced at Lynn. "It would give us time to talk."

Lynn and Beth had been separated for a few months, and Beth had made it clear on several occasions that she wanted to move back home. Maggie knew Lynn had decided to ask for a separation because Beth spent more hours at work than she did at home. The perils of being a doctor's wife. Carrie had been caught in the middle of their discussions, and Maggie was her sounding board.

"No. Tonight's not a good night for that. My head already hurts," Lynn said, her voice firm.

Maggie darted her gaze from Lynn to Beth. "I don't mind staying, really. Parties aren't my scene. I'll just hang out here and watch a movie or something." Pulling her lips into a light smile, she glanced over at Lynn. Something with Lynn would definitely be the preferred distraction.

Beth flattened her lips. "Okay then. We'll have all the fun without you two."

"Thanks, Mags. Don't worry. I'll make sure Beth doesn't drink too much," Carrie said, turning to give Lynn a hug.

"I think you have that backward," Beth said.

"Either way, both of you girls be careful." Lynn watched them go out the door, then popped the top off the ibuprofen bottle and slid the pills back into it.

"You're not going to take them?"

"I don't really have a headache. I was just trying to avoid going out and have some alone-time tonight." She put the bottle on the shelf and slapped the cabinet closed. "That certainly backfired on me."

"Why didn't you want to go out?"

Lynn shot her a look.

"You didn't want to go out with me?" Maggie didn't hide her disappointment. She'd hoped Lynn had at least some interest in being with her, even if it was just platonic.

"Yes. I mean, no." She moved around the counter to where Maggie was sitting. "I know you have some kind of crush on me and don't want to encourage you." She let out a heavy breath. "I thought, as time went on, you'd get over it."

"I have," she lied. It was much more than a crush, and since her mother's abandonment, her feelings for Lynn had only grown deeper.

"Maggie, don't think I haven't noticed what you've been doing all day."

"What?" Maggie played dumb, giving her a puzzled look.

"The flirtatious comments and those little looks you were shooting me in the car. Not to mention the way your hand brushed across my thigh every time we went around a corner."

"I was just trying to keep my balance."

"Maggie." Lynn frowned. "I'm not stupid."

"Was I that obvious?" Maggie laughed at herself. "I'm sorry I lied. But I can't help it. You seem to bring that out in me." Lynn studied her for a moment, and Maggie wasn't sure how to take her scrutiny. "I wasn't trying to make you uncomfortable. Honest."

"Your flirting should be harmless." Lynn let out a breath.

"But?" Every inch of Maggie waited for Lynn to finish her sentence, hoping she had the slightest of chances.

"Maggie, you're a beautiful girl, and any woman would be lucky to have your interest, but tempting as it is, I can't be attracted to you. Even though Beth and I are separated, we're still married."

Maggie pushed out of the barstool and stood up. "You're tempted?"

Lynn smiled nervously. "It's hard not to be. You're the perfect package. Sweet, funny, beautiful." She let out a heavy breath. "Believe me, if you'd come along at another time in my life, you'd be in big trouble right now."

Maggie locked her gaze and didn't falter. "Big trouble?" She quickly closed the space between them, not about to miss this opportunity. She needed to feel Lynn's soft lips against hers, just once.

She'd dreamed about it so many times, and when it happened, she wasn't disappointed. It was everything she'd imagined, only better. Lynn fell into her and seemed to relax as the kiss grew deeper, tongues mingling softly, breaths ragged, lungs fighting for air. She let her hands roam up Lynn's sides, feeling their way to her soft, billowy breasts. Suddenly the kiss was broken, and Lynn was staring blankly into her eyes.

"That shouldn't have happened." Lynn put her fingers to her lips.

She brushed the hair from Lynn's forehead and let her fingers trail across her cheek. "But it did." Maggie locked the front door before she took her hand and led her toward the bedroom.

Lynn took a few steps with her before she stopped, let her hand drop, and created more distance between them. "No, that is definitely not happening." Tears welled in her eyes. "I think you should go."

"I don't want to." Maggie felt the stabbing in her heart. She'd crossed the line, and Lynn wouldn't meet her on the other side. She didn't want whatever she had with Lynn to end. Not this way. "I'm

sorry. I shouldn't have done that. Can we just hang out on the couch and watch a movie? Please?"

Lynn had let her stay, but it was torture sitting so close to Lynn and not being able to touch her. However, she'd done something stupid, and the distance between them was clear. Now Lynn was within reach again, but still just out of her grasp. She turned back to the bar and ordered a shot of whiskey. Not a wise move, but considering the circumstances, she needed something more to calm her nerves.

❖

Maggie didn't feel a bit of pain when Pam slid the needle for the IV into her arm. She'd held perfectly still in hopes that her head would stop throbbing soon. As soon as Pam had gotten a look at her this morning, she'd swept her into an exam room and hooked her up.

"You don't drink much, do you?" Pam asked as she checked to make sure the fluid was moving in the IV.

"No." She spoke softly, trying not to let her voice disturb the monster with the sledgehammer currently living in her head.

"Where'd you go?"

"Lafferty's."

Pam pressed her lips together. "I was there for a bit last night. Didn't see you."

"I saw you...and Lynn."

"You should've come over and said hi."

"Absolutely not. I mean, you two looked pretty involved in conversation. I didn't want to disturb you." It was already hard enough. She refused to socialize with Lynn and her girlfriend and should've left as soon as she spotted them.

"So, I'm assuming you stayed at the bar much later than we did last night and drank much more than you anticipated."

Maggie nodded.

"You don't seem like the type to have to unwind after work. So why'd you do it?"

Maggie pried open an eye. "Something from my past crept up on me."

"Something or someone?"

"I should hate you."

"But you don't." Pam spoke with conviction, and she was right.

"No. You're too nice to hate." She let her eyes close to avoid the blinding light filling the room. "Promise you'll be good to her." She opened her eyes and stared up at Pam. She was still a little drunk, and her filter was completely broken.

Pam rolled her lips in and took in a breath. "So, listen. I'm going cover for you this time. I'll tell Dr. Baird I pulled you to assist me today. Don't ever do this again, or I'll make sure you get fired."

"Thank you." The woman was a saint. Maggie had just told her she should hate her, and she still planned to help her.

The door flew open, and Lynn came into the room. "What's going on?" She rushed to her side and felt her forehead. "Are you sick?" She rushed around the bed to check the IV bag, then stared at Pam. "She's drunk?"

Pam tilted her head and gave her a flat smile.

"What the hell is wrong with you?" Lynn's voice had lost its concern and gained a whole lot of anger. "If you're serious about being a doctor, especially a peds doctor, you can't just go get blasted whenever you feel like it. These children depend on *you*, not someone else, to give them your very best all of the time."

She didn't need a lecture this morning. "Don't worry. I know exactly what it takes to be a doctor. I don't need you to tell me." Maggie sat up and took in a deep breath to silence the hard-rock drum solo in her head before she reached to pull the needle out of the back of her hand.

Pam stopped her and pushed her back onto the bed. "Don't touch that until the bag is empty. After that, come find me." She turned to Lynn. "*You*, I need to talk to, *now*." She took Lynn into the hallway just outside the door, but Maggie could still hear them.

"Why is she drunk?" Lynn still sounded angry but totally baffled. Maybe the feelings Maggie had were truly not mirrored by Lynn. "She knew she had a shift this morning."

"She was in the bar last night. We didn't see her, but she saw us."

"So she got this drunk?"

"You have to tell her," Pam said, and Maggie knew there was no chance for them now. They were probably already living together and on the road to pure marital bliss.

"I can't. That would only make things worse."

"Look at her. She's a drunk, lovesick puppy, and that's your fault. Get the situation under control, or she's going to fail. You don't want that on your conscience, do you?"

"No. I don't want her to fail. That's not my intent at all."

"Then take care of this."

"Okay, but I can't talk to her when she's drunk."

Pam seemed to be satisfied with that response, because the conversation ended. Maggie wiped the tears from her eyes and rolled to her side. She hadn't wanted anyone to see her like this, especially not Lynn. Total fail.

Lynn closed her eyes, and her stomach rumbled as she thought about the last time she'd seen Maggie. Four years ago, the last time she'd seen her before Maggie left Baltimore and never looked back. It had all been prompted by Carrie finding them together the morning after her graduation and assuming something that hadn't actually happened.

"What the fuck?" When Carrie's voice came through the sleepy haze, Lynn struggled to open her eyes, and when she did, she found Carrie, eyes narrowed, standing just on the other side of the coffee table.

She was warm but couldn't feel her arm. In fact, she couldn't move. Maggie lay draped across her like a blanket. She shot up, and Maggie rolled to the floor like a log falling from a timber truck. The warmth Lynn had been feeling quickly vanished as fear raced through her.

"This is why you stayed home last night? So the two of you could—"

"No. Absolutely not." Lynn straightened her clothes. Thank God she still had them on. How had they ended up like that? What had happened last night?

Maggie stood and rubbed at her eyes before she picked up her phone and looked at the screen. "It's only nine thirty."

"Does that really matter?" Carrie asked.

"I didn't think you'd be home until later."

"And wouldn't interrupt this cozy little picture," Carrie said, the words coming out in a deep sort of growl.

"It's not at all what you think." Lynn moved around the table to Carrie.

"It's exactly what I think." Carrie backed up. "You weren't even sick last night, were you?"

She shook her head. "No. I didn't want to go out with Beth and knew you'd have a better time if I stayed home."

Carrie's eyebrows flew up. "You mean you'd have a better time. I knew you and Aunt Beth were having issues, but sleeping with Maggie?" She glanced at Maggie and tilted her head. "And you, my best friend... did this?" The betrayal in Carrie's eyes was clear.

"We are not sleeping together." It didn't matter what she'd wanted last night. Nothing had happened. She'd made sure of it.

"Really? Sure looks like something's going on to me." Carrie turned and rushed out the door.

Lynn couldn't stop the tears that came next. "Oh my God. How am I going to fix this?"

Maggie spun her around. "I'll fix it. I promise."

"You can't." Lynn couldn't look at her. Everything in her world she knew to be true had been shattered. "I made promises—vows. I have to try to make it work."

"But Beth is a horrible wife, and you clearly don't love her anymore." Maggie's voice wavered. "Do you?"

"That doesn't matter. Only Carrie matters now." She pointed toward the door. "Did you see her face?" The look of betrayal flashed in her mind. "She would never understand."

"You can't say you don't feel anything for me." Maggie closed the distance between them and took her in her arms.

"I can and I will." Her lips trembled, and she pushed Maggie away. "Fuck! I can't do this. Any of it." She should've left well enough alone, made Maggie leave last night, but she was weak and liked the warmth Maggie provided. A total delusion that she was going to have to wipe from her mind.

Maggie grabbed Lynn's shoulders, holding her in place. "You don't have to leave her. We'll work something out."

She snapped her gaze back to Maggie. "I can't be that person, Maggie. Lying, cheating, leading two lives. That's not me."

Maggie let her hands drop to her sides. "So, we're just done here? There's no future for us?"

The hurt look on Maggie's face cut right through her. "There can't be." She picked up her phone and hit the button for Carrie. "I need to find Carrie."

"I'll find her." Maggie didn't say another word as she slid on her sneakers and tied them.

Lynn thought of Beth. She'd been a good partner in life, providing her a home and more things than Lynn had ever thought she'd have. She *had* loved Beth, but she'd never had the desire for Beth that she felt for Maggie. Eventually she realized her life was incomplete and she'd always yearn for the kind of love she couldn't have as long as she was married to Beth. In truth, Lynn and Beth had been dealing with several issues, but after Maggie came into Lynn's life, lack of desire had moved to the top of the list.

❖

Stacy stood at the nurses' station reviewing charts when Maggie got there. She glanced at her watch. "Where have you been?"

"I..." She thought about what Pam had said, about keeping her secrets. "I was helping Pam, I mean Dr. Davidson, with a laceration."

"Ooh, so you're on a first-name basis with the doc now, huh?" Stacy chuckled. "Lady-killer."

"Don't even start that rumor." She took a tablet from Stacy and scrolled through it. "Not that I'd mind, but I think she's already taken."

"I don't have to start it. Anyone who saw you last night is gonna be way ahead of me."

"Shit. Was I that bad?"

"Let's just say you've set your sights pretty high."

"There she is." Russell's voice echoed through the hall as he came their way. "Miss Let's-have-another-shot."

"Why didn't either of you stop me?"

"We tried. Multiple times. Where's the object of your affection this morning?"

Maggie reached in front of Stacy and grabbed Russell's arm. "Don't say another word. That is top secret."

"I thought it was cute," Stacy said.

Cute, right. It might have been if she could envision a good ending to this whole scenario—one where she and Lynn rode happily off into the sunset. But with Pam around, that wasn't likely to happen. "If you tell another soul, I will make sure neither of you ever has another on-call room to yourselves again."

The look of panic Stacy and Russell exchanged was comical. "Got it," they said in unison. "At least we didn't let you follow her home."

She put her palm to her face. "Did I try?"

"You don't remember anything, do you?" Russell leaned on the counter and raised an eyebrow.

"Not after the second shot."

"Lightweight." He swiped a tablet and started to walk away, but spun back around and whispered, "Just an FYI. The doctor is already married, so you might put your efforts into someone else."

Maggie held the counter for balance as the room grew smaller and her whole body heated. *They're married?* She was too late. Lynn had moved on with her life and found happiness with someone else.

CHAPTER SEVEN

A s soon as Maggie had arrived home from her shift, she'd gone straight to bed and crashed for several hours. Stacy had picked up another shift and wouldn't be home until late, so when she'd woken later, Maggie had opened a bottle of wine, ordered a pizza through the app on her phone, and settled on the couch for a night of binge-watching the new show everyone at the hospital was raving about on Netflix. She'd only taken her first sip of wine when she heard the knock on the door and grumbled. It couldn't be the pizza. She'd just ordered it a few minutes ago, and it usually took at least thirty minutes for it to get here if they weren't busy.

Closing one eye, she looked through the peephole and squealed when she saw Carrie. "Why didn't you tell me you were coming?" she asked as she jerked open the door.

Carrie dropped her bag in the hallway, rushed in, and swept her into a hug. "I wanted to surprise you."

"Mission accomplished," she said with a huge smile.

"Yay." Carrie picked up her bag and entered.

Maggie reached to take Carrie's bag from her. "You're staying here, right?"

"Yep. Lynn's busy, so I'm all yours." Carrie grinned. "Did you know she lives in the same building as you?"

Maggie's mind spun. Multiple apartment buildings surrounded the hospital. What kind of a crazy serendipity was it that they'd chosen the same one? This development added a whole new layer of complication to their situation. "Awesome," she said as she took the bag into her bedroom, wondering what was keeping Lynn so busy that she couldn't make time for Carrie. "So what's Lynn up to?"

"She and Pam had a trip scheduled to a cabin upstate. They go every year just to get away from work."

"Just the two of them?" Maggie's stomach knotted at the thoughts running through her head. Lynn and Pam alone together in the wilderness, loving life, loving each other.

"No. I think about five or six of them go. It's a big cabin. They invited me, but I'd rather hang out with you."

Maggie smiled. At least that was something. It didn't relieve her pining for Lynn, but being with Carrie would keep her mind off reality for a while. Or would it? The ultimatum Carrie had given her four years ago flashed through her mind.

Maggie had called Carrie multiple times and still no answer. She didn't want to talk, but she had to find her and explain what had happened, or, more accurately, what hadn't happened.

Maggie stood at Deidre's door, a mutual friend from college, and waited for her to answer. The door swung open, and an immediate roadblock stood in front of her. Deidre.

"You certainly came out in a big way." She shook her head. "Did you really sleep with her aunt?" Deidre and Maggie had slept together on more than one occasion to relieve stress.

"I did not." Given the chance, she would've, but Lynn had shut her down. "Is she here?"

"She doesn't want to talk to you," Deidre said firmly.

"Well, I need to talk to her," she said as she pushed through the door. She found Carrie sitting on the couch, and the scowl on her face let Maggie know she was in no mood for any explanation.

Carrie bolted off the couch and came at her hot. "I can't believe you'd do something like that to me."

"I didn't do anything, at least not what you think."

"You were wrapped around my aunt on the couch like a fucking flour tortilla on a burrito. What am I supposed to think?"

Maggie slapped her hand to the back of her neck, trying to suppress the heat tingling across it. "I don't know." And she didn't. If Lynn had let her, she would've taken her to bed and done everything she'd sworn to Carrie that they hadn't. "I'll be honest. I tried, but Lynn wouldn't."

"You can't treat her like one of your college fuck-buddies." Carrie threw her hand up and looked past her at Deidre, then stared back at her.

Maggie would admit to a few of those, including Deidre, but it wasn't like she slept with a different woman every night. "It's nothing at all like that with her. You know she means much more than that to me."

"Do I? If she meant more, I think you'd be more worried about her needs than yours."

That comment hit Maggie right in the gut. She knew how Lynn felt about Beth, but she couldn't tell Carrie that. "Maybe Lynn's needs have changed."

"That's not your concern. She's still married to my Aunt Beth, and they're going to get back together. Beth wants it and said she's going to try harder to make it work."

"Right." She hated the words as they came out of Carrie's mouth, but they were true. Lynn had told her the same thing just a little while ago. Her decision had been clear, and Maggie couldn't do anything to change her mind. Whatever Maggie had thought the circumstances were, Lynn had chosen to stay with Beth, and she wouldn't stand in the way of that.

"Besides that, we're going to Boston, and she'll still be here, six hours away."

Carrie was right. Her life was getting ready to be busier than it ever had been. She wouldn't have time for romance with anyone, let alone someone long-distance. "What do you want me to do?"

"I want you to stay away from her. Then I'll see if I can forget it ever happened."

"Okay." To save her friendship with Carrie, she would steer clear of Lynn and never speak of her feelings for her to Carrie again.

Did Carrie still expect Maggie to avoid Lynn now that they were working at the same hospital? Now that she was divorced from Beth? Tonight would be the perfect opportunity to test those waters.

Carrie unzipped her bag and dug out some clothes. "So, unless you were planning to go out, which it doesn't look like you were, I'm gonna change and get comfy."

"Nope. Just slumming around here and watching TV."

Carrie's eyebrows rose. "Pizza?"

"On the way," she said as she left the bedroom. "You want a glass of wine?" she shouted as she swiped her glass from the coffee table and then rounded the corner from the living room into the kitchen.

"Of course," Carrie shouted back.

Maggie met Carrie on the way to the couch with a newly filled glass of wine and a refilled glass for herself. They each took a corner of the couch, their places being set since college. Maggie exchanged her glass of wine for the remote and began clicking through shows on Netflix. She stopped on the one everyone was raving about.

"Season one of this was my plan for the next couple of days. Thoughts?"

"That's good. I've been wanting to watch it too."

"Awesome." Maggie clicked on episode one and let it start.

They were only fifteen minutes into it when the pizza arrived. Carrie sprang from the couch to answer the door. "Did you already pay?"

"Yep. Tipped too."

Maggie grabbed some paper plates and napkins from the kitchen and met Carrie back at the couch. She didn't use real plates often. They weren't practical for how little time she spent eating at home, and paper plates were easy cleanup.

They'd watched two episodes of the show before Carrie popped up off the couch and announced, "I have to go to the bathroom." She held up her empty glass. "And I need more wine."

Maggie swiped the glass from her hand. "Go pee. I'll get the wine." She gathered the dirty plates and wineglasses on top of the pizza box and carried them into the kitchen as though she was a skilled restaurant server, which she had been for a time in college. Something that she didn't miss, considering the sometimes lousy customers and tips. At least this life lesson had taught her how to talk to strangers, a skill that came in handy as a doctor.

After she tossed the paper plates into the trash and put the leftover pizza in the refrigerator, Maggie filled their wineglasses and set them on the coffee table before she hit the bathroom in her room. When she came back into the living room, Carrie was back in her spot sipping her wine. It was now or never, time to feel out how thin the ice was.

"So, hey. I've met someone and am not sure what I should do," she said as she flopped onto her corner of the couch and picked up her wine.

"What?" Carrie slid her glass onto the table. "That's the first thing you should've told me when I got here." She pulled one of her legs up under the other and gave Maggie her full attention.

"Right?" She laughed, rolled her eyes, and shook her head. "What's wrong with me?"

"Why don't you know what to do? Is it the beautiful blue-eyed brunette from your first day? Is she married, in a relationship, or just a dangerous choice altogether?" Carrie bulleted her with questions.

"No. She is not the blue-eyed brunette and probably a dangerous choice altogether."

Carrie's eyes widened and she leaned forward. "Ooh, I was hoping for that. Now I need all the details."

"You're incorrigible." She shook her head. "There aren't any *details* yet. She doesn't even know I exist in that way."

"Where did you meet her?"

"Where do you think? The only other place I ever go besides here."

"Another doctor? An intern?"

Maggie nodded. "Yes, but no. Not an intern." She could see the relief in Carrie's eyes. She'd lied because she didn't want to give Carrie any specific details that would make her suspicious. And technically, even though she wished for something with Lynn in the future, nothing was going on between them. Especially since Lynn was currently off gallivanting in the woods with her wife. She shook the thought from her head.

"You're thinking about her right now, aren't you?"

Maggie nodded, and heat rose to her cheeks. Just the thought of having anything with Lynn made warmth spread throughout her. "She's really special, and I don't want to screw it up."

"Well, then don't, dummy. Does she at least know you like her?"

"She may have an idea. She's beautiful, sweet, and super-smart. I can't help but get a little gaga whenever she's around." She tried to calm the butterflies swirling in her belly.

"Oh my God. Look at you. You're blushing. I don't think I've seen you act this way about anyone before. Not even Brenda."

"*Never* Brenda. That was all about convenience. Love never entered into that relationship at all." *At all.*

"Did Brenda know that?"

"Oh, yeah. It was the same for her. We've never had anything in common besides sex. Which, don't get me wrong, was amazing, but you can only base a relationship on sex for so long before you get on each other's nerves." And Brenda had been getting on Maggie's nerves all the time before she left. Maybe Maggie's state of mind was pushing her away, the knowledge she was moving back to Baltimore where she'd left her heart so many years ago. Even so, when Maggie wasn't studying, all she wanted to do was stay at home and chill. Brenda never got that. She was a talker, which went along with her huge circle of friends and active social life. Maggie wouldn't miss being dragged to parties and places she didn't want to be.

"I'm guessing you were at that point, or she'd be coming to see you."

"It was a clean break. I'm sure she's already involved with someone else." Brenda wasn't the kind of girl to stay single for long. She hated being alone. Maggie, on the other hand, valued her privacy and alone-time, and she didn't get much of it when she was living with Brenda.

"I think she is." Carrie smiled slightly. "I wasn't going to say anything, but you seem to have moved on yourself."

She smiled lightly and shook her head. "That's not surprising." And it wasn't. Brenda was a flirt and liked attention.

Carrie shifted in her seat. "So back to the doctor…what's holding you back?"

"I think she might be seeing someone. I don't know." She didn't tell her that the beautiful blue-eyed brunette was her competition.

"Well, find out." Carrie took a drink of wine. "Married puts her off-limits, but only seeing someone means she's fair game."

Maggie relaxed into the couch and took a drink of wine. "I'm not going to stalk her." Her stomach churned as the image of Russell's face flashed in her mind as he said *The doctor is married.* It had happened only a week ago, and she was still stunned by the news. She hadn't had a chance, nor had she wanted to get more information yet, so that fact was still unconfirmed.

"Okay, so just think about it. Who does she interact with?"

"Everyone. She's very friendly." Thoughts of Lynn's beautiful smile floated through her head.

Carrie pulled her eyebrows together. "Hmm. Does she come to work alone?"

"I think so."

"Does she leave with anyone?"

"Yes. The person she may be involved with." She'd seen her leave the hospital with Pam several times.

"Damn it, you're not making this easy."

Maggie chuckled. "Correction. *She's* not making this easy." Pam was an awesome woman and would be stiff competition if Maggie decided to push forward.

"Why don't you just ask her out?"

"It would be really awkward if she says no. I pretty much have to see her every day." After having Lynn reject her years ago, Maggie didn't know if she had it in her to make the first move again.

"Jesus, Mags. Stop playing it so safe, or you're never going to find the right girl. When will you see her next?"

"When I get back to work day after tomorrow, and there's a softball game scheduled one evening next week."

Carrie's eyes widened. "She's in the hospital softball league? Perfect." Her voice rose. "You're awesome at softball, so dazzle her with your skills."

"The suspected girlfriend plays on her team, and she's really good too."

"Fuck. That's an obstacle." Carrie shifted on the couch. "Okay, then get your flirting game going. I know you can do that. I've seen you in action."

"Uh, not in a long time."

"Stop. If I were into women, you'd have had me a long time ago."

"Really? I had no idea." She raised an eyebrow and leaned forward. "You're sure you're not into women? I can teach you some things."

Carrie leaned forward and stared into her eyes. "Ooh, you think so?"

Both of them laughed and fell back into their corners. That would never happen. Maggie had lost any interest she'd ever had in Carrie once she met Lynn. Not that anything would've ever happened between them anyway. They were best friends, and Maggie wanted it to stay that way. Her biggest worry about starting a relationship with Lynn was that it would upset Carrie again. But she had to take that risk, or she'd never know if Lynn was the one, and she'd never get over her. Four years in different cities had already proved that getting over her was impossible.

"So what about you?" Maggie needed to move from the subject, or she'd end up spilling more information than she intended. "How are things going with super-smart and gorgeous Scott?"

A dreamy glimmer appeared in Carrie's eyes, and she looked up at the ceiling. "He's absolutely awesome, Mags. I want to spend the rest of my life with him."

"Oh my God. Have I been replaced?" Maggie had seen that coming since the first time Carrie had told her about him.

"I'm sorry," Carrie said as she put on her best puppy-dog face. "You knew it'd happen sooner or later."

"So, are you two actually together?"

"Well, we're not totally together, but we have a lot of sleepovers and spend a lot of time in the on-call room. You know those times when you need a certain type of stress relief?"

Maggie nodded as memories of the bare-bones room with a single twin bed at Boston Hospital flew through her mind. She'd spent a bit of time there herself. No-strings-attached mid-shift commingling with some of her fellow medical students and one or two very experienced residents relieved a lot of stress. She'd learned a few things about how her body worked, what turned her on, and what didn't, as well as how to satisfy a woman and make her come back for more. The call rooms at Johns Hopkins weren't much better, but she hadn't had the opportunity to use them in ways other than napping. Had Lynn ever used them for the same kind of stress relief? She shook the thought from her mind and tried to focus on Carrie's romance with Scott.

"Are you listening to me?"

"Yes. Sorry. I just came off an overnight call shift, and I'm still a little wiped out."

"Gotcha. Let's hit the sack, and we can continue this conversation in the morning." Carrie got up. "I need a pillow and blanket."

"Just bunk with me. Stacy will be home in a couple of hours, and she's all kinds of noisy." Maggie dropped the wineglasses off in the kitchen before heading to the bedroom. "Besides, I don't want her to freak out about a stranger sleeping on the couch."

Carrie raised an eyebrow. "A stranger?"

"You are strange." She glanced over her shoulder and winked. "She's a little nutty about people she doesn't know."

"Noisy and nutty. Can't wait to meet her."

"She's in lust with Russell, one of the other interns on our service, and that's making her worse."

"I thought you weren't going to do the roommate thing again."

"I kinda got trapped into it, and this place is a little pricey."

Carrie climbed into bed, fluffed her pillow, rolled to her side, and tucked her arm underneath it. "Think that'll work out?"

"What? Stacy or Russell?" She hadn't let anything slip about Lynn, had she?

"Stacy and Russell."

"I don't know. Russell's really focused. I'm not sure he's even getting the hint."

"He's probably forgotten how flirting works. Too much medicine will do that." Carrie grinned. "Maybe he'll have a reawakening, like you."

Back to her again. She needed to get off the subject. "So tell me, romance queen. How did it unfold between you and Scott?"

"It was a total glass-slipper moment. I told you I initially met him at the gym, right?"

Maggie nodded.

"So, one night after shift, some of us went to the usual place after work to screw our metabolisms by eating some over-fried food and drinking too much."

"Hmm. I can almost taste the wings now. Is it weird that I miss that place?"

"Totally, but they still have the best ones."

"Sorry. What happened after you ordered and slammed down a pound of wings?"

"Buffalo sauce and ranch dressing on the side."

"Of course." Maggie missed having Carrie close by. The things they'd experienced together made everything flow between them so well.

"Nothing happened while we were there, but I drank a little too much and forgot my phone on the table when I left."

Maggie propped up on her elbow. "And he brought it to you?"

"He followed me out of the bar and gave it to me." Carrie rolled her lips in and looked at the blanket between them. "And I thanked him with a kiss."

"Oh my God," she said, covering her mouth, unable to contain her laughter. "Alcohol always did make you push your boundaries."

"Only it didn't backfire this time. He kissed me back and then walked me home." The dreamy look in Carrie's eyes was unmistakable.

Maggie raised an eyebrow. "Did you two?"

"No, not that night. He's a ridiculous gentleman." Carrie grinned. "He did kiss me again, though. It took everything I had not to pull him inside and tear all his clothes off."

"Sooo?"

"On our next night off we went on an actual date, and we haven't really spent a night apart since."

Maggie smiled. "I'm so happy you got your fairy tale." She closed her eyes, and her thoughts floated to Lynn. Maybe one day she'd be able to have hers as well.

She had just drifted off to sleep when she felt Carrie slide closer and snuggle her back against her stomach. Carrie reached back, took Maggie's hand, and laced their fingers together before she tucked it close to her belly.

"Are you sure you're straight?" she asked, her eyes still shut.

"Absolutely. But I miss Scott. So shut up, share your heat with me, and keep your hands to yourself."

"I'll do my best." Maggie chuckled. "Tell me more about your Prince Charming."

Carrie continued with the details as Maggie tried to focus on her and Scott, but her mind wouldn't let her. All she could think about was how fate had brought her full circle. When she'd received her hospital assignment on Match Day, no one had been more surprised than Maggie to learn she'd be going back to Baltimore. Even though Carrie hadn't said anything, she knew Carrie had concerns when she'd told her Brenda wasn't coming with her.

It was noon on the third Friday in March. Match Day. Students dressed surprisingly alike—men in pants, colorful shirts, and vibrant ties, and women in brightly spring-patterned dresses, tights, slacks, and blouses—stood in a room decorated with red and white balloons and streamers. The hum of excited conversation filled the room as Maggie and one hundred and forty or so others drank champagne just a few feet from the tables where plain white envelopes that dictated the next three to seven years of their futures lay taunting them.

Maggie stood with the rest of the Boston University School of Medicine fourth-year students waiting to receive her internship assignment. She'd applied to fifteen different hospitals, including Boston Children's, Children's Hospital of Philadelphia, and Johns Hopkins. She'd been invited to interview at more than half of those where she'd applied.

Her first choice was to remain in Boston, where she'd lived and studied for the past four years. She'd completed a visiting rotation there, as well as a few other East Coast schools. Maggie had become accustomed to the changing seasons and loved the way people kept to themselves when necessary, but as any medical student would, she'd be happy with anything offered. She'd considered returning to Baltimore closer to her family but felt it wasn't the best option due to her still-strained relationship with her mother.

The conversation in the lounge lulled when the dean entered and made a short speech. Everyone joined in the countdown to noon, starting at the number ten. The number one had barely slipped from her lips when everyone rushed the tables and searched for their names on the hundreds of envelopes. Maggie swiped hers, which had been lying amongst the others, and opened it. She was stunned. The vibrant pink of Carrie's dress caught her eye as she rushed across the room toward her. She looked gorgeous, as always, and Maggie's stomach dipped. In recent years, Carrie had begun to look more and more like her aunt. Specifically, her smile, but that smile wasn't glowing at this moment, and Maggie couldn't read her face. She wasn't jumping up and down and hugging people like some of the others were. Neither one of them was.

"Where'd you get?" Carrie asked.

She showed her the letter stating she would be interning at Johns Hopkins Children's Hospital. Crazy feelings of disappointment mixed with excitement filled her.

"Seriously?" Carrie blew out a short breath.

She nodded. "You?"

Carrie handed her the letter. Boston Children's. "You've got to be kidding?" She chuckled. "How did that happen?"

"Not my first choice," Carrie said as she swept her long, dark hair from her face. "I guess it could be worse." She folded the letter and placed it back in the envelope. "At least I know the commute." Carrie had chosen Johns Hopkins as her number one because she wanted to go back home to be closer to her aunts. Maggie had chosen the exact opposite. She'd hoped to remain at Boston Children's because she had a nice apartment, a girlfriend, and had become attached to so many people here. They'd become her family, and starting all over would be difficult. And then there was Lynn, which meant avoidance would become central in her life again.

"You'll always have a place to stay with me if you get tired of your aunts," she said. Even though she and Carrie had cultivated different circles of friends due to their medical specialties, Maggie in pediatrics and Carrie in neonatology, they'd remained friends throughout medical school.

"You know I'll take you up on that." Carrie swept her into a hug. "I'll miss you, though."

"I'll miss you too." She would miss her much more than she let on. "You can always text, FaceTime, or even call me." She rolled her eyes. "Any time."

Carrie gave her a slight smile. "I know, but it'll be different knowing I can't just come over when I want."

"I'll definitely miss your late-night pizza deliveries," she said with a grin.

"Now I know why you've put up with me for all these years." Carrie chuckled. "Do you think Brenda will go with you?"

"I doubt it. Her job here is pretty solid." Maggie folded her letter and slipped it into the envelope.

"You don't seem sad about that." Carrie always had a way of reading her.

Glancing up at the ceiling tiles, Maggie studied the ridges that formed the checkered pattern as she thought about the discussion between her and Brenda a few nights before. She shook her head and refocused on Carrie and shrugged. "I'm not. She's a sweet girl, but we just don't have the connection I want. Plus, she's really high *maintenance, and I won't have time to make sure she's happy in a new place."*

"Sounds like you've already thought this through."

"We've had the conversation. She doesn't want to leave Boston because her family is here." Maggie tapped the envelope in her palm. "I don't know how she's going to take this, though. I was so sure I was staying."

"Same. I was sure I was going." Carrie took Maggie's hand before she leaned in and whispered, "Maybe we can secretly trade." They both laughed loudly and squeezed each other's hand before a few of their friends raced across the room toward them and pulled them back into the crowd of happy graduates.

One of the benefits of going to Boston for medical school was that she was too busy to think about what she'd left behind. Maggie didn't look forward to starting over again, but she'd made the best of it. At least Baltimore was familiar. Now if she could just keep her mind on medicine instead of the huge distraction it presented. Getting Lynn out of her heart was more difficult than anything she'd ever come up against. She'd feared she would never forget what had happened between her and Lynn and never be able to move on to someone else, which was absolutely true.

CHAPTER EIGHT

Lynn sat outside on the deck taking in the faint sounds of birds whistling, along with a chorus filled with the long, high-pitched, vibrating call of the American toads and the siren-like trill of spring peepers gathered near the lake. Each sound on its own would probably be annoying, but together they formed the most beautiful symphony. Teamwork at its best.

She'd loved this place from the first time Pam had invited her along on the yearly girls' trip, which didn't seem like that long ago. They'd barely met, and Lynn had been working for Heather in her practice for only a short while when Pam had included her. But they seemed to get each other and hit it off right away. Pam was a constant at the office, visiting her and Heather whenever she could escape from the hospital, and they'd become immediate friends.

The cabin was large, containing six rooms—two downstairs and four upstairs. Although others paired up and shared rooms, she and Pam hadn't. The weekend was a planned clandestine getaway for some of the couples.

Her first trip here had been what seemed like the possible beginning of something, but when Heather had showed up unexpectedly single, the spark between Heather and Pam was noticeably visible and undeniable, something Lynn herself had experienced with only one other person. It seemed Pam had just been patiently waiting for Heather to become unattached. She didn't know why she hadn't seen the attraction between them before, but knew immediately she and Pam were only destined to be best friends, which was okay with Lynn. Pam was her advisor and confidant, so she couldn't ask for a better friend.

Annoyed with herself that she couldn't get Maggie out of her thoughts, she sprang up and paced to the end of the deck. She loved the serenity of the forest. It could break through the constant hospital noise filling her head the moment they arrived at the cabin, but Maggie— her smile, her voice—had found a presence in her head and wasn't leaving so easily. Maybe that was because she felt a calmness around Maggie she'd never experienced before, even when they were at the hospital. Her marriage to Beth had always been filled with turmoil. They did everything on Beth's terms or had a lengthy discussion, which ultimately ended in them doing what Beth wanted. Lynn eventually avoided the discussions and just let Beth run the show.

The door slapped shut, and Heather strolled onto the deck with a cup of coffee in each hand. "What's going on with you?"

"Nothing. Just enjoying the peace and quiet." She crossed the deck and stood next to Heather at the railing.

Heather handed her a cup, then set hers on the railing and looked out at the lake as she stretched her arms up over her head and twisted from side to side at her waist. "Don't give me that. You enjoyed the *quiet* the whole way up here."

"Did I? Sorry. I didn't realize." She'd been in her head a lot lately.

Heather nodded, then walked over to one of the many natural-wood Adirondack chairs lining the cabin exterior and sat. "Even Pam noticed the usual chatty you didn't have much to say. I expected an earful of new-intern stories."

She sank into one of the chairs next to Heather. "I was just thinking."

Heather's eyebrows pulled together. "About what?"

Maybe Heather could offer some advice. Lynn certainly hadn't been giving herself much that did any good. "If you had the chance to capture an opportunity you thought was long gone, would you?"

"I'm assuming we're talking relationship here," Heather said as she sipped her coffee.

She nodded. "Yes."

"Was it a good one?" Heather asked.

"I don't know. I didn't explore it. I wasn't at a place in my life where I could let it happen, but I think it might have been."

"Then hell, yes." Heather didn't mince words. She was always straight with people even when it wasn't easy, which came along with being in medicine.

She took in a deep breath and blew it out slowly.

"I expected more of a happy response," Heather said.

"It's really complicated." So many factors filled her head: age, career, Carrie. The impact on Carrie would be huge and was her main concern.

"Tell me about her." Heather raised her eyebrows and smiled. "Maybe I can help you figure it out."

She tried to calm the butterflies swarming her stomach. "She's sweet and beautiful, and smart."

"Have you told her that?"

"No. She can't know I have feelings for her because that will open a door I don't think I can close." She took in a deep breath. "I don't have the strength."

Heather looked at her thoughtfully. "Do you really have to close it?"

"She's so much younger than me." It didn't feel like they were different ages when Maggie was near or when they talked, but the reality was still there.

Heather took another sip of coffee and licked the tiny residual drops from her upper lip. "How much younger?"

"Eight, maybe nine years." It was twelve, but for some reason she couldn't bring herself to say the number.

"That's nothing. Pam and I are almost nine years apart. If you have feelings for her and she has feelings for you, does that really make a difference?"

"But you two met after your careers were set. She's just starting hers."

"Oh. I gotcha." Heather chuckled and pulled her lip up to one side. "She's an intern. The forbidden fruit." She glanced over at Lynn. "Well, not for you." The rules were different for nurses than for doctors, but such relationships were still frowned upon, and the rumor mill would take it and run the full-mile track.

She nodded. "She really kind of is. I've known her since she was in college. She's Carrie's best friend."

Heather's eyebrows rose. "Ack. That is a complication."

"Right?" She shook her head. "I don't know how Carrie would

handle it, and if she doesn't react well, it could throw all our lives into turmoil. I've already had enough of that in my life." It would be complicated at best. She worried that Carrie might perceive the relationship as Lynn loving Maggie more than she loved her. But that was silly. They were totally different kinds of love, and she could never replace one of them with the other.

Heather stared at her thoughtfully. "But you really want to be with her, don't you?"

Was she really that transparent? She sighed. "Yes. It's hard to see her every day and not want her."

"Does said intern want it too?"

"It seems like it."

"Then I say, go ahead. Carrie loves you. She'll get over it eventually." Heather always had a way of cutting through the crap.

"My life is good right now, stable. This would really complicate it."

Heather reached over and touched her hand. "You've already had one shitty marriage. Do you want to settle for stable?"

She looked up, saw the concern in Heather's eyes, and thought about Maggie. Her heart raced and she shook her head. "No."

The screen door slapped open, and Pam appeared with the coffee decanter and stared at Heather. Lynn watched the look they exchanged. The unspoken zap between them was unmistakable, and the way they knew exactly what each other needed was uncanny. She'd never had that with Beth and wasn't sure she'd ever have it with anyone. Maybe it would be possible with Maggie.

Pam smiled, then veered her gaze to Lynn. "Whatcha talking about?"

"Work."

"I know that's not true. Heather shuts that down immediately when we're here."

"People at work."

"Oh, the intern," Pam said, and Heather lifted an eyebrow.

"You sent her out here to talk about it." Lynn shook her head. It wasn't like it was a secret, but Pam could've at least let her know she'd told Heather.

Heather rolled her eyes. "Don't be upset. I didn't know the particulars. I only knew there was someone."

"It's okay. I appreciate the opinion from a non-biased party." She leaned forward and stared at Pam. "That one is already planning my wedding."

"She's a hopeless romantic," Heather said.

"And a fine wedding it will be." Pam circled Heather and refilled Lynn's cup with coffee. "You know I don't keep anything from Heather, and it was sort of necessary since she thinks I'm your girlfriend."

"I'm sorry. She just assumed, and I let her." It was the easiest way for Lynn to make sure Maggie kept her distance.

"That doesn't bother me in the slightest. It just makes you hotter." Heather bounced her eyebrows at Pam as she held up her cup for Pam to fill.

"Hey. I just want you to get your happily-ever-after, exactly like us." Pam filled Heather's cup and then looped her hand around the back of Heather's neck and kissed her fully on the lips. The steaminess that existed between them made Lynn look away. Their chemistry was off the charts, and on more than one occasion Lynn felt the need to leave them alone to explore it.

"Good morning, love," Heather said softly as she stared into Pam's eyes.

"Good morning." Pam let her hand trail from Heather's cheek down her neck and across her shoulder. "We'll discuss that 'hotter' comment tonight."

Lynn gave them a backhanded wave. "Please go. Discuss it now if you must."

They both chuckled. "No. We're good. We did that before the sun came up."

She shook her head and smiled. "You two." What she wouldn't give to be in love like that. Maybe Heather was right. Maybe something with Maggie was possible after all. She'd know only if she let Maggie into her heart and gave it a shot.

After Pam returned the decanter to the kitchen, she came out and sat next to Heather. "Jackie called. They're not coming."

"What? Why not?"

"Jen is close to eight months and isn't up for the drive. Especially with the kids."

"Well, shit." Heather let out a huge sigh. "If I'd known, we could've picked up the kids and given them some alone time. I was really looking forward to seeing them and taking them out on the boat."

Pam took Heather's hand and squeezed it. "We'll get there, honey."

Lynn saw the sadness in Heather's eyes and knew immediately what she was thinking about. They hadn't had any luck on their last round of in-vitro fertilization, and that was their second try. Lynn wished she could make it easier for them, because the disappointment was crushing. IVF treatments were more successful than ever these days, but the odds of getting pregnant were low to begin with for someone in their twenties or thirties, and Pam was close to forty. Heather was the older of the two, which was why they'd decided Pam would carry the child. That and she embraced the experience more than Heather had. Heather loved kids of any age and, from the start, was good with adopting, but knowing how hard it was to find a baby for adoption, Pam wanted to try IVF first. They'd recently completed everything necessary to become foster parents and had been approved, but hadn't acted on it yet. Forming a bond with a child and then having the birth parents change their minds wasn't a blow Heather wanted to experience.

"What about Terra and Jo?" Heather asked, seeming to want to move away from the subject.

"Nope. Jo just started a new job and has to work. She asked if maybe we could set up another one of these in a few months." Pam sipped her coffee. "I told her we'd have to look at our schedules."

"You up for that, Lynn?"

"Sure. I'm always up for this place. I love it here." It was so peaceful and serene. When she was here, she seemed to always be able to let go of the outside world. Except this time, she couldn't seem to get Maggie out of her mind.

"Maybe you can bring the intern." Pam winked.

"So are you two going to tell me the intern's name?" Heather smiled at Pam and then looked back at Lynn. "I mean, I'd hate to blow your cover." That wasn't likely to happen, since Heather was a partner in a family practice that resided in a separate building from the main hospital. She kept up with who was on staff but only frequented the hospital if and when one of her patients was admitted.

"Maggie Randall."

"Hmm." Heather tightened her lips. "Definitely beautiful and seems to be smart as well."

"You know her?"

"She treated one of my asthma kids a couple of weekends ago. She was thorough and did all the right things." Heather drank down the rest of her coffee. "You could do worse." She stood. "Anyone up for pancakes?"

"Always." Pam pushed out of her chair.

"I'm in," Lynn said and followed them inside. Heather's assessment of Maggie didn't appear to be clouded by Lynn's feelings, which lessened her anxiety for the moment. Her life had been uncomplicated until now, and suddenly she had Maggie to consider. So many thoughts were running through her head. Maggie wanted to be a pediatrician, so she'd want children, but Lynn had already raised her child. Was she too old to go through it all again? Would she be able to trust Maggie not to leave all the parenting to her the way Beth did? She didn't have answers to any of these questions, and until she did, she couldn't move forward in any way with Maggie.

CHAPTER NINE

Maggie felt like she'd been asleep for only a few minutes when she heard the bedroom door swing open. She opened one eye to see Stacy staring at Carrie, her face turning redder by the second.

"Oh, shit. Sorry," Stacy said when she made eye contact and started to back out of the room.

"It's all right. What's up?"

"I need some Russell advice." Stacy tilted her head to get a better look at Carrie. "Who's that? What about—"

"Shh." Maggie held her finger to her lips and glanced over Carrie's shoulder to see if she was awake. "I'll come out." She slipped out of bed and pulled on her hoodie as she crossed the room. Then she glanced back to see if Carrie was awake before she went out into the living room.

"What's up?"

"Who's that in your bed?"

"My friend, Carrie." She rubbed her eyes, trying to clear the fog from her mind, and rounded the corner into the kitchen.

"Carrie is *cute*. Where'd you meet her?"

"College. She was my roommate."

Stacy was right behind her. "You didn't tell me you had a thing with anyone from college."

"I didn't. I don't." She looked at the clock on the oven—seven a.m. "Did you just get home?" she asked as she filled the coffeemaker with water.

"Yes, and don't change the subject. Why is your college roommate in your bed spooned into you?"

She could practically feel Stacy's eyes boring into her back. "I need caffeine," she said as she scooped a few spoonfuls of coffee into the maker and pushed the start button. Once the coffee was brewing, she leaned against the counter. "Because you live in the other bedroom and she was cold. She's my best friend *and also* Lynn's daughter."

Stacy's eyes went wide. "Oh, shit."

"Exactly."

"Did you tell her how you feel about Lynn?" Stacy lowered her voice.

"No, but you almost did." She lowered her voice to match Stacy's. "You need to think before you talk, here *and* at work." Stacy had a bad habit of saying things out loud before she fully processed them in her head. Not the best thing when dealing with sick people already upset by the circumstances they'd been stricken with.

"Sorry. I'm working on that. It surprised me."

"Me too." She chuckled. "She just showed up last night. I had no idea she was coming."

"Did she come to see Lynn?"

"Nope. Apparently Lynn's out of town having all kinds of fun with Pam and a few other women. It's some annual trip they take." The coffeemaker beeped, and she took a couple of cups from the cabinet.

"Feeling left out, are we? A little jealous, maybe?" Stacy had been teasing her nonstop since she'd told her about her feelings for Lynn.

"Shut up." She poured herself a cup of coffee and jammed the decanter back into the machine. She was ridiculously jealous right now and didn't know how to get past it. She needed to accept the fact that Lynn was with someone else, an admittedly sweet woman who seemed to make her happy. Why couldn't she just be good with that? She wanted Lynn to be happy, right? She really did, only Maggie wanted to be the other half of that happiness. "So what was so important that you had to wake me at the crack of dawn?"

"Russell."

She rolled her eyes. "Russell is not an emergency."

"He wants to take me to dinner tonight." The excitement in Stacy's voice wasn't unusual, but this time it was different.

"Where?" Dinner was dinner, but the location would set the mood for the evening.

"An Italian place near the hospital he wants to try."

Carrie appeared from around the corner. "If it's Dino's, you're his buddy. If it's La Scala, then ooh la la. Be ready for some action," she said and bounced her eyebrows as she came into the kitchen. "But they're both good."

Stacy's face broke into a huge smile. "It's La Scala."

"Nice," Carrie said as she got a mug and poured herself a cup of coffee. "I'm Carrie, by the way, and you must be Stacy."

Stacy nodded.

"Are you off tomorrow?"

Stacy nodded again. "We both are."

"Well, then you'd better get some rest. It sounds like you have a big night ahead of you." Maggie winked. "Whatever you do, don't bring him back here. I don't want to hear any of that going on in there." She pointed toward Stacy's bedroom.

Carrie leaned against the counter and blew on her coffee. "You should take that chickie you're interested in there. I've been there a few times. Believe me when I say it's a sure win."

Stacy's eyes widened. "You should. I bet she'd love it."

"So, you know who Maggie's crushing on?"

"I do." Stacy nodded rapidly. "At least I think I do, and she's awesome."

The look Carrie gave Maggie was nothing short of devious as she stood between her and Stacy and said, "Tell me more."

"I already told you she's a doctor and involved with someone else." Maggie looked over Carrie's shoulder and narrowed her eyes at Stacy.

Coffee spilled onto Carrie's hand, and she hissed as she spun around and said, "You, shut it. I want an impartial opinion from Stacy." She reached for a kitchen towel and then spun back around. "Is this woman involved with someone else?"

She could see Stacy's throat move as she swallowed. "She appears to be, but that's not confirmed."

"Does she wear a wedding ring?"

"No ring," Stacy said.

Carrie glanced over her shoulder at Maggie and raised an eyebrow. "Well, then what are you waiting for?"

She needed to head this discussion off before Stacy got flustered and spilled the beans. "A lot of doctors don't wear jewelry."

"And a lot of doctors do."

"Right?" Stacy's eyes went wide. "That's what I've been telling her."

The sigh that escaped her lips wasn't intentional, but it was huge. "Honestly, I'm not ready to make my life awkward on the daily. If she's married, that's guaranteed."

Carrie shrugged. "She'd probably just be flattered."

"You can always do what you told me to do," Stacy said to Maggie.

"What's that?" Carrie asked.

"Be present all the time, but not annoying. She'll notice you."

Maggie chuckled. "That's horrible advice. Did I really tell you that?"

Carrie laughed along with her. "Definitely horrible advice, but it'll keep you in her thoughts one way or another. She'll either fall in heavy like with you, or you'll annoy the fuck out of her." She drank the last of her coffee, put her cup in the sink, and pulled open the refrigerator. After rummaging through the minimal contents she said, "I'm starving. Let's get some breakfast." She headed out of the kitchen. "Stace, you want to come?" Carrie spoke as though she'd known Stacy forever. She was good about making people feel comfortable, a trait of a great doctor in the making.

"Thanks, but I'm going to bed." Stacy smiled at Maggie. "I have a date tonight," she said as she pushed away from counter and dance-walked her way across the apartment to her room.

Maybe she *should* take her own advice. It seemed to have worked for Stacy. She'd definitely have to turn on the flirty charm she'd engaged in the past regularly before her mind became a vault of medical knowledge. If she remembered how.

CHAPTER TEN

The days away at the cabin had been good for Lynn. She'd organized her thoughts and, with a little help from Heather and Pam, realized relationships didn't have to be so complicated. She'd been overthinking the whole thing. Every worst scenario had been swirling in her head from the first moment she'd seen Maggie again. Well, no more of that. Today was the start of a new chapter in her life, and it might very well contain a little happiness, which might just be Maggie.

She glimpsed Maggie in the hallway and raced to accidentally bump into her on purpose. "So I heard Carrie was in town last weekend while I was gone. Did you two have a good time?" Lynn asked.

"Yep, except she hogs all the sheets and wants to cuddle all night."

"What?"

"You don't have to worry about my bad influence. She's still as straight as they come."

"I wasn't worried, and I've never considered you a bad influence on Carrie. In fact, I've always thought you were good for her."

"Really?"

She smiled. "Yeah, really. A good influence for both of us."

"Well, then maybe you and I should spend more time together." Maggie lifted an eyebrow and gave her a sexy smile. "I could change your thoughts on that subject if you'd give me a chance."

"I'm sure you could." Lynn was frozen for a moment, realizing the conversation was changing into banter that both excited and terrified her. "We already spend a lot of time together."

Maggie leaned near and whispered in her ear. "I mean fun stuff away from here. Carrie mentioned that you and I live in the same apartment complex. Maybe I could come by your place after work?"

A jolt shot through her as she considered this new development of their living proximity. "Really? I had no idea."

"Yep. Second floor, apartment fifteen." Maggie remained close as she spoke.

Lynn could smell the subtle scent of lemon and sage body lotion that she remembered and took in a deep breath. She hated to admit it, but she'd missed everything about Maggie—her beautiful, light-blue eyes, her silky, blond hair, her quick wit. And her laughter. But she'd missed her positive attitude the most. With a little twist of her tongue, Maggie could turn any bad situation into something better. Her optimism had brought a shining light into Lynn's life so long ago when she'd first come home with Carrie. Having any kind of relationship with Maggie had been so far out of reach then, Lynn had never thought she'd have the opportunity to be close to her, yet here she was right back in her life again, closer than she'd ever imagined. Possibly closer than she should be.

Something caught Lynn's eye, and she forced her stare from Maggie's vibrant blue eyes to glance over Maggie's shoulder. Beth stood not far away in the hallway, watching them intently. Lynn suppressed the shudder that ran through her. It always amazed Lynn how the vision of Beth dressed in a suit perfectly tailored to her figure could make all sensible thoughts jumble in her head. She never debated the fact that Beth was a striking woman physically—six feet tall with short, silvery hair that had morphed from blond in her late thirties, trimmed neatly on her neck, cobalt-blue eyes, and a smile that could melt Lynn in an instant. Just one look from Beth always made her body do things she, to this day, couldn't prevent. None of that made up for Beth's inability to form an emotional connection, something Lynn needed for her own well-being and couldn't live without.

She immediately stiffened and squared her shoulders. Maggie seemed to notice her sudden discomfort and swung around to see what she was staring at.

Beth strode closer, nodded, and said, "Lynn, Maggie," in her monotone doctor voice that Lynn remembered hearing when Beth wasn't happy about something. Lynn shrugged it off. She didn't answer to Beth anymore and had nothing to feel guilty about. She was allowed to enjoy herself at work.

"Hi, Dr. Monroe. It's good to see you." Maggie offered her hand, and even though Beth's stare was intimidating, she made clear eye contact. They quickly shook hands, and Maggie focused back on Lynn, touched her shoulder, and smiled. "I'll see *you* around the floor," she said without hesitation, then turned and rushed off in the other direction, not giving Beth another look.

"What are you doing here?" she asked.

"Is that really the question that begs for an answer in this situation?" Beth asked, raising an eyebrow.

The back of Lynn's neck burned with heat. She'd known Beth wouldn't let the contact, although minimal, go without comment. "We're not married anymore, Beth. I don't have to explain my actions to you." She didn't have to justify them either.

Beth pulled her eyebrows together. "She's Carrie's best friend, and you were overtly flirting with her."

"She's an intern at this hospital, and I was not flirting." She wasn't, was she? It was just an everyday conversation about Carrie. She'd tried to stop the banter.

"I disagree, and that little display I just witnessed leads me to believe she may be more than just an intern to you." Beth narrowed her eyes.

Lynn put her hands on her hips. She didn't have the time or desire to discuss her feelings about Maggie with Beth. "Listen. Whatever is going on in my personal life, whether it's with Maggie or anyone else, is none of your business." She looked Beth up and down. "Why are you dressed like that?"

"I just met with the hospital board about the CEO position."

"You're thinking of moving out of surgery?"

"Possibly. It would mean a considerable raise and give me some of my life back."

"You did lose a lot of that," she said softly, wondering if things would have turned out differently for them if Beth had made different choices earlier in her career.

Beth touched her on the cheek. "Maybe I could get some of it back?"

She covered Beth's hand with hers, closed her eyes briefly, and took in a breath to settle herself. "Not that part." She shook her head. "Not from me." Beth had made many promises in the past that she'd never kept, and Lynn couldn't depend on anything from her. Especially not future promises that had always gone unfulfilled.

Beth removed her hand and remained silent for a moment. "You can't blame me for trying." She gave her a soft smile.

She could blame her, but she wouldn't today. "No, I guess I can't." That was a line she would never cross again. Lynn had severed any emotional connection she'd had with Beth long ago, and she wouldn't act on the physical attraction ever again. Beth had no idea how hard it was for her to stay once she'd made up her mind to leave their marriage the first time. The last year of their relationship had been nothing more than existence for Lynn. Once Beth had moved home again, all the effort she'd been expending to be more present in the relationship had stopped. Beth had gone back to being the person she truly was, a person who should've never had a family and honestly didn't deserve one.

Beth began spending more and more time at the hospital, and Lynn went back to work being a full-time nurse. Lynn had cultivated her own set of friends at the hospital outside of those she and Beth were usually friendly with and soon realized nothing had changed in their life together. It wasn't long before Lynn knew she couldn't continue being second best to Beth's career. It was like someone had flipped a switch within her, and everything she'd ever felt for Beth suddenly vanished. She was finally free.

"Just remember that intern won't have any more time for you than I did." Beth raised an eyebrow and smirked.

The heat on the back of her neck flamed again. Lynn wanted to smack that know-it-all look right off her face, but she'd be damned if she'd give her the satisfaction. "Go back to surgery, Beth. There's nothing in this department for you."

Beth's expression changed, and she seemed sad, almost sullen, like Lynn had taken away her favorite teddy bear. Maybe she really did regret her choices in life. She touched Lynn on the shoulder lightly before she strode toward the elevator but then turned back momentarily. "Wish me luck?"

She shook her head. "No. I won't do that. As I recall, you never thought luck had anything to do with the things that mattered." It was all about dedication and skill.

"True." Beth smiled slightly and turned and walked down the hallway.

Lynn suddenly felt sick to her stomach. She remembered everything about their life together clearly—the homework, the events, the horrible nights when Carrie was sick that she thought she'd never get through. She'd done it all alone, without a single bit of help from Beth. Doctors did miraculous things for other families, but not all of them took the time to do the same for their own.

Lynn had been the one to make all the sacrifices when Carrie had come into their lives. She'd loved her as though she were her own child. She hadn't been given a choice of whether to take her and raise her. The irresponsibility of her own sister had brought Carrie into their lives. She was a gift born from tragedy, and Lynn cherished the beautiful girl she'd been given. Nothing would ever change that fact.

From the corner of her eye, Maggie watched Lynn and Beth interact. She wasn't sure what that vise-grip handshake from Beth was about, but she wasn't about to lose eye contact with her during it, no matter how much it hurt. She wasn't Beth's surgical lead or even on her service, but the woman was intimidating as hell, and Maggie wouldn't let Lynn know that she made her nervous under any circumstances. Beth would have to do a lot more than crush the bones in her hand to make her give in to any intimidation.

Beth's surgical skills had always impressed her, but her personal skills left a lot to be desired. Maggie had sworn she'd never be like that: never send an intern to deliver news that begged for more questions or leave a patient worried about anything she said and definitely never let the woman she loved wonder if she was the most important aspect of her life. When Maggie had a family in the future, her wife and kids would have no doubt about the way she felt about them. She loved medicine, but she didn't intend to let it overshadow her happiness. Maggie wanted it all—the white picket fence, the wife, the kids, and the career.

What am I thinking? She shook her head. She was getting way ahead of herself. Kids were a long way off, and she was barely into her first year of residency. She had many long days and nights ahead of her. Not nearly enough spare time to start a relationship, let alone a family. Lynn immediately popped into her head, and she thought maybe she could make room for someone in her life.

Stacy dropped a tablet in front of her. "Can you look at this and give me a diagnosis?"

Maggie shrugged out of her thoughts and picked up the tablet. "Sure. What's going on?"

"Fifteen years old, heart rate's up, and she's presenting like she has the flu, but without fever now."

"But she had fever before?"

"Yep. The mother said it spiked at 102 three days ago."

"Light sensitivity?"

Stacy shook her head.

"So, what are you thinking?" she asked as she handed the tablet back to Stacy.

"Probably mono."

"That's what I'd look for. Doesn't present as meningitis. Did you get the blood work back?"

"No. Just sent it off a few minutes ago."

"You didn't really need my consult, did you?"

Stacy smiled. "I saw you talking to Lynn and her ex. What was that about?"

"Just trying to show me who's boss."

"Did it work?"

"Fuck, no." She flattened her lips. "If anything, it made me even more determined to stay present."

"Good choice," Stacy said with a grin. "What's your next move?"

"Not sure, but it'll happen soon. You coming?"

"Nope. I have another date."

"Wow. That's really working out for you."

"Seems to be. Good luck tonight." Stacy spun around and waved over her shoulder.

Maggie gripped the counter and took in a breath as she glimpsed Beth leaving Lynn in the hallway. Another factor she'd have to deal with if she continued down this path. Lynn was a spectacular woman, and it seemed everyone knew it.

CHAPTER ELEVEN

After being on her feet for a good ten hours straight, Maggie had ducked into the doctor's lounge to take a quick break because her feet were killing her. With them resting on the coffee table in front of her, she'd just cleared the images of the trauma from her mind when she heard the door open and then felt the couch cushion sink as someone sat next to her. She opened one eye slightly to see who had disturbed her zen and found Stacy staring at her.

"Great. You're awake."

"I am now."

Air whooshed out of a bag of potato chips as Stacy opened it. After taking a few, she held the bag out to Maggie.

"Thanks. I'm starving." She couldn't remember the last time she'd eaten. Maybe breakfast? The trauma had come in around lunchtime, and she hadn't stopped for anything until now.

"I just wanted to tell you how impressed I was with your triage and diagnosis out there earlier."

"You didn't do so badly yourself. How'd the surgery go?"

"It was awesome." Stacy twisted to face her and pulled her leg up underneath her on the couch. "We found a liver laceration while we were in there, and Dr. Cozzi let me stitch it up." Again, Stacy held out the small bag of chips she was eating from, and Maggie took a few more. The salt would do her good. "Is it weird that I'm so happy about that?"

Maggie chuckled. "Kinda, but I know what you mean." And she did. In order for any of the interns to get the education they needed and the satisfaction of performing well, someone had to get injured.

"You're going to love the surgical rotation."

"I'm sure I will, but I plan to go into general pediatrics, not trauma or surgery. I don't want a crazy schedule like that. I want a life."

"Well, you're not going to get much of that until you finish your internship and residency." Stacy looked at her like a lightbulb had gone off in her head. "Hey, maybe we can start a practice together. You handle the everyday stuff and I handle the surgery."

Maggie chuckled. "You're getting way ahead of me, Stace. Let's get to fourth year and then discuss it." Stacy was an amazing doctor, with her quick hands and great instincts. There would be worse doctors to go into practice with, but Maggie didn't want to limit her options just yet. She didn't know if Baltimore would be the right place for her if it meant having to get used to seeing Lynn living a life without her.

Lynn stuck her head in the room and glanced around the room.

"Hey, guess what, Lynn? Mags and I are going into practice together when we're done here."

Lynn's smile lit up the room, as usual. "That sounds awesome."

"Right? I'm going to handle surgery, and Mags will handle the kids in the office." The excitement in Stacy's voice was ridiculous, seeing as how that would happen, if it happened, at least four years from now.

Lynn focused her gaze on Maggie. "No surgery for you, Maggie?"

"Nope. I don't want to spend all my time at the hospital." Maggie was dedicated to the patient side of care. She wanted to make a difference in kids' lives by interacting and getting to know them as they grew from infancy through adolescence and then on to adulthood. That was the magic of pediatrics that enchanted Maggie. You didn't have a whole lot of continuity like that in surgery.

"Oh." Lynn hesitated like she was processing the information and then seemed to brush it away. "Have either of you seen Dr. Coz?" she asked. The experienced nurses never referred to the doctors by their full name. They either shortened it to the most common syllables or came up with some sort of nickname that fit their personality. Doctors came and went, but nurses usually stayed, and most of them had been there longer than any of the doctors. Lynn had probably used the respectful doctor prefix only because she was talking to first-year interns.

"Haven't seen him since the trauma came in earlier." The coffee table screeched against the floor when Maggie pulled her legs from it and stood. "Anything I can do to help?" She wouldn't pass up a chance to impress Lynn, no matter how big or small it might be.

"No, but thanks. I just need clarification on post-op care for the boy he took up to surgery earlier from the car accident."

"I can help," Stacy said as she popped off the couch and went to Lynn. "I assisted." She took the tablet from Lynn's hand, made a few extra notes, and handed it back. "How's that?"

Maggie crossed the room to the refrigerator, grabbed a soda, opened it, and took a sip as she watched Lynn interact with Stacy.

"Great. Thanks," Lynn said and glanced at Maggie.

A few minutes of silence passed, and Stacy seemed to notice the tension between them. "How about I check on him really quick?"

"Uh…Okay, thanks." Lynn handed her the tablet, and Stacy rushed out of the room. "No surgery, really?"

"No. I like kids. I want to interact with them."

"Beth always found surgery so exhilarating. I'm surprised you don't."

"I'm nothing like Beth." She set her soda on the coffee table and shortened the distance between them. "Don't you know that by now?"

"I haven't seen you in so long, Maggie. I don't really know much about you at all now."

Maggie moved closer and touched Lynn's hand with her fingers. "We can change that."

"You're so young, Maggie. You have a whole lifetime of people and experiences ahead of you."

"Don't do that." She shook her head but kept eye contact. "Dismiss me like I'm a child. I've known who I want to be since I was ten. And as for who I want to experience my life with, I've known that since the day I met you in the garden behind your house." Maggie touched her cheek. "I still remember the clothes you were wearing and the way the wind tousled your hair. That sweet smile and pink cheeks that the sun kissed softly. Your beautiful, welcoming, green eyes."

Lynn closed her eyes as she leaned her face into Maggie's hand and placed her hand on top of it. "That was long ago, Maggie."

"Seems like just yesterday to me." Maggie's heart pounded against her ribs as she stroked Lynn's cheek with her thumb, absorbing the softness of her skin. "I want that back." She'd held her feelings in long enough, and it felt good to let go. They were so close now, Maggie could feel Lynn's breath on her lips. All it would take was one more inch to put them together, and Maggie took it.

Lynn moved quickly, and Maggie's lips landed on her cheek. "I can't go back to that place in my life," she whispered into her ear. "You have no idea how hard it was for me to get past it. I'm happy with my life now."

"I know." Maggie let her hand drop to her side, backed up, blinked a few times, and glanced across the room to keep her eyes from welling. "You're married to Pam now, and she's wonderful."

"I'm not married to Pam." Lynn blew out a breath. "She's very happily married to someone else."

"What?" Maggie snapped her eyes back to Lynn. "I thought the two of you were a solid couple."

"I let you believe that because I thought it would be easier for you to let go."

"Are you fucking kidding me?" Maggie spun around and paced across the room. "Do you have any idea how knotted up I've been since I got here because I thought you were in love with someone else?" It had been the most miserable few weeks of her life. She couldn't even enjoy the news that Lynn wasn't involved with Pam because she was so angry right now.

"You just assumed and I let you." Lynn chewed on her bottom lip. "I shouldn't have, but when I realized what had happened, I thought it would be best to just go with it."

"And here I thought you didn't want anything to do with me because you'd fallen in love with someone else." She blew out a breath. "I guess I know where I stand now." It seemed Lynn didn't want to be with her, period. No other reason than that.

"Friends, Maggie. Can we just be that for now?"

"Yeah, sure. Friends. I can do that." She wanted to say so much more but couldn't. She would only push Lynn further away. "So work is the extent of your willingness to see me?" Now that she knew Lynn was free, it would be gut-wrenching at best to see her and not be able to touch her, like trying to hold lightning in a bottle, but she had no choice.

Lynn nodded. "Yeah. That and softball. If it makes you feel any better, I'm not interested in anything more than that with anyone. I like my life the way it is now. Uncomplicated."

Softball would be only once every few weeks. "Well, thanks for finally letting me know." She couldn't remember how many people she'd commented to about Pam and Lynn, trying to gain more information, but it was enough to make everyone think she was crazy for sure, since absolutely nothing was going on between them. She'd probably started a whole lot of rumors that Pam had to contain. Her wife must be either really understanding or totally pissed off by now.

❖

As the day continued, this newfound information had Maggie stewing herself into a ridiculous frenzy. She was angry that Lynn had let her go on believing she was involved with Pam, yet thrilled that she wasn't in a relationship. Also, Lynn hadn't given her a firm no on the future, hadn't said something between them was out of the question.

The tablet slapped against the counter when Maggie dropped it. "They're not married."

"Who?" Russell asked.

"Lynn and Pam."

"Not to each other." From the smile on Russell's face, it was clear that he enjoyed delivering the news. Maggie really liked him but was realizing he could be a real ass sometimes.

"Did you know that too?" she asked, giving Stacy her attention.

"Not until the other day. Russell got pulled in to assist with one of Pam's surgeries. He had to get her wife on the phone during the procedure to let her know she was running late."

"Her wife's a pediatrician and has a practice in the physicians' building." Russell chimed in again before he headed off to see another patient.

Stacy moved closer and whispered, "I also heard Lynn is divorced from the head of surgery, but I don't know if she's involved with anyone else."

"She's not." She closed her eyes and thought about what she'd said to Pam the morning after she'd gotten drunk and what she'd overheard her and Lynn saying outside the room. Pam was telling her that she needed to tell her the truth, that they weren't involved. "This is so embarrassing. Everyone must think I'm crazy."

"No worries. We've all been there, right? I mean I was there just last week with Russell." Stacy rubbed her back. "At least now you have a shot."

Did she really? This whole time, she'd thought Pam and Lynn were involved. Lynn hadn't told her differently. She'd just let Maggie go on believing it was true. Why? Was the thought of being with Maggie so terrible?

"Maybe, but now I need a plan."

Stacy rubbed her hands together. "I was hoping you wouldn't give up."

"She only wants to be friends."

Stacy's eyebrows flew up. "Did she say that?"

She nodded. "Won't spend any time with me outside of work except for softball."

"Is she involved with someone else?"

"No. She says she's happy with it that way, doesn't want to complicate her life."

"I say, you prove her wrong. Make her want to complicate it, make her want to complicate it with *you.*"

Maggie leaned against the counter and smiled. "You look so sweet on the outside, but you're a devious rule breaker, aren't you?"

"Any chance I get when it doesn't involve my own love life." She slid the tablet back into its slot. "I'm hungry. Let's grab a snack and do a little plotting."

Maggie soaked in the air-conditioning while the sunlight beamed through her windshield as she sat in her car in the softball-field parking lot. Stacy's plotting made her realize that every decision wasn't created in stone. The sculptor could chisel away at an incomplete sculpture and create something completely new.

Maggie would find a way to change her visibility in Lynn's life. She would do just as Stacy suggested and be the best complication Lynn could ever imagine. She'd started by checking the softball schedule to see when and where Lynn's team played, which just happened to be tonight. She planned to be at each of them. She wasn't about to fade into the black death of friendship.

"Are you playing today?" Andi's dark ponytail swung as she looked at the field and then back at Maggie.

"No. Just here to watch." As she headed to the bleachers, Maggie watched Andi run into the dugout and caught a glimpse of Lynn watching her. She waved, and Lynn waved back before she sat down on the bench.

The ballgame was a blur, and by the time Maggie arrived at the pizza place, the table was packed. Andi saw her enter and waved her down to the end where she was sitting with her group of friends. She stood up and prompted the girl next to her to move to the chair at the end of the table. Andi had already decided where Maggie sat, without any input from her, which was fine. At least someone wanted her company. It wasn't like Lynn had saved her a seat. Maggie took the chair Andi offered between her and one of her friends and introduced her to them all. Bev, Jamie, Rhonda, and Rita. She recited the names in her head, but she was distracted and knew the names would be lost in her memory by the end of the night. She could forget names, but not the way Lynn looked in her softball gear tonight. Her baseball pants were just tight enough to let Maggie's imagination run wild about what was underneath. She had perfect form as she vaulted from a squat, arm muscles flexing as she fired the ball back to the pitcher.

"Beer?" Andi asked.

"Sure." Maggie tried her best not to turn her head and glance at Lynn.

Andi filled the last empty mug with beer from the pitcher and slid it in front of her. Maggie took a gulp and let the cold brew cool her. The field had been hot today, and sitting in the stands had been almost unbearable. She could only imagine how hot it had been in the dugout. Women who oozed the pungent scent of sports surrounded her, and that was okay. She loved being part of a team sport, and that odor came with it.

The game had been pretty one-sided. Bat Intentions was good, with a combination of doctors, nurses, and paramedics on the team. All the women varied in size, which gave them great hitters and fast runners. Their normal pitcher, The Heater, as Andi had referred to her before, was there tonight. She was also known as Heather, Pam's wife, which was very apparent from the way they interacted.

"You're on the Heavy Hitters, right?" Andi asked.

She nodded.

"So what brought you to the game tonight?"

She glanced down at the other end of the long table, where Lynn, Pam, and Heather were seated.

"Oh, that's right. You're a friend of the doc's."

"I'd call her more of a mentor. She's been good to me." She was interested in Andi but having a hard time keeping her eyes from drifting toward Lynn. "So, what made you want to become a paramedic?"

"My dad was a firefighter, and I always admired the way he helped people even when he was off duty."

"So you're a firefighter and a paramedic?"

"No, just a paramedic. Having the courage to run into a burning building is impressive, but I could never do it on a regular basis. So I left that part to my dad."

"Still, handling medical situations on the fly in all kinds of conditions is impressive as well."

"Not really." Andi shrugged. "It's just what I do."

Maggie smiled at her humbleness. "What's your favorite part of the job?"

"Honestly?"

"Of course."

"Having the ability to help someone."

"I know what you mean about the helping-people part, but doing it anywhere sounds stressful."

Andi chuckled. "It was at first. I was terrified. But after a lot of practice I got used to it, and now it's kind of second nature."

"Well, Andi, I have to say I admire you for that."

Andi's cheeks reddened, and she looked away before she took a drink of her beer.

"I'll be right back." Maggie went to the bathroom and was surprised when Lynn met her at the door as she came out.

"Andi seems to like you. You should take advantage of that possibility," Lynn said softly as she propped her shoulder against the wall in the small hallway.

She leaned against the wall as well and stared into Lynn's eyes. "Should I?"

Judging by Lynn's body language, she didn't seem too certain of her advice.

"Why not? She's cute, sweet, and around your age."

"Really?" She rolled her eyes and shook her head. "I don't need a matchmaker, Lynn." She pushed off the wall. "I'm not looking for relationship advice from anyone—especially you. If you think Andi's so special, why don't you hang out with her for a while."

"Calm down." Lynn glanced over her shoulder. "Why are you so angry?"

"I don't want to calm down. You have no idea how hard this is for me."

Lynn's eyebrows flew up. "I have a pretty good idea."

"Then stop trying to push me into something with someone else." She raced past her to the door and left the place as quickly as she could. Once she was outside she braced herself against the building. How horrible of her. What would Andi think of her leaving like that, without even saying good-bye? She didn't have anything against her. In fact, Andi had been nothing but super-sweet to her the whole evening. She'd just made up her mind to go back inside and tell her she was leaving, when Andi came out the door.

"Lynn said you left. Are you okay?"

"I've been better." She sighed. "Listen. I really like you, Andi, and you may not have anything else in mind for us besides friendship, but I have to let you know that my heart isn't open to anything but that right now."

Andi scrunched her eyebrows. "Bad breakup?"

"No. It's something that never really got started, and I can't let it go just yet."

Andi rolled her lips in and shook her head. "Friends it is." She hooked her thumb over her shoulder toward the door. "You want to come back in and have another beer?"

"Thanks, but I'm just going to take off."

"Okay. I'll walk you to your car."

"You don't have to do that."

"Yeah, I do. It's getting dark, and you're kind of tiny."

Maggie chuckled, and they walked the short distance to her car. It *was* getting dark, but Maggie wasn't really that tiny. Well, maybe compared to Andi. She stopped in front of the silver Honda Civic. "This is me."

"Will I see you at the next game?" Andi opened her arms in front of her.

"Count on it." She moved into Andi's arms, and Andi gave her a long hug. Once she was in her car, she watched Andi go back inside and cursed herself for not being able to move on. Lynn was right. Andi was cute and sweet, and from her reaction a few minutes ago, it seemed she was interested. But Maggie just couldn't follow that path until the other one ran its course.

CHAPTER TWELVE

Maggie was late, the game was almost over, but it had been a hell of a week at work. Having Lynn purposely avoid her the past few days had topped it off. It was probably for the best, considering the conversation they'd had after the last baseball game, but she had committed to being present and in Lynn's line of sight whether she liked it or not, and that was exactly what she planned to do.

After the way Maggie had left the previous game's after-pizza get-together, she hadn't expected the frantic wave Andi gave her as she strolled toward the field. Andi had been very sweet about the whole situation. She sprinted out of the dugout and met Maggie halfway, swept her into a hug, and squeezed her.

"How are you doing today, champ?" Andi asked with a huge smile as she dropped her to the ground.

"I'm better now." She couldn't stop the grin from taking over her face. "I should schedule a hug from you every day."

"That's what I like to hear." Andi pointed to the bleachers behind the dugout. "The game's almost over, but we're going for pizza after."

"That's why I'm here." And to keep herself present in Lynn's mind. Maggie glanced into the dugout. She'd never seen this particular look on Lynn's face before and thought it best not to explore it right now. Unintentionally, she was stirring up the jealousy demons in Lynn, and it felt good to know she really did care. She waved and headed up the bleachers, finding a seat so she could watch the last inning of the game.

When she arrived at the restaurant, she didn't hesitate to enter, and even though she spotted an empty seat next to Lynn, she chose to take one with Andi and her friends. She needed a safe zone right now. The pizza had already been ordered, and a mug of beer was waiting for her in front of the empty chair next to Andi, who immediately stood and pulled out the chair for her. She kind of liked being pampered.

Maggie enjoyed the weird stories about what happened to Andi and her friends on ambulance calls, and after her third slice of pizza, she was afraid she might explode. She heard laughter from the other end of the table and saw that Pam had gotten up from her chair and was mixing with others still seated on her side of the table. When she made her way to the end where Maggie was sitting, Pam leaned down, patted her shoulder, and whispered in her ear. "You seem to be having fun, and you're doing a hell of a good job of keeping someone's interest."

"I *am* having fun." She glanced to the other end of the table to find Lynn watching them. "That's good to hear, but it's not my intent."

"Why don't you come join us for a few minutes?" Pam asked.

She smiled. "I really am having a good time at this end of the table, so maybe next game?"

"You're playing with fire, girl. I hope you can juggle it." Pam chuckled as she walked around the table and back to her seat.

Maggie forced herself not to look that way. She didn't want to drop everything she was doing and everyone she was with when someone sparked an interest romantically. Even if it was Lynn. She wasn't lying to Pam or herself. She really did like Andi and her friends Bev, Jamie, Rhonda, and Rita. They were beautiful people who made her feel comfortable without any strings attached. She felt part of something and hadn't had anything close to that feeling since she'd entered medical school. Even though other students had taken the journey with her, it was a solitary adventure, and the loneliness could be unbearable at times. She'd been invited in and wanted to be part of this softball tribe.

"The doc?" Andi scrunched up her nose. "Really? You know she's married to The Heater." The Heater was Heather's nickname because she could fire a fastball pitch harder than anyone else in the league.

"You don't think I should go after her?" Maggie said with a chuckle.

Andi smiled widely. "She'd be a challenge, but hey. If that's who you're stuck on, go for it."

Maggie laughed out loud. "You're such a team player. You know that?"

Andi shrugged. "I do what I can."

"Although Pam is all-around adorable, it's not her."

Andi glanced over her shoulder. "Ooh. It's the nurse." She stared down the table.

Maggie couldn't stop herself from glancing over her shoulder as well. Pam had taken her seat next to Lynn and was whispering in her ear. When Lynn looked Maggie's way and stared back at her, the disappointment on her face was clear, and Maggie didn't know how to feel. Hadn't Lynn told her more than once she only wanted to be friends? Did being available whenever Lynn wanted her company constitute friendship? Maybe all this being-present stuff was actually working. She forced herself to stay seated and focused on Andi again. It was bad of her, but Maggie found the feeling very satisfying in an odd sort of way. Lynn must've expected her to jump up and run to her like a little puppy dog.

"Whoa," Andi said. "Something's clearly going on between you two."

She let out a sigh. "Only in my mind. A one-sided romance does not a couple make."

"From the look you just got and the daggers I'm feeling now, I don't think it's all one-sided." Andi leaned back in her chair and smiled. "You want to talk about it?" She was the sweetest person ever. She'd totally backed off romantically, and here she was wanting to help with whatever she had going on with Lynn.

Rita came back to the table with a new pitcher of beer and filled everyone's mug except Maggie's. Andi glanced up at Rita, who was eyeing her, and immediately took the pitcher and filled Maggie's mug.

"Looks like you've got something of your own going on there."

"Only on her terms." Andi shook her head. "She's jealous."

"Seriously?"

"Well, you are kinda hot."

"Oh my God. Stop." Heat was rushing up her neck.

"Lookie there. You don't even know it." Andi winked. "You want to get out of here? I suddenly feel like we're in a fishbowl."

Maggie rolled the suggestion around in her head for a minute as she glanced around the table and caught the masses of suddenly averted eyes. "Sure," she said, and stood. She and Andi were good on the friendship thing, but did she expect more?

"Hey," Rita said. "Where you going? It's early, and you haven't finished your beer."

"I've had enough for the night," Andi said as she put her hand on the small of Maggie's back and guided her in front of her. She put up her other hand, waved, and said, "See you guys next game."

Various people at the table said their good-byes, including Pam. Lynn said nothing. She only stared. All eyes were on them as they left. The fishbowl was getting smaller. Maggie hoped she wasn't making a huge mistake.

"That was awkward," Maggie said as they crossed the parking lot to her car.

"They're just used to having things the way they've always been." Andi opened the door for her and held it while she got in.

"And you've always been with Rita?" Strange. Maggie hadn't seen any romantic interaction between them to indicate they were in a relationship, except the subtle passive-aggressive move of not filling her mug with beer tonight.

"On and off. She doesn't want to commit, and that's hard for me." She flattened her lips. "Follow me," Andi said before rounding the car and going to her truck.

She put the car in reverse and backed out. Andi obviously wanted more with Rita, but the situation sounded just as frustrating as her own.

Within a couple of minutes, they'd pulled into a parking lot of a nearby park.

As Maggie opened the car door, Andi rushed over and grabbed it. Chivalry wasn't as dead as everyone claimed, at least not in Andi Denison's world.

"There's a nice spot out here by the pond where we can relax and watch the ducks."

Once they found a bench to sit on, they lingered in silence as the ducks swam slowly around the pond, back and forth. They mesmerized Maggie.

"How long have you and Rita been on and off?"

"A couple of years."

"Want to tell me about it?"

Andi pulled her lip up to one side. "That's my line."

"How about we tell each other?" Maggie went on to explain how she'd fallen in love with Lynn when she was still married to Beth and the complication of being best friends with Carrie. Andi seemed to understand much better and to get the connection Maggie felt with Lynn.

The lights came on in the park, and Maggie glanced at her watch. She hadn't realized they'd been talking for close to two hours. They both looked ahead, focusing on the lights illuminating the pathway back to the parking lot. Maggie slid into her car and fired the engine as she watched Andi cross behind her to her truck.

The night hadn't started out well, but her conversation with Andi had made it better. She wasn't the only one in the world pining for something she couldn't have, and for some reason, that eased her mind a bit. She just needed to relax and wait it out, but in the meantime the two of them could help each other. The idea of a pairing between Andi and Maggie seemed to bother both Lynn and Rita. She liked spending time with Andi, and if that became a catalyst to her happiness in any way, then all the better.

❖

When Maggie had arrived at the hospital this morning, no one was more surprised than her when she received a page to report to Beth's office. Their unexpected encounter the week before had been chilly at best.

The assistant looked up from the note she was writing and raised her finger, signaling her to wait. She stood patiently outside the chief of surgery's office while the assistant finished the phone call she was handling. Once she was done, she got up from her chair, rounded the desk, and opened the door. "Dr. Randall is here."

She heard Beth say, "Send her in." And the assistant moved aside and motioned her in.

"Dr. Randall. Come in and have a seat," Beth said as she finished signing a document and sliding it into a manila file folder. "I'm sure you're wondering why I've asked to see you."

Maggie nodded. "Actually, yes."

"I've lost a first-year in surgery and need to move you over for your first rotation." Beth spoke matter-of-factly, as if Maggie didn't have a choice, which she didn't. Even though she knew why Beth was switching her, refusing to cooperate would be political suicide. Beth could end her time at Johns Hopkins immediately.

"Dr. Monroe, may I ask why me? I mean, as you can probably see from my file, I'm not looking at surgery for my field of medicine."

Beth studied her for a moment. "I've been watching you and have, indeed, checked your records from Boston. You're the top of your year, and I need that in surgery right now." She relaxed into her chair. "Lynn speaks highly of you as well."

Had Lynn really been talking to Beth about her? Although she knew she could do it, she wasn't expecting a surgery rotation right out of the gate, especially not when she'd already started another. Maggie slid her hands down her thighs, smoothing the cotton scrubs covering them. When her fingers reached her knees, she held them there. "When do I start?"

After Maggie exited the elevator, she went straight to rounds. She'd barely made it to the floor before Lynn tracked her down.

"You're switching to surgery?"

"Jesus, word travels fast here. I literally *just* left Beth's office."

"Why would you switch? You told me you didn't have an interest in surgery."

"It's not like I had a choice. When the chief of surgery asks you to do something, you do it."

"Beth changed your rotation?"

She nodded. "She said you speak highly of me."

Lynn opened her mouth and then closed it again. "I'll take care of this."

She grabbed Lynn's arm and pulled her into an on-call room. "No. You *will not* take care of this. You won't do anything. I'm going to have to complete the surgery rotation at some time, so it might as well be now."

"She's doing it because—"

"Because she's jealous, right? Wants to keep me busy and away from you?"

Lynn nodded. "She saw us together and made an assumption."

"We can always make that assumption true." She moved closer.

"Maggie." Lynn shook her head. "This is not the time for that."

She raised her eyebrows and smiled. "So there may be a time for that?"

"No."

Maggie's heart sank, and from the look on Lynn's face she could see her reaction.

"I mean, maybe. I don't know."

Her stomach did a somersault, and her heart raced. It wasn't a no. She suddenly had hope. "I'll take that for now." She ran her hand down Lynn's arm before she spun around and bounced out of the on-call room. If she was switching services in the morning, she had some patients to hand off this afternoon.

CHAPTER THIRTEEN

Maggie slid the simple black scoop-neck, spaghetti-strap dress over her head and smoothed it with her palms. She turned and looked at the back, which had a reinforced cross-back with a cutout that would keep her boobs seated firmly in the front. It would be perfect for tonight—not too hot, not too cool, just long enough to cover her knees, and just a little bit sexy. She wasn't trying to attract anyone, but she still liked to look good when she went out. She sat on the edge of the bed and slipped on her black open-toed, strappy heels. They'd probably come off halfway through the night, but they set off the dress perfectly. She draped her bolero sweater over her arm and picked up her clutch as she left her apartment.

During their long talk at the park, Maggie and Andi decided to help each other. Rita had declined to go to Andi's cousin's wedding with her, so Maggie had agreed to be her date for the event. She knew what it was like to go to weddings alone, to be the person people flocked to only because they thought you were unhappy and lonely. She was happy to help Andi. She'd have a nice dinner, a few drinks, and some great conversation with Andi. Life could be worse.

The wedding wasn't until seven thirty, but since Maggie's apartment was in the opposite direction, she was supposed to meet Andi at the ballpark at six. Time was tight, so Maggie would then take Andi to her place to shower and get dressed. Andi had messaged Maggie and told her she'd just come off her shift at the firehouse and caught a ride to the game with Rita.

She pulled into a spot at the end of the row closest to the field and got out of her car. Andi must have been watching for her because she sprinted from left field to the fence as she walked closer.

"We're almost done. The inning's almost over, they have one at-bat left, and I think The Heater's going to put her to bed quickly," Andi said with a grin.

She grinned and raised an eyebrow. "That almost sounds fun, and a little dangerous."

Andi laughed as her gaze floated down Maggie's body. "You look spectacular, by the way." She ran back to the field, and at that moment she heard the commotion at home plate. She turned to see that Lynn had thrown off her catcher's mask and was scrambling for the ball and then launched it to first base.

"Maybe you should wait in the car," Andi shouted. "Apparently, you're distracting the catcher."

Maggie almost couldn't contain her excitement as she caught Lynn looking her way. She waved before she spun and walked back to the car. *She missed the catch because of me.* That was definitely a good sign. Her night had officially been made. No matter what else happened tonight, it would be insignificant compared to that information.

She watched from the driver's seat as Andi gathered her softball gear and came out of the dugout. Suddenly Rita was right behind Andi, grabbing her by the arm. The conversation didn't look friendly, and when Andi broke away, Rita watched her walk the full way to Maggie's car. She popped the trunk so Andi could stow her bag before she slid into the passenger side of the Civic.

"You okay?"

"Yep," Andi said with certainty.

"She's pissed you're taking me to the wedding."

"She has no say in who I take. I asked her first." Andi took in a deep breath and glanced over at her. "But hey. You and that dress got some attention."

Maggie chuckled as she backed out of the parking spot. "Looks like it."

"Good move."

"If you haven't noticed, I know how to play this game, and I'm pretty competitive." She pulled to the exit. "You're my navigator, so which way?"

Andi's apartment was only about a fifteen-minute drive from the field. She'd given Maggie the game play-by-play as they drove and explained that The Heater threw fast and hard, and Lynn was the only catcher who could handle her pitches. She'd also said that Lynn had asked where she was, and it had surprised Maggie that Lynn had let anyone know she was curious about her. Maggie had thought she'd wanted to keep their interactions to a minimum. She'd see how long that lasted. Her resolve seemed to be weakening.

❖

The wedding venue was located on Baltimore Harbor, right on the water. The short ceremony had been held on the harbor's outside patio on a glorious day. The sun was shining and the humidity at a minimum, thankfully. After they stepped inside for the reception, they stopped in the doorway, waiting in line to enter. From where they stood, Maggie could see windows spanning one side of the room. The venue had been beautifully decorated with elegant cream linen tablecloths on each of the twenty tables that surrounded the wooden dance floor centering the room. Eight padded, gold, wicker-back dining chairs, which seemed to be just the right amount for the size, encompassed each round table. A lit pillar candle surrounded by cream-colored roses and leafy greenery centered each tablecloth. Maggie took a deep breath. She wanted something similar someday—with not nearly as many guests, but a venue just as beautiful.

When they finally reached the head of the line, a woman standing by a table located by the door asked for their names and told them their table number. Andi rushed directly to theirs to assess the name tags lying in front of every place setting. She immediately picked up theirs, went to a table by the window, and traded two of the name tags with theirs.

"I like these seats better," Andi said as she pulled out the chair for Maggie and then rushed back to the other table and dropped the tags in front of the place settings.

Maggie couldn't help the grin that came across her face as she watched Andi walk to the bar to get their drinks. Dressed in a snug-fitting black suit with a double-breasted jacket, white shirt, and leather-and-turquoise bolo tie around the collar, she was heart-stoppingly handsome. She oozed confidence and definitely knew what she wanted, at least around her family. A glass of white wine magically appeared from over Maggie's head and landed in front of her before Andi slid into the chair next to her.

Andi pointed to the wineglass in front of Maggie. "I hope that's okay. I thought I remembered you told me you liked pinot grigio."

"Thank you. I do." She took a sip and then set her glass on the table. "You're sneaky."

"If I have to be here, I'm going to at least enjoy the view." Andi grinned and leaned closer. "I mean the view outside as well as the view sitting beside me."

"Wow. You *really are* a charmer." She sincerely hoped Andi was just flirting harmlessly, because she wasn't up to giving her the friends spiel again.

"That's no lie. You're absolutely beautiful tonight." Andi smiled and then veered her attention to the center of the room. "My cousin put us at the table with all her single friends." She took a sip of the amber liquid in her highball glass. "She's always trying to set me up."

"I take it you don't like that?"

Andi shook her head. "Not at family events. These are sacred times when you shouldn't have to be on display."

"Gotcha." She was glad Andi didn't think she had to put on a show for her. Maggie liked that Andi seemed to be a genuine, caring person, and Maggie found her interesting to talk to about anything and everything. "So, who did you stick at the singles table?"

"Aunt Sylvia and Uncle George. She's the matchmaker of the family. I can't speak for George or the singles, but Sylvia will have a great time there."

Maggie laughed. "I'm impressed. You've thought this out carefully."

"Always." Andi lifted her glass in cheers, and Maggie clinked her wineglass against it.

After dinner, Maggie stared out onto the harbor as the sunset glistened off the water. Andi had gone to get them dessert, but Maggie was full. The broiled lobster had been delicious, so much so that she'd eaten the whole tail plus the creamed potatoes and asparagus that had accompanied it. Even though her full stomach was making her regret eating it all, she would forgive herself the indulgence this time, since she rarely got to experience that kind of meal.

"We have three choices of cake. Can you believe that?" Andi asked as she took multiple plates with slices of Bavarian-cream-filled yellow, chocolate mocha, and red velvet cakes from the tray she held and set them on the table in front of everyone. "I got several of each." She'd brought enough for everyone at the table, another sign that she was a great catch, if only Maggie were fishing right now.

She'd been watching the other couples at the table, made up of Andi's older cousins and aunts and uncles, interact all night. They all seemed to be very attentive to each other and genuinely happy to be together, something Maggie had dreamed of having with Lynn but would probably never happen. Her life would go on, but she couldn't conceive of having that kind of bond with anyone other than Lynn right now.

"What's up with you?" Andi's voice broke through her thoughts. "You look like you're thinking about something serious." She raised an eyebrow. "Don't tell me it's about work."

"No. Not at all. Just love." She sighed. "And how ridiculously complicated it is." She took a gulp of water and set it next to her almost-full glass of wine. She didn't dare drink any more wine for fear that Andi would fill her glass again. She was an excellent date, but Maggie had abandoned the wine after her second glass since Andi was on her fourth glass of whiskey and seemed to be having a great time.

"I hear that." She drank the remaining whiskey in her glass. "I've never asked anything of Rita other than to be exclusive, and she won't. It's not like I'm trying to change her life." She rubbed her face. "I just love her so much. I wish she could see that."

"I'm sure she does, and that's probably what scares her."

"I know. It's hard for me to detach and just be one of her girls. I want to be *the only* girl in her life."

"Seems to me like you've done a good job of backing off." Maggie smiled slightly. "I wouldn't be here with you tonight if you hadn't."

"It's not like you have any romantic interest in me," Andi said, moving her head closer.

Maggie met her halfway and leaned forehead to forehead with her. "If circumstances were different, I definitely would. You're such a great person. Just tonight, I've seen so much more of how special you are. I'm sorry Rita isn't here to see it too."

Andi broke the contact and raised her glass. "Friends?"

Maggie clinked her glass with Andi's. "Always."

Only a drop of whiskey was left in Andi's glass as she put it to her lips. Andi cleared her throat of emotion and said, "I need a refill." She got up from the table and headed across the room.

As Maggie watched her weave through the tables to the bar, she couldn't help feeling sad for her. She was in the same boat, only different, in that at least Rita gave Andi some of her time. Lynn wouldn't give Maggie any of hers. Maybe that was better. Once she got a taste of what her life would be like with Lynn, she didn't know if she'd ever be able to return to not having her be a part of it.

❖

Andi fumbled for the keys in her pocket and handed them to Maggie. The drive had been interesting. Andi had repeatedly opened the window for fresh air, and Maggie had closed it each time. Maggie's hair was now windblown beyond belief. She brushed it from her eyes as she tried to key the lock. Once she had the key in, she turned the knob and pushed open the door.

The sight of Andi's lips coming at her when she looked up had been unexpected and unwanted. Their lips met softly, but she wasn't moving Andi out of the friend realm, and that meant all sexual activities and any kind of actions that might lead to sex were off-limits.

Maggie put her hands on Andi's chest and urged her back. "Although that was nice, we both know nothing's going to happen here."

Andi chuckled. "You're so practical."

"I am." She opened the door. "Now get inside before your neighbors start complaining."

Andi weaved her way around the living-room furniture to the kitchen. "You want another drink? Wine? Beer?" She took a bottle of whiskey from the cabinet.

She rushed to her, took the bottle, and slid it back onto the shelf. "No. And you don't need one either."

"No one wants me. I need to drown my sorrows." Andi retrieved the bottle.

"Stop that right now." She swiped the bottle from Andi's hand and held it out of her reach. "If I wasn't so screwed up about Lynn, I'd take you up on anything you had to offer. Plenty of women would kill for a chance to be with you. Rita must be crazy."

Andi leaned against the counter and raised an eyebrow. "As soon as you leave, I'm going to get that bottle."

"Then I guess I'll stay." She took Andi's hand and pulled her forward. "Where's your bedroom?"

Andi chuckled. "You're the first woman who's ever dragged me to bed."

She laughed. "Just stop," she said with a laugh as she pushed Andi's jacket from her shoulders. "You looked very dapper tonight."

"Did I?" Andi grinned.

"You did." She pushed Andi onto the bed and raised her feet to the bottom of it. "Too bad there weren't any lesbians there to notice."

"Yeah. My family doesn't attract them. Totally straight." Andi smiled up at her. "It's a curse."

Maggie glanced around the bedroom, looking for any type of extra blanket or throw. "I'm gonna a grab a blanket from the..."

"Hall closet."

The closet had multiple sheet sets and blankets. She reached for one of the blankets and then peeked into the room across the hall, which was furnished with another queen-sized bed.

"You're coming back in *here*, right? I want to talk more," Andi shouted from the bedroom.

She sighed. "I'll be in after I go to the bathroom."

"There's a new toothbrush in the drawer." Andi's voice carried loudly through the small two-bedroom apartment.

She washed her face and then found the toothbrush in the drawer and brushed her teeth. By the time she got back to the bedroom, Andi was asleep. She covered her with the blanket she'd taken from the closet and then slid under the bed covers next to her and felt her chest. Still breathing. That was good. She'd never seen someone drink so much whiskey. Even though there was only a finger's worth in the highball glass, Andi had downed many of them. Maggie would've been drunk by the second glass. Andi was larger than she was and seemed to have a tolerance for alcohol, but she'd probably have a helluva hangover in the morning.

❖

The smell of bacon filled the bedroom. Maggie opened her eyes and saw that Andi was gone. Some watchdog she was. Maggie hadn't even heard her sneak out. She rolled out of bed, went to the bathroom, peed, washed her hands, brushed her teeth, and checked herself in the reflection. The minimal makeup she'd been wearing last night was now smudged under her eyes. That plus her lack of sleep had created dark circles under them that removing the makeup would minimize only slightly. She wet her hands again and raked her fingers through her hair to fluff the flattened areas created from sleeping on one side, watching Andi, most of the night.

Once completely satisfied that she wouldn't scare anyone, Maggie went to the kitchen, stopped at the entrance, and watched Andi, now dressed in dark-blue shorts and a gray T-shirt, cook. The bacon was already done, and she was scrambling eggs. She whisked some kind of seasoning she'd taken from the cabinet into the bowl and then poured the eggs into a pan on the stove before she turned to set the bowl in the sink.

Maggie grinned. "Good morning, sunshine."

"Good morning," Andi said with a sheepish smile. "Sorry I drank so much last night."

She raised her eyebrows. "Are you feeling okay?"

"Yeah. I'm good. Just need some protein." She picked up the plate of bacon and held it in front of Maggie.

She took a piece, bit the end off, and moaned. "Do you know how long it's been since I've had home-cooked bacon?"

"I made plenty." Andi took the plate to the table. "Coffee?"

"I'd love some." That would be her only saving grace today. She didn't have to work, but there was cleaning and grocery shopping to do. Once Maggie got home, she wouldn't want to go out again, but she couldn't stop at the store dressed the way she was. She'd call Stacy on her way home to see if she could do the shopping. The two of them hadn't lived together that long, but they'd found a grocery phone app they could share to make sure they didn't buy too much or too little food for the week.

Andi handed her a cup of coffee and pointed to the table. "Sit. The eggs will be done in a minute."

The table had already been set with plates and silverware and a glass of orange juice by each of the plates. Maggie had to admit the food smelled wonderful when Andi brought it to the table. In addition to the bacon, Andi had cooked eggs, toast, and a couple of small steaks that Maggie hadn't noticed when she was in the kitchen. Maggie never ate like this at home alone, but since Andi was a paramedic and lived at the fire station during her shifts, it was probably the norm for her.

The chair screeched as it slid across the linoleum floor when Andi pulled it away from the table. "I've got milk if you want it."

"Juice is good." She picked up the glass and took a gulp. "Does your family know about Rita?"

"Yeah. They've met her, but they're not too keen on her. She acts weird when she comes to family events," Andi said as she took the seat across from her. "They can see she hasn't gone all in on the relationship."

"Friends and family are pretty perceptive about those things."

"I'm not sure how to make that happen." Andi chuckled. "Aren't we a pair?"

Maggie nodded as she chewed the bite she'd just taken and then wiped her mouth. "Right? Forever destined to pine for women we can't have."

"At least I'm in good company." Andi stared at her plate as she filled her fork and shoveled another bite into her mouth.

"You're an awesome cook." Another reason Andi would be a good catch. Why couldn't she just move on to someone like Andi? She studied her long lashes and full lips, and caught herself moving her gaze down to her strong arms and imagining the muscled abs underneath her T-shirt. That needed to stop right now, or both of them would end up getting hurt.

Andi finished her breakfast and looked up from her plate. "You want to shower and change into one of my T-shirts and some shorts? You'll probably swim in them."

"Thanks, but I'm just gonna go home and shower there." She ate a last forkful of eggs. "These are really good."

"Secret spices for special guests." Andi winked. "You'll have to stay over again sometime."

"I just might do that." She grinned. Andi was so sweet, she just wished she had someone to come home to. Maggie wasn't ready to let go of her hopes for Lynn, or she'd definitely take a chance on romance with her.

Andi insisted on walking Maggie to her car, and just as she opened the door for her, Maggie glanced over Andi's shoulder and caught a glimpse of Rita's blacked-out Dodge Charger parked farther down in the lot. She gave Andi a hug and held on for a few minutes until she heard a car start and saw the Charger drive away, Rita staring out the window at them. Maybe Rita cared a little more than she wanted to let on.

She'd had a great time with Andi at the wedding, even with all the questions she'd had to field from her family about who she was and how they knew each other. They'd finally accepted the fact that they were friends after the umpteenth time both she and Andi had told them. Andi had said not to worry and had reaffirmed throughout the night that she knew where they stood, even though it was fun having Maggie as her date for the night. The whole night and morning had been an absolute pleasure. Rita should wise up and see what was in front of her.

CHAPTER FOURTEEN

Lynn rolled over and looked at the large red numbers of the alarm clock on her nightstand. It was almost six, but the sun wasn't up quite yet. Daylight savings time always wreaked havoc on her sleeping habits, and this morning had been no exception. She'd finally drifted off to sleep around three but had been ridiculously restless. She'd been so focused on Maggie, she hadn't gotten more than a couple hours of sleep. At the game last night, when she'd seen her drive up and get out of her car, her mind had filled with so many thoughts, and she couldn't take her eyes off her. The sexy spaghetti-strap dress showed her every curve, and the legs peeking out below the bottom were gorgeous. Lynn hadn't even seen the ball until it hit her in the chest. Thank God she wore a thick pad for protection, or her girls would be super-sore today.

The thing that hurt more than the hit was that Maggie knew she'd missed that play because of her. She had to have noticed Lynn's error. When Maggie had waved and gone back to her car, all she wanted to do was follow her and stop her from going out with Andi. But that would involve telling Maggie how she felt about her, and she still had too many unknowns, too many life choices to make for that.

Since going back to sleep was out of the question, she got up, went to the kitchen, and rummaged through the cabinet. There she located the ingredients for a pound cake and got started. Baking soothed her when she was stressed, and she'd found herself doing a lot of that lately. Once the cake was in the oven, she showered and threw on some sweatpants and a T-shirt before making a pot of coffee.

By the time the sun came up, the cake was out of the oven and cooled somewhat. She found herself cutting a couple of slices and wrapping them in foil before she refilled her coffee cup and then did the exact opposite of what she should. She left her apartment and took the elevator down a floor, went to Maggie's apartment, and knocked on the door. Then she knocked again, only harder this time. No answer. She glanced at her watch. It was after seven, so she'd probably already gone out for her run. Lynn headed to the elevator and went to the lobby to see if she could catch her when she got back. Her life had been turned completely upside-down since Maggie came back to Baltimore, and the constant struggle she was battling within wasn't getting any better. Who knew a single kiss that had occurred years ago could linger for so long? She had to get her feelings for Maggie under control, and having Maggie's participation seemed to be the only way to resolve them.

Many people had come in and out of the lobby since Lynn arrived. Seated close to the elevator in the lobby, not reading the paper, for at least an hour, she was beginning to wonder if Maggie was still upstairs in her apartment and just hadn't heard the knock. But then Maggie rushed through the front door of the complex, and Lynn's stomach bottomed out when she glimpsed her. She was still wearing the same dress she'd showed up in at the softball field last night, her shoes swinging in her hand, held only by the straps. *She went home with Andi.* So many thoughts swarmed her mind. Did they have sex? *Probably.* Was she going to do it again? *Of course she is.* Had she lost her only chance with Maggie? *Absolutely.* Her heart pounded. She hadn't realized until now how deep her feelings for Maggie went.

Maggie stopped when she noticed Lynn staring, glanced around the lobby, and then seemed to take a deep breath, straighten her shoulders, and press forward. Sitting here, waiting for Maggie this morning was a bad idea, and seeing her come home from her date only confirmed that Maggie belonged with someone else. Someone her own age.

She glanced up from the paper she held as Maggie passed and said, "You certainly jumped all in on that one." *Did I really say that?* Where was her even-tempered restraint when she needed it? She cursed herself for noticing how good Maggie looked and for becoming uncontrollably jealous.

Maggie stopped like someone had hit her square in the back with a water balloon, balled her fists like Lynn had seen her do many times before when she was preparing to stand her ground, and turned around. "Isn't that what you told me to do?" she asked, her eyes narrowed and focused.

"The dress, the hair…" Lynn looked her up and down. Even fourteen hours later and disheveled, Maggie was still beautiful. "Everything was probably hard for Andi to resist."

Maggie's hand went to her hip. "You told me you didn't want me, so sue me for looking good for someone else."

She wasn't just looking good. She was looking spectacular. "You're right. I did say that." Lynn swallowed and rolled her lips in. "I take it all back." And she did. Her heart was pleading with her to tell Maggie how she felt, but her head was still hesitating.

The strappy shoes cut through the air as Maggie swung them over her shoulder. "Because you're jealous?"

The vision in front of Lynn had just become even sexier, and her mind scattered. "No. Yes. I don't know." She folded the paper in her lap and tossed it onto the table next to her.

"That's not an answer I can accept. I need you to know why." She stared into Lynn's eyes, obviously waiting for more, but Lynn didn't say another word. "Listen," Maggie said and let out a heavy breath. "I'm tired and I need to shower, so can we continue this conversation another time?"

"No need to continue. It's not my business." And it wasn't, but damn it. She wanted it to be more than she ever had before.

Her stomach swirled as she watched Maggie walk to the elevator. She ached to follow her, run her hand across the bare skin peeking out from the open spot on the back of her dress. She took in a breath and picked up the paper. She would read the same line she'd read a thousand times already this morning again before she headed up to her own apartment in a few minutes.

❖

Maggie's shift was halfway over, and she hadn't seen Lynn at all again today, just as she hadn't seen her over the past few days after their encounter in the apartment lobby. She didn't know where she was in the hospital, but it seemed as though she'd been avoiding her since they talked Saturday morning. It had been a bad idea to make Lynn jealous.

The only thing letting Lynn think she'd slept with Andi did was let her know Maggie was looking for casual sex with anyone to fill the void, and that was far from the truth.

She didn't want Lynn for a quick fuck. She wanted her for a lifetime. She wasn't sure what had actually happened during their conversation in the lobby. It was clear that Lynn was upset. She'd said things that had made Maggie defensive, and she hadn't come clean about not sleeping with Andi. She'd only fueled the jealousy Lynn was displaying. She'd gone over their conversation many times in her head since it had happened and knew she'd screwed herself by letting her feelings get the best of her and being irrational. Now she felt bad about the whole situation and didn't know quite how to fix it, but Lynn had been nowhere to be found to clear it all up.

She heard Andi's voice from down the hall and turned to find her accompanying a patient in on a gurney. She waved and then said something to her partner, and he went on with the patient as Andi came Maggie's way.

Andi swept her into a hug. "I owe you a huge thank you for the other night."

She held on to Andi's shoulders as she lifted her off the floor and squeezed her. "For what? Hiding the alcohol or pouring you into bed?"

"Yes. All of that and so much more." Andi laughed and set her free.

She tilted her head and leaned against the wall. "So much more?"

"Rita was in the parking lot that morning. She'd come to see me and got all jealous when she saw you leave. Now she wants to be exclusive."

"That's awesome," she said with a grin. She'd seen Rita but hadn't mentioned it to Andi. Maggie was happy that the date had prompted Rita to take action and only wished she'd gotten the same reaction from Lynn. Their conversation that morning had seemed to do just the opposite. Running into Lynn as she crossed the lobby to the elevator was the last thing she'd expected that morning. Had she been waiting for her? No. She couldn't have known she hadn't come home the night before. *Damn it.* She was sure she'd looked horrible from sleeping in her dress and with her makeup smeared. She'd glanced around for another path to the elevator but hadn't found one, so she'd straightened her shoulders and padded across the floor to accept the consequences.

"How are things with the nurse? Any movement there?" Andi asked.

"Nope. None at all. I think she's avoiding me." Lynn seemed to be going out of her way to be elusive since then, switching shifts and floors with other nurses.

"You sure got her attention the other night." Andi fanned her face with her hand. "You were hotter than hot in that dress."

"Did I?" She thought she had, but it hadn't seemed to make much difference in Lynn's interest. Any interaction they'd had since had been minimal, and even then she seemed cold and reserved. All business.

"I've never seen Lynn miss a catch. So, yeah."

She bit her lip and smirked. "Well, I guess that's something." She didn't know what, but she must be in Lynn's head, or she wouldn't be going to so much trouble to avoid her.

Lynn walked around the corner and jolted to a stop when she saw Maggie in Andi's arms. A rush of heat flashed through her. She'd been doing her best to avoid Maggie for the past few days and hadn't expected to run into her this morning, let alone while she was flirting with her new paramour. The sight of her wrapped in Andi's arms made her both jealous and sad. This whole situation was her fault. She'd pushed her into seeing other people to save her own sanity, only it hadn't done anything close to that. She thought about Maggie more now than she ever had. Why was it so difficult for her to accept the attraction and just go with it?

Maggie glanced her way over Andi's shoulder as she leaned against the wall smiling and caught her staring. Lynn spun and headed back in the direction she'd come, running straight into Pam and almost knocking her off her feet as she rounded the corner.

"Sorry," she said and tried to angle past her.

Pam grabbed her shoulders for a moment and glanced down the hallway as Lynn maneuvered around her. "Hang on a minute," Pam said and followed her. "Are you crying?"

"No." Only she was and didn't want to explain her reasons to Pam right now. She just wanted to get to a place where no one could see her.

Pam grabbed her arm and pulled her into a vacant room. "What is going on with you? I thought you said you didn't want to be involved with Maggie."

"I did." She wiped the tears from her eyes.

"So why the tears?"

"You saw her." She scrubbed her face with her hands. "All happy with Andi."

"Oh, honey." Pam swept Lynn into her arms. "If she's what you want, then tell her. I know she'd rather be *all happy* with you."

"Would she? Really?" Lynn broke free of Pam's embrace, shot to the other side of the room, and paced back.

"That girl is totally in love with you. She looks at you like I look at pie. Have you been there with her...to the pie stage?"

Lynn nodded. "Still there, I'm afraid."

"Then stop pretending she doesn't matter to you and do something."

"I'm trying to be practical. Andi's her age, and they seem to get along well."

"We both know there's nothing practical about love when it happens." Pam's voice was deep and full of strength, the way it always sounded when she got serious.

She continued to pace. "What if she wants kids?"

"Then you cross that bridge when you come to it." Pam tilted her head and smiled. "She'd make pretty babies."

She shook her head. "I know she would, and she'd be a great mom too. I just don't know if I can do it again."

Pam looked into her eyes and smiled lightly. "I know you *can*. It's the *want* you have to work out."

She broke eye contact and paced across the room again. "I did everything for Carrie. Beth was never there."

Pam followed her. "She's not Beth, and if that's why you're holding back, then stop. You're comparing her to a very low standard. Get that out of your head. She's so much more than Beth ever was." She took her by the shoulders. "Listen to me. She's still got a long way to go in her career until she reaches a place where she'll have time for kids, so why not enjoy yourself until that decision pops up?"

"What will the other nurses think? What will Carrie think?"

"Does it matter what anyone else thinks? Can you be happy with her? I mean, really, what do you have to lose?"

"Besides my heart? Everything." She could hear the desperation in her own voice. It was ridiculous, but she'd never been so unsure about anything before. "You think I should?"

"Jesus. Yes. For your own sanity *and* mine. Stop fighting it and give her a chance." Pam chuckled. "Stop thinking so much and start following your heart." She poked her in the chest. "You've been miserable since she started hanging out with Andi—even though you encouraged it. Not to mention that you've been a huge pain in everyone's ass around here."

"I have not."

Pam rolled her eyes and tilted her head. "Is the 'no drinks near the computer' sign at the nurses' station really necessary?"

"I guess I have been a little anal about things lately. I've been trying to keep myself distracted."

"All the more reason to let yourself have some fun. If it doesn't work out, I'll take the blame for pushing you into it. Not that you need much of a push. A little nudge will do."

Lynn laughed and let go of the stress plaguing her. She felt so much better now that she had direction. She was going to do exactly as Pam said and go for it. Suddenly her future was so much clearer. What did she have to lose besides her heart? She took in a deep breath. "I can't just go out there and tell her now. I need a plan."

"Yes, you can. You don't need a plan. She may be having fun with Andi, but she hasn't given up on you. Just let it happen."

She blew out a breath. "Okay." She went into the bathroom and splashed her face with water. The avoidance stopped now.

"Ready?" Pam asked.

"Ready," she said as she followed her out of the room. "I hope you're right about this."

"Am I ever wrong about these things?" Pam sliced her a sideways glance and lifted an eyebrow.

"Nope, never." She chuckled. Pam knew all the romantic happenings in the hospital, and when she matched people, sometimes even before they'd met, it always happened. "Well, maybe that time with—"

"That was not my fault." Pam raised an eyebrow. "I didn't know either one of them was married, and they still get along great."

She raked her fingers through her hair and walked to where

Maggie was standing near the nurses' station. No sign of Andi or any other paramedic in the hallway. "Hey. How's it going today?"

Maggie glanced up from the chart she was studying. "Good." She focused on Lynn. "Is everything okay? I mean, I saw Pam whisk you around the corner. I came to see what was up but couldn't find you."

"I'm fine. Everything's fine." She stilled her nerves.

"Okay, good." Maggie went back to studying the chart.

"You want to grab some dinner after shift?" she blurted.

Maggie seemed surprised, the deer-in-the-headlights look she gave her unmistakable. "Yeah. I'd love to." A smile crept across her face.

"I'll meet you in the lobby later?"

"Okay," Maggie said softly, still staring at her. "Wait. Is this some kind of trick? Are you going to give me another lecture about what I'm doing with my life? Because if you are, I'm going to decline."

She smiled slightly, trying to keep it all in, but failed as a grin burst across her face. "No. No lecture. I miss you, and I'm tired of avoiding you." She watched Maggie's smile broaden before she turned and walked away, realizing she hadn't felt that good in a long time.

CHAPTER FIFTEEN

The emergency that came through the door just before Lynn's shift ended was going to put a kink in her plans to have dinner with Maggie. When she saw that the patient was an infant, she knew Maggie wouldn't leave without seeing it through.

Jonathan was on ER rotation and caught the case as it came in. While he was in the exam room assessing the baby, Maggie rushed out of the elevator and headed straight for the nurses' station. She spun and headed to the parents for more information. Lynn watched as a little girl, probably the older sister, stood just behind the mother's leg clutching her hand. Maggie listened to the mom for a minute and then bent down and smiled at the child before she spoke. The child nodded, and Maggie immediately sprang up and rushed to the exam area.

"Wait. There may be something in the airway." She pushed Jonathan out of the way and placed her ear close to the infant's mouth.

"That's not what the mother said when she came in."

"New story." She swept the child onto her arm and popped her swiftly on her back. A small piece of plastic flew to the floor. "Medicine 101, check the airway first." Maggie placed the baby on the gurney, put her stethoscope on her chest, and listened. "Distinct wheezing." She held the baby's hand in hers, assessed her palm, and glanced at the parents. "Her skin isn't pink. The pallor is growing pale, almost blue." She checked the baby's mouth and airway but couldn't see the object. "Pulse-ox is below ninety percent, so there must be something else. I can't see anything, and she's still wheezing badly. She might need surgery to remove the object."

Endoscopic surgery using specialized instruments to remove the foreign body from the esophagus or breathing passages through the mouth wasn't all that common, but necessary in cases like this. This procedure would be done under general anesthesia, and Lynn knew the parents might be reluctant, as would she be if she wasn't well aware of how this scenario could end without it.

Lynn had no idea why Jonathan hadn't checked her history and talked to the older sister. She got the attention of the father, who was holding the sister in his arms, and took them outside of the exam area. "Did the baby put more than one thing in her mouth?"

The child, who could have been five years old at the oldest, looked at her father as though she might get into trouble. So many times children don't disclose things because they're scared.

He immediately kissed her on the forehead. "It's not your fault, honey. We just need to know, so we can make Kylie better."

The little girl nodded, and Lynn rushed back into the exam area. "The sister confirmed that she swallowed more than one object."

Maggie didn't waste any more time. She pulled up the rails and started moving the bed out of the room toward the elevator, then turned back to Lynn. "I need to get the consent form signed."

Lynn shoved a clipboard into her hand. "I'll take her and meet you in CT," she said and watched Maggie rush back to the parents. Maggie had made the right call, and hopefully the second object would be easily removed. Otherwise it was going to be a long night for both of them.

❖

Lynn was lingering near the surgery waiting room watching, when Maggie came through the door. She wanted to be there in case there wasn't a good resolution. A smile broke across Maggie's face as she rushed across the room to the parents and spoke before she dropped down and brushed the hair from the older sister's eyes. The little girl hugged Maggie, and the weight lifted from Lynn's shoulders. Everything was okay.

She'd never waited for Beth after surgery. Beth had always been so confident and sure of herself that she'd never let Lynn see any vulnerability, *ever*. She wasn't sure if Maggie would be the same, but she hoped not. Long ago Lynn had found she needed a partner who would share the joys and fears of life with her. Beth hadn't done that with her, or anyone. Her bottled-up emotions made Beth cold and impersonal as the years of their marriage continued. How had Lynn survived it?

When Maggie returned to the elevator and pressed the button, Lynn clearly saw the blanket of panic take over Maggie's face. Maggie was second-guessing herself. She rushed to her side but didn't make eye contact. "Helluva job you did with that baby."

"Was it? Really?" Maggie asked as the elevator doors opened.

Lynn grabbed her arm and tugged her inside. "Stop doubting yourself. To succeed in pediatrics, you have to have lightning-fast critical-thinking skills, good instincts, and the ability to follow your gut." Tears were brimming at the edges of Maggie's eyes as she stared straight ahead, and Lynn's stomach clenched.

"The CT scan wasn't clear. I only suspected something was still trapped in her airway. What if I'd been wrong?" Maggie's voice cracked as she spoke. "I would've performed an unnecessary procedure on a tiny body."

"You weren't wrong." Lynn's voice softened, and she took her into her arms. "If you have a hunch that something doesn't look quite right, you always need to consider it. Pediatric patients can go from awake and talking one minute to completely unresponsive the next—with absolutely no warning."

She released Maggie and took a step back, reminding herself of the boundaries she'd set for herself. "Unlike adults, children are great at compensating for whatever's going on until, all of a sudden, they crash." The elevator doors opened, and they walked to the recovery room where the baby lay sleeping. She took Maggie by the hand and led her to the corner of the room, where they couldn't be seen behind the curtain. She reached over, wiped the moisture from Maggie's cheeks, and then held her face in her hands. "Also unlike adults, kids have an uncanny ability to bounce back." They glanced over at the bed when she heard the baby stirring. Kylie opened her eyes and immediately smiled. "And the optimism is palpable."

Maggie let out a laugh, the relief in her eyes clear now. This incident could've ended many different ways. Jonathan had been too confident in his decision earlier, but Maggie had kept her cool and assessed the situation appropriately. As it was, Lynn had been impressed by Maggie and had glimpsed a vulnerability that Maggie rarely revealed. That glimpse made her feel needed.

❖

The elevator stopped at Maggie's floor, and she started out.

"I'm sorry we didn't get to go out to dinner, but what you did for that baby tonight..." Lynn closed her eyes, and a tingle ran through her as she remembered what had happened. "The way you took charge and saved her was amazing."

Maggie held the door for a moment, then spun around inside and let the elevator doors close. She scrunched her forehead. "Jonathan will probably be pissed at me forever."

"Do you really care if he is?"

Maggie shook her head. "No. Not really. He's an asshole."

"He really is." Lynn chuckled. "You're going to be a great pediatrician, Maggie."

"You think so?" Maggie asked, staring into her eyes.

She nodded. "I really do. Jonathan, on the other hand, has a lot more to learn."

"Yeah. He always seems to be looking for the obvious and doesn't rely on his gut much. He's a little full of himself, but I think this one really might have hit home."

"Good, because someone's going to get hurt if he doesn't pay more attention."

Maggie walked with her to her apartment, but Lynn had promised herself she wouldn't invite her in. It was too soon. If she did, they wouldn't be able to stop the chemistry between them from exploding into a huge pile of regret. She would regret it, wouldn't she? The proximity between them was making her wonder. She'd been ridiculously impressed earlier and was quickly rethinking her decision to keep her distance tonight. But she still needed time to process the path she wanted to take with Maggie and didn't want to screw it up by rushing anything.

"I'm not letting you come inside."

Maggie moved closer and put her hands on Lynn's hips. "Are you sure?"

Lynn closed her eyes and took in a breath. "I'm sure."

Maggie hovered closer. "Okay. Then I'll leave you with this."

Lynn leaned against the door for some distance but, instead, found herself pressed up against it, being kissed with such power and tenderness that all her doubts faded away. She tingled as their tongues mingled, touching and baiting each other in a dance that she'd imagined thousands of times. Literally holding on for dear life, she wrapped her arms around Maggie's neck and pulled her closer. The sensations coursing through her had never been so strong. The heat between them hadn't faded. Seemingly stoked by their days apart, each day was another flaming log thrown on top, and the blaze was raging out of control. Maggie could still make her feel a thousand days younger than her years, and she reveled in the sensation. The confusion overwhelmed her, but clearly nothing had changed from the first time they'd kissed so long ago. Lynn couldn't get past the wonder of how incredible it felt for Maggie to hold her.

The kiss ended as quickly as it had begun, and Lynn felt cold when Maggie backed up, stared into her eyes for a moment, and then turned and walked slowly to the elevator, her hips swaying ever so slightly. As she watched Maggie get into the elevator, Lynn pressed her palms to the door, holding herself in place for fear she might bolt that way, chase her down the hallway and beg her to come back.

Lynn finally managed to slide the key into the lock and get inside her apartment. She closed the door and leaned against it for a moment. She hadn't expected anything like that to happen tonight. In fact, a week ago she hadn't expected to ever let it happen. When she knew she'd be entering the elevator with Maggie, she'd immediately sent a text to Pam that simply said *SOS*. After watching Maggie perform today, her resolve to venture forward slowly was crumbling, and after the kiss she'd just received it had disappeared entirely. They both knew it was a game-changer.

❖

Maggie entered the elevator without looking back. She couldn't, or she would never be able to leave Lynn standing there. She couldn't keep hiding the feelings she'd kept locked away in the vault of her past for so long. Knowing that Lynn had been watching her and thought she was a good doctor had broken the seal, and they'd tumbled out in full force. Lynn's confidence in her had made Maggie braver than she'd ever been in the past, so she'd taken a chance and kissed her. She'd been unsure of Lynn's reaction at first, but when she'd leaned closer, she'd felt the rhythm of her hammering heartbeat and knew it matched her own. She'd gripped her hips tighter, and when Lynn had pressed into her, she'd forged ahead. The slow, erotic, body-tingling kiss she'd received in return had confirmed that Lynn still had feelings for her, and she could build on that certainty.

When she reached her apartment, she hesitated. She wanted to go right back up to Lynn's and kiss her again—let whatever would be happen. Instead, she slid her key into the lock and went inside. The last time Maggie had pushed her, Lynn had returned to Beth. No, she'd have to be patient and let Lynn realize how good they'd be together. She just hoped to God she'd do it soon.

She flopped onto the couch and typed a text to Lynn.

Thanks for the confidence.

You'll always have that from me.

I'd like to have a whole lot more from you, she typed. Then erased her message and instead typed, *Dinner Friday night?*

She watched as the bubbles appeared on the screen, and it seemed to take forever for the message to finally appear.

Yes. My place @ seven.

The thrill that ran through her was electric. She quickly typed *Good night* with a smiley face after it, got up, and danced around the living room. She'd been hoping for a yes and that Lynn hadn't changed her mind since this morning. Suggesting her place as the location was unexpected and filled with so many opportunities. The possibility of something between them was quickly becoming a reality. She went into the bedroom and put on her running gear. It was still light out. No way would she get to sleep any time soon. Only running could help her wind down from this high.

"Whoa. Sorry." Maggie clutched the woman she'd barreled over as she came out of the elevator, surprised to see it was Pam. Pam seemed to be just as surprised to see her. Evidently both of them had their minds on something else. "Hey. What are you doing here?"

"Just thought I'd stop by and see Lynn." Pam wore yoga pants, a blue tank, and a red hoodie, and Maggie still couldn't get over what a beautiful blue her eyes were. Whoever had married those would be lost in them forever.

"Really? Why aren't you at home cuddling up with Heather?" Maggie aspired to someday have the relationship she'd seen between Pam and Heather.

Pam hesitated, moving from side to side on her sneaker-clad feet before she answered. "I probably shouldn't show you this." She held up her phone to see the text from Lynn that simply said *SOS! My place in 15 minutes.*

Maggie panicked. She'd left her only ten minutes ago. "What?" She grabbed the phone from Pam's hand. "When did she send this?" She spun around and hit the up elevator button.

The phone chimed, Pam took it back, and shook her head as she read the message.

"Is that from Lynn?" Maggie reached for the phone, but Pam slid it into the pocket of her jacket before she took Maggie's arm and moved her away from the elevator, where others could overhear their conversation.

Once they were in an area free of inquiring ears, Pam sat down on the lobby couch and continued. "Apparently, someone thoroughly kissed her just a little while ago. Do you know anything about that?"

Maggie's cheeks warmed at the memory as she took the spot on the couch next to Pam. "Possibly."

"Lynn hasn't told me everything that's happened between you two, but enough to get that you make her very vulnerable."

"Hmm." Maggie smiled as she thought of the way she'd just left Lynn—definitely vulnerable. "Is that a bad thing?"

"It scares the hell out of her."

"Why? I'd never hurt her."

"Not intentionally. You're twenty-six and she's thirty-eight." Pam held her hand up, spacing her thumb and forefinger about an inch apart. "Lil' gap there." Her tone made her comment sound like she thought it was a no-brainer.

"I don't care how old she is, and she knows that. Why's she so worried about it?" And she didn't care, not then and not now. In fact, Lynn's maturity only solidified the attraction. Maggie was tired of dating women her age, women who never looked at the big picture, who only whined about things that didn't matter to her.

"Carrie, for one," Pam said.

She sank into the couch. "Yeah. I'm worried about that too, but that's not about age. It's about Carrie being a stubborn ass sometimes."

"Plus, she's already raised her family. Don't you want kids?"

"I do, but…damn it." She blew out a breath because she didn't have a counter for that comment. She loved kids and wanted at least a couple to raise herself. "I've never clicked with any woman the way I do with Lynn, and I don't want to let that go without at least trying to make it work."

"I get that, and I'm sure sometimes you feel this will be your only chance at happiness."

"Not sometimes. All the time. How do I make her feel that too?"

"You deal with her concerns. Don't brush them off, and don't ignore them. Truly deal with them."

"That means I have to tell Carrie."

Pam's hand flew up in the air. "Hold on. You can't do that without Lynn knowing. That'll just piss her off and push her farther away. Talk to her about *everything*—present, future, and past. She needs to trust that everything will work out if she chooses a life with you."

If she chooses. Maggie didn't have any other choice. "Are you working for or against me?"

"Oh, honey." Pam took her hand and squeezed it. "I'm totally working for you. I want Lynn to be happy, and I think you can make that happen." That was a relief. At least Pam saw the relationship as a good thing, even if most others might not. Pam glanced at her watch and stood. "I better get up there before she talks herself into a frenzy."

Maggie stood and hugged her. "Thanks for being in my corner."

Pam nodded. "Just don't fuck it up and hurt her, okay? She's my best friend."

"I won't. I promise." She waved to Pam as she entered the elevator to go up to Lynn's apartment. She definitely had to slow things down and concentrate on gaining Lynn's trust. She checked the heart sensor on her Apple Watch. It was already higher than normal, a wonderful remnant of the kiss she and Lynn had shared. Her run was going to be much longer than she'd intended this evening. She had a lot to think about.

CHAPTER SIXTEEN

Lynn had almost finished preparing dinner—baked chicken with rice and summer squash. She'd made a small salad for each of them as well and would complete the meal with chocolate-fudge cake. She'd decorated the table with flowers and candles, much too romantic. She picked up the candlesticks and hesitated. That's what she wanted, right? To let the evening lead them wherever it would? She took in deep breath as a tingle ran through her.

Yes, she'd thought about what might happen a lot since the earth-shattering kiss she'd shared with Maggie, and that was exactly what she wanted. She set the candlesticks down again before she flattened the linen tablecloth as she set the table with silverware, two place settings adjacent to each other. If she had to look at Maggie directly, they might not make it past the salad, and dessert would end up being much more delicious than cake. Her apartment was spotless. She'd spent most of the morning cleaning and doing laundry. She'd also washed her sheets, just in case something else happened. She'd been telling herself no for so long, she didn't know if she could hold off any longer.

When her phone chimed and she saw the text from Maggie, disappointment hit her square in the chest.

Been paged to surgery. Not going to make dinner. I'm so sorry.

She slumped down into the dining room chair. Maggie wasn't coming.

She typed back *I'm sorry too*, and left it at that. Anything else might be incredibly hurtful. Everything she'd tried to forget about her relationship with Beth sped into her head: long days and lonely nights, vacations taken alone with Carrie, forgotten birthdays and anniversaries, and eating so many dinners in front of the TV by herself. It was a bad idea to get involved with another doctor, no matter what kind of promises Maggie made.

The oven timer beeped, so she walked into the kitchen, took the chicken out, and slid it onto the stovetop to cool. Even though it smelled wonderful, she wouldn't eat the meal she'd prepared. Her appetite had vanished. The cork popped as she pulled it from the bottle of chardonnay she'd had chilling in the refrigerator.

She'd just finished her first glass of wine when she heard a knock on the door. Maybe Maggie's surgery had been canceled. Her heart raced as she rushed to the door and pulled it open. When she saw Beth standing in the hallway, she immediately had the urge to close the door again.

"Oh, hi, Beth," she said, unable to contain her disappointment.

Beth seemed to notice her reaction. "I was hoping for at least a smile."

"Sorry. I just wasn't expecting you."

"Can I come in?"

She stepped aside and allowed her to enter. "Sure."

"Something smells awfully good in here."

"Chicken," she said softly. "I baked a chicken."

When Beth got to the dining room, she stopped and turned. "Looks like you were expecting someone else. Maybe I should go."

"I thought Carrie was coming to town this weekend, but her plans have changed," she said. It was the only thing she could think of that wouldn't prompt an argument.

Beth's brows shot up. "And she waited this long to let you know?"

She nodded and hoped Beth would let it go.

"Well, that's rude. I'll have to talk to her about disappointing you like that."

Since when did Beth worry about anything that happened between her and Carrie? "No. Don't. I'm sure she has a good reason."

Beth walked into the kitchen. "Do you mind if I stay? It'd be a shame to waste all this wonderful food," she said as she surveyed the chicken. "It's been a while since I've had a home-cooked meal."

"Sure. Why not?"

Beth picked up the bottle of wine and poured herself a glass. "Should I carve the chicken?"

"You're the surgeon." She smiled as she spoke. They'd shared this running joke for years. Even though Lynn was fully capable of carving the meat, and did quite often, on the few occasions Beth made it home for dinner, she insisted on doing the carving. The surgeon in her always came through in everything she did.

"That I am." Beth took the knife and fork from the block and used them to move the chicken to the cutting board before she began slicing the breast into perfectly equal quarter-inch slices.

"Still as precise as you've always been."

"A benefit of the job I cannot restrain."

"Among other things."

Beth didn't respond to her comment as she placed a few slices of chicken on both plates and proceeded to fill the bare spots with rice and squash.

"Would you mind bringing my wine?" she said as she carried the plates to the dining room and set them in each spot. She glanced around the room, walked to the pass-through counter, picked up the lighter, and went to the candles.

"Those aren't necessary."

Beth lit them anyway. "Maybe they'll improve the mood." She smiled lightly and then pulled Lynn's chair out for her.

She took in a breath and let it out. Everything in her was warning her she should tell Beth to leave, but what could it hurt? She'd prepared a nice meal, and Maggie wasn't here to eat it with her. She really didn't want to be left alone to wallow in her disappointment. If nothing else, Beth was a good conversationalist as long as they kept it impersonal.

Maggie tried to walk quickly to her apartment building, but it had been a really long day, topped off with an unplanned surgery. Her shift had just ended when Beth had called her back to assist with a minor surgery. She'd been disappointed about missing dinner with Lynn, but also excited about the surgery, since she hadn't performed one like it before. Beth seemed to be including her in most of the unique cases as they came in, so much so, that when she'd entered the operating room this evening, Dr. Able, a fourth-year surgery resident, had said something indicating that Beth must either have a history with her or see something special in her work. Maggie didn't know what to think at this point.

Maggie had been in the locker room when her beeper had gone off. She'd rushed to the surgery unit and found Beth at the desk making notes on the chart. Apparently she'd already done the patient exam.

"What do we have?" Maggie asked.

"An appendectomy." Beth looked over her notes. "Seems pretty routine." She handed the chart to Maggie. "I have plans tonight, so I'm going to leave this one in Dr. Able's capable hands, with you assisting."

"Oh, wow. Really?" She couldn't suppress the excitement in her voice. She'd seen only one or two appendectomies and was eager to get another surgery under her belt.

"I hope you didn't have plans," Beth said as she added an additional note to the chart and handed it to Maggie.

"Nothing that can't be rescheduled." A total lie, but medicine was her life right now, and she hoped Lynn would understand. When she'd received the page, she'd texted to apologize about missing dinner, and the response she'd received had been short. *I'm sorry too.* Maggie had responded with *Can I come by after?* But Lynn hadn't replied, which probably meant she was upset. Something she'd have to deal with later.

"Good, because I might be able to convince Dr. Able to let you take the lead on this one." Dr. Able was Beth's go-to surgeon for difficult cases most of the time and was in line to be chief resident next year.

The surgery had gone well but had taken longer than Maggie had anticipated because the appendix had ruptured and the patient was septic. They had to remove the appendix and clean all the infection from the patient's abdomen. Dr. Able hadn't let her do more than assist, which was completely understandable. Still, she ached all over, and her feet were killing her. She wanted to go home and get into a nice hot bath but decided to stop by Lynn's place first and apologize in person. Hopefully, she understood.

Maggie knocked on the door and waited. Lynn opened the door, and Maggie immediately said, "I'm really sorry about tonight."

"It's fine." Lynn's voice was low and without emotion.

Maggie rolled her lips in to wet them. It wasn't fine. "I just came by to apologize before I head home and go to bed. I'm beat."

"Okay." Another short answer.

Fuck. Lynn hadn't asked her to come in, so now she knew she was angry. Maggie heard noise coming from the living room and glanced over Lynn's shoulder. "Who's here?" She scrunched her forehead.

"Beth."

She shook her head. "What the hell? You had dinner with Beth because I couldn't make it?" Was she that interchangeable?

"She just showed up. You weren't coming, and the food was ready." Lynn's tone was firm.

"And you just let her in. Had a nice romantic dinner with her?" It was a shitty thing to say, but she was hurt and upset and ridiculously jealous. Beth had eaten the dinner meant for her, enjoyed the wine and romantic ambiance meant for her, and now she was enjoying Lynn's company. All instead of her.

"Is that what you really think?" Lynn seemed to straighten her stance. "She came by and…well, she pretty much invited herself."

She knew exactly what was going on. "For your information, I was almost out the door when *Beth* assigned the surgery to me." She must have somehow gotten wind of Maggie's dinner plans with Lynn and purposely destroyed them.

Beth came to the door carrying a glass of wine. "Got that surgery wrapped up? Everything go well?" She tilted her head and smiled.

Maggie wanted to slap the smug, veneer-toothed smile right off her face. "Everything went great." She took in a breath to calm herself. "Just stopped by to let Lynn know I talked to Carrie on the way home. Now I'm planning to go take a long, hot bath." That was the lamest reason in the world to stop by, but she couldn't think of any other excuse.

"Okay, then. We'll let you go do that." Beth put her hand on Lynn's shoulder, letting Maggie know that she had no intention of leaving soon.

Lynn moved forward, and Beth's hand fell from her shoulder. "We'll talk tomorrow, okay?" Lynn said.

"Yeah, sure. Tomorrow." She glanced at Beth before she turned and headed toward the elevator. She wasn't talking to anyone until she got this jealousy under control. She hated herself for what she'd just said to Lynn, and it was all because of Beth.

On her way to her apartment, she thought about the events that had occurred earlier. Beth had purposely assigned her the surgery and Maggie, thinking she was special, dove right in. Beth had tricked her so she could be alone with Lynn, and she couldn't do a thing about it. She had to work with her until her surgery rotation was done, which still had a couple of weeks to go, and Beth had all the control.

❖

Maggie held the box of doughnuts in one hand and the tray of coffees in the other as she pushed the doorbell button to Lynn's apartment. She hoped the peace offering would lessen Lynn's anger. They'd both said unnecessary things the night before, and Maggie attributed her own remarks to jealousy. On the other hand, she could attribute Lynn's words only to disappointment. Either way, the situation had clearly hurt both of them. She hoped she could make that up to her.

The door swung open, and Lynn appeared in the doorway still dressed in her pajamas.

She held up the box of doughnuts. "Peace offering."

Lynn didn't take the box or the coffee. She didn't move, just stood there and stared.

"I was an ass last night. I'm sorry."

"You were an ass." Lynn accepted the doughnuts and went into the kitchen.

She followed her. "I said I was sorry. I'm not sure what else I can do."

"You can trust me to know who I want in my life and who I spend time with."

"I can't believe you're letting Beth back in after all she's put you through."

"That's not your business."

"Isn't it? I mean it will be if…" She closed her eyes briefly. "I don't want her to hurt you again."

Lynn's eyebrows pulled together. "You're jealous."

"Fuck yes, I'm jealous. Do you have any idea how I felt last night when I found her here with you eating the dinner you planned for me?"

"The dinner you didn't show up for."

"That wasn't my fault. I fully expected Beth to perform the surgery and was totally surprised when she gave it to me. Don't you see? Beth set that up. She must have found out about our plans somehow."

"That's ridiculous." Lynn picked out a doughnut and bit into it.

"Why else would she have shown up here last night? Or is that a habit I'm not aware of? Do you have some kind of friends-with-benefits thing going on? Because if you do, we have a problem."

Lynn seemed to contemplate what she'd said. "No. I rarely see her outside of the hospital." She sighed.

"I'm an intern on Beth's service. She has complete control of me at work right now."

"I'll talk to her about it."

She shook her head. "No. That'll only make it worse."

"Then what? We just suffer through Beth's control?"

"It's only for a couple more weeks." Maggie moved closer and pushed a stray hair from Lynn's forehead away with her fingers. "Can you handle that?"

Lynn nodded "I don't really have a choice if I want to continue on this path with you." She took in a deep breath. "And I do want to see where it leads."

She smiled. That was what she wanted to hear. "Can we try again this week?"

"Thursday after shift. Tell no one," Lynn said as she raised an eyebrow.

"I promise." Maggie kissed her, and the sweet taste of sugared doughnuts exploded in her mouth. Soon she had Lynn pressed against the refrigerator with her hand on her breast, wanting to do so much more, but she stopped herself, broke away, and took a breath. Lynn stared, her eyes dark and glassy, and Maggie knew she could have her right now if she wanted. God help her, she wanted her more than anything else.

But not this morning. Not this way. Lynn fell into her arms and held her near, and she knew she'd made the right decision.

CHAPTER SEVENTEEN

The week hadn't gone fast enough for Lynn, and with the way her day had turned out, she couldn't wait for it to end. It had been disappointing that her work week had ended with such a crazy day. She'd ended up working late and was going to have to cancel dinner with Maggie. Maybe they weren't meant to be together. All the forces around them seemed to be working against them. When she'd texted Maggie to cancel, she'd immediately texted back.

Absolutely not. I'll have dinner with you at midnight if I have to.

Lynn smiled at her response and typed back, *That's a possibility. Come here when you're done. We'll eat with the vampires. Will you be alone?*

Lynn knew Maggie's roommate, Stacy, was on a different service. Lynn had seen her now and then but had no idea what shift she worked and when her days off were scheduled. The bubbles appeared as she waited for Maggie's response.

Completely alone, and possibly naked. Get here soon.

The sentence was punctuated with a wink face, but Lynn knew she wasn't kidding, and the thought of seeing Maggie completely naked sent a jolt through her that she almost couldn't contain. This was happening tonight. She glanced around to see if anyone was watching her, and thankfully no one had seen the heat rush to her face.

When her last patient had been discharged and sent home, Lynn couldn't leave fast enough, so it was nowhere close to midnight when she showed up at Maggie's door. She'd texted her when she'd gotten home and told Maggie she was stopping by her place to take a shower first. She didn't want to smell like the hospital and needed to relax for a few minutes to wash off her day.

Maggie opened the door looking absolutely breathtaking. A pair of sweatpants and a tank top had never looked so good. It was amazing how she could do things to Lynn without even trying. "I thought you might want this." She handed her the glass of wine in her hand and moved aside to let her in. "The pizza just arrived. Sausage and mushroom, right?"

"Right." She glanced at the box and saw that it was from her favorite pizzeria, the one she'd always ordered from when they'd lived in the house on the other side of town. She couldn't believe Maggie had remembered after all these years. Maybe she'd just taken a wild guess. No, she'd ordered from there specifically instead of from one of the many other pizzerias and restaurants nearby.

Maggie led her into the living room of the small apartment and sat down on the couch before she opened the box, snagged a couple of pieces, put them on a plate, and handed it to Lynn before she did the same for herself.

She immediately took a bite, savoring the taste. It had been a while since she'd had this particular pizza, and the sauce was just as perfect as she remembered. She took a sip of wine before she said, "I'm so sorry I got hung up."

"No worries." Maggie devoured her first slice. "We can't avoid our jobs or the shit life throws at us, but we can navigate it together if you'll just stop worrying and let whatever happens, happen."

"You underestimate the power of our circumstances. The last two times we've tried to have dinner have been disasters."

"Only one disaster. Tonight is still looking good, if you ask me." Maggie gazed over her glass at her before she took a drink. "You want to tell me about your day?" She set her glass on the coffee table and snagged another slice of pizza.

Lynn smiled. Maggie seemed to be starved. She must have waited for her to get here before she ate. Beth would've eaten and already been asleep. The two were so different, almost exact opposites. Beth was all about herself and never asked Lynn about her day. She might have inquired a few times when they'd first started seeing each other, but as their relationship progressed, it was one of the little things Lynn needed that had gone missing, along with everything else.

As she went through all the ups and downs of her day, Maggie listened and commented when Lynn felt down about something she'd done or that might not have come out right, which happened daily.

The curiosity in Maggie's eyes and voice comforted Lynn. So many things about her job just spilled out, things she'd learned to keep bottled up. Maggie had a fantastic aura of care that made Lynn want to tell her everything. Almost an hour later, she realized how much she'd been talking while Maggie's attention hadn't strayed. She was still watching her intently, waiting for whatever words came out of Lynn's mouth next.

"I'm sorry. I've just been running on about things you probably don't even care about."

"Not true. I care about everything that happens in your life."

"You are so…"

Maggie's head tilted as though she was waiting for the rest of the sentence to come out of Lynn's mouth. Lynn took a deep breath and glanced around the room. "I don't even know where to start with what I need to say."

"How about the beginning?"

"You are so not what I ever expected you to be. Not then. Not now."

A slight smile crossed Maggie's face, and she shifted to face her. "The reason you've been avoiding me?"

"I'm so sorry, Maggie. I just didn't know what to do. I thought you'd moved on, and I certainly didn't want to complicate your life during your internship."

"What does that mean? Complicate my life how?"

"By letting you know how I feel about you."

"How do you feel about me?" Maggie's eyes were wide and curious. Did she really not know?

"Very few days have passed that I haven't thought about you since you left for medical school. I've been ignoring my feelings for so long that having you here in front of me seems surreal."

"Really?" Maggie seemed to be more able to keep a handle on her emotions at this moment than Lynn did.

Lynn nodded, and her heartbeat drummed in her ears. "I never stopped feeling it. I tried seeing other women after my divorce, tried to put you out of my mind, but I never could. And trying to avoid you since you came to Baltimore has been exhausting. I can't get you out of my system."

Maggie's lips twisted into a quirky half-smile. "You don't need to avoid me."

"Oh, but I do." Lynn shook her head. "You have so much ahead of you. Your career, kids, a family. I don't want to ruin your life." The words came out of her mouth in a firm, strong voice, as though Lynn was trying to convince herself.

"Ruin my life? That would never happen, and if that's what you think, bring it on. I want you to ruin it in the best way possible." Maggie moved closer, took Lynn's face in her hands, and kissed her.

Every rational thought flew from her mind as she kissed her back with everything she had. It was still a wonder how one kiss from Maggie could do things to her that no one else had ever been able to. When Maggie's lips went to her neck, she could think of only one way to resolve her reactions.

"We can't tell anyone about this," she whispered.

"What?" Maggie immediately stopped kissing her, batted her eyes as though trying to focus, and backed up. "Why? Are you ashamed to be with me?"

"No. Of course not. I just want to figure this out without other people watching and giving us advice."

"Okay. That makes sense." Maggie returned to kissing her.

"And we have to consider Carrie." Would Carrie mind if she were involved with a younger woman other than Maggie? Did that make it better or worse?

"Right, Carrie."

"And Beth."

"Fuck Beth."

"Do you think Carrie will be okay with this? I'm essentially her mother, and you're her best friend."

Maggie growled into her neck. "For God's sake, stop talking about Carrie. It's really killing the mood."

"I'm sorry, but I worry about it."

Maggie sat up and created some distance between them. "Okay. Then let's look at all the scenarios." She threaded her fingers through her hair and swept it out of her face. Several blond strands immediately flopped back across her forehead.

It was hard to focus with Maggie sitting so close. Her cheeks were pink and her hair mussed perfectly around her face. She was beautiful and vibrant, and unbelievably sexy. Maggie was so much more than Lynn had ever expected to have in her life. She pushed off the couch and went to the kitchen to get some water. They had quickly drained the wine bottle after dinner, and Lynn definitely needed to clear the fog from her mind.

When she returned, she handed Maggie a bottle of water and sat in the corner of the couch. Maggie attempted to move closer, and Lynn put her hand up in front of her. "Stay there until we figure this out." She pulled one leg up under the other on the couch, creating a barrier between them.

The deflated breath that whooshed out of Maggie's chest sounded pitiful. "Then can we continue?"

"Yes."

Maggie raised an eyebrow as she slid her fingers lightly across Lynn's leg. "What if I don't remember where I was?"

She took her hand and held it. "I'll remind you."

"Okay, then. First scenario, we tell Carrie, and she's ecstatic about us being together."

"Optimistic, and I'd love that, but…" Carrie would not be thrilled about it at all.

Maggie frowned. "You're right. Carrie's probably going to be a hard sell."

Lynn nodded. "It took her a while to accept my divorce from Beth."

"Did she ever tell you why? I mean, did the two of you talk about it?"

"She said she hadn't seen it coming." They'd put on such a good show of being happy on the outside that everyone was surprised.

Maggie raised her eyebrows. "But you'd separated at one point. I remember that."

"I believe she just always thought we'd work things out. She's fine with it now. We've talked, and she understands the reasons."

"So we need to ease her into the idea of *us*."

"Right. How do we do that?" she asked, sure it would be a slow process.

"Well, she's already aware that I'm seeing someone."

"You told her that?"

"You know how she is. Twenty questions right up front whenever we talk."

Lynn chuckled. "Yes, I do."

"Have you told her you're seeing anyone or are even testing the dating-pool waters?"

She shook her head. "No. She asked, but I haven't told her."

"Okay, first step, let her know you're interested in dating. Or at least going out with friends."

"I can do that."

Maggie inched closer and kissed her.

"We didn't go through the bad scenarios," she said in a breathless whisper.

"But we have a plan," Maggie said against her neck as she tickled it with her lips. "We can revisit the scenarios if something goes awry."

This wouldn't stop with only a kiss. It took everything she had to push Maggie away and move to the edge of the couch. "No. I need to have everything straight before we go any further." She drank another swallow of water and stood. "I need to go."

"Seriously?"

"Maggie." She shook her head, trying to make sense of the feelings swarming her. "I need to think."

Clearly disappointed, Maggie blew out a breath and sank into the couch. "Okay. You set the pace."

"Thank you," she said and went to the door. Maggie didn't follow, only watched her go like a sad puppy being left alone for the day.

As she sprinted to the elevator, all she could think about was the disappointment in Maggie's eyes and how much she'd wanted to make it go away. The more she thought about it, the more confused she got. Maybe she was wrong about trying to make sense of it all and should just let it happen. God knows she wanted it to. Carrie would be all right as long as she was happy, right?

She changed her mind several times, pacing back and forth in the hallway, and had been standing outside Maggie's door when it suddenly swung open. She looked into Maggie's beautiful blue eyes, and all her willpower vanished. She couldn't put the lightning coursing through her back in the bottle even if she tried. She wanted Maggie with everything she had. She'd waited so long for this moment and had completely resigned herself to it never happening. Now, here she was standing in front of her, practically begging her to love her. They absolutely couldn't turn back now. Not with the way they were looking at each other.

CHAPTER EIGHTEEN

Lynn knew she should turn and walk—no, run away, but the decision was out of her hands now, and she quickly closed the space between them. She exploded in need as Maggie took her in her arms and each of them explored the other's mouth with their tongue. She wanted to feel every part of Maggie against her, had dreamed about it so many times. She wasn't disappointed. Everything she'd imagined sprang to life. The soft, tender kiss began slowly, and then suddenly the intensity made her stagger. Unbidden feelings swept through her as the union turned into a firestorm that Lynn knew she might regret.

Suddenly she heard the door slam shut and was pressed up against the wall inside, thankful for the support it supplied. Maggie's soft, warm hands crept up under her shirt, and she shuddered. She dragged her lips away and saw the want in Maggie's deep-blue eyes.

"I've been waiting so long for this. For you." Maggie's eyes were dark and full of desire. She'd thought for sure Maggie would've moved on, at least found someone her own age in medical school.

"You have?"

"Uh-huh. Since the moment I saw you. The first day I came to your house."

"When I was in the garden? Oh, God. I was all hot and sweaty." She remembered the day perfectly. Maggie hadn't been the only one who felt the connection.

"Were you? I didn't notice. All I remember is that when you turned around and smiled at me, my world shifted." She moved up to her ear and whispered, "God, you were gorgeous."

"That was so long ago."

"It seems like an eternity." Maggie buried her face in her neck, painting it with her tongue. "No wonder I want you so much." She stroked her thumb across the silky cup of her bra, and Lynn shuddered.

Maggie slipped her hands underneath Lynn's shirt and skimmed her finger over her ribs. The touch, even though soft and tender, made Lynn quiver. When Maggie traced the valley between her breasts with her fingers before slipping her thumb beneath the underwire of her bra and flicking her nipple, Lynn shook, the most incredible jolt coursing all the way to her center.

"We shouldn't do this." She arched when Maggie fell to her knees and slid her tongue across her midsection.

"You want me to stop?" Maggie asked as she continued to caress her belly.

"No," she whispered and let out a moan as Maggie's tongue dipped into her belly button. "I don't want you to stop. I might die if you do."

Maggie chuckled and then popped back up and kissed her again.

She broke the kiss, and Maggie's forehead creased. "What?"

"I want every bit of you, but not here in the entryway." She shook her head. "I'm way too old for sex on the floor."

Maggie smiled and held out her hand. "Every bit of me is yours. Always has been."

Every word that came out of Maggie's mouth was perfect. She couldn't make Lynn want her more at this point. Her heart raced as she reached for Maggie's hand and let her lead her into the bedroom, where Maggie immediately took her face into her hands and kissed her until she felt weak. She slowly, methodically pulled her shirt up over her head and then went right back to kissing her. Jesus, she could kiss. Every pulse point on her body was thrumming and waiting to be touched. When she reached for the button of her jeans, Maggie stopped her. It was completely clear who was in control tonight. Maggie popped the button loose and slid the zipper down slowly, letting her fingertips graze the skin underneath. Chills ran through Lynn as she fought to maintain herself. Once her jeans were on the floor, Maggie lifted each foot out of them, one by one. The kiss Maggie placed on her inner thigh sent a red-hot bolt of electricity through her, and Lynn had to grab hold of Maggie's head to steady herself.

Maggie let out a soft chuckle and continued her journey up across Lynn's hip and then her belly. "You are so beautiful," she whispered before their lips met again. She kissed her with such tender power, Lynn forgot all time and space. She pressed into her and felt Maggie's clothes instead of bare skin.

She pulled at Maggie's tank top. "Take this off." Then she pulled at her sweatpants. "These too. Now." The desire that had been building inside her for the past few months was topping out.

Maggie stopped kissing her long enough to do exactly what she asked and then pushed Lynn onto the bed and began to touch, explore, take her to levels of pleasure she'd only dreamed of visiting. She reveled in the feel of Maggie's skin against hers—breasts, stomach, thighs that were all so perfect. The light graze from Maggie's fingers fleeting over her center made her jump, and she laughed.

"You like that, huh?" Maggie asked.

She sucked in a breath as Maggie did it again. "I like everything you're doing."

"I like that you like it." Maggie moved downward, sucked Lynn's nipple into her mouth, and let it pop back out before she covered it again and swirled her tongue around it.

Lynn squirmed beneath her as the jolt zapped through her. If she kept this up, she might explode before she even got between her legs. Maggie seemed to sense that possibility and gave her nipple one more twirl before she abandoned it and moved lower. The heat of Maggie's mouth on her center had Lynn on the verge of letting go, and when she pushed her tongue inside, Lynn did just that and tumbled into orgasm. Maggie held firm, stroking her until she couldn't take anymore and reached to stop her. Maggie rested her head on her thigh momentarily before she crawled up next to Lynn, kissed her gently, and tucked her under her arm. This relationship was going to complicate her life in a huge way, but right at this moment, she didn't care.

Contentment rolled through Maggie as she opened her eyes. The warmth she felt lying here holding Lynn in her arms was wonderful. She could remain in this very spot for the rest of her days. Loving Lynn had been everything she'd imagined it would be. Feeling her squirm with pleasure and writhe beneath her drove Maggie to want even more, and she drank in every sensation she'd produced in her.

She circled the spot right below Lynn's belly button with her finger. She'd kissed it repeatedly during the night and fully intended to kiss it a thousand times more before the sun came up. She moved her hand farther, hovered there, letting the soft curls of Lynn's center tickle her palm before she traced the entrance to the hidden treasure it covered.

Lynn shifted and lifted her head. "Oh my gosh, I fell asleep. How long have I been out?"

"A couple of hours." Maggie pressed her lips to the top of her head. "It's okay. You had a long day."

"No. It's not okay." Lynn quickly rolled on top of her. "I've been waiting forever to do this."

A jolt zapped through her as Lynn kissed her and slid her leg between her thighs, rocking against her. Maggie lifted her hips and pressed into her harder. Her breath caught as Lynn took a nipple into her mouth, swirled it with her tongue, and let it drag out of her mouth, and she couldn't help the moan that escaped her lips. She heard Lynn chuckle as she kissed her way to her other nipple and captured it between her teeth, nipping it gently. When Lynn's hand tiptoed down her side to her hip and then between them and into her folds, Maggie almost couldn't take it and thrust her hips up for more. She'd been ready for this since the first moment she'd seen Lynn again.

"Slow down, love. I have many places yet to taste," Lynn whispered as she began a slow rhythm with her fingers and dragged her mouth from her breasts to her belly, bathing her with her tongue.

Maggie squirmed beneath her, begging for more. The glorious caress was almost too much. She wanted her inside, now. She was soon rewarded as the heat of Lynn's mouth came down on her center. The control in her hips was completely gone as she bucked into her and Lynn pressed harder, licking, sucking, enjoying her completely. The orgasm took her, spreading throughout her midsection, then to her limbs with lightning speed, zapping each one of her senses as it heightened. She'd just started the descent when then next one hit, and she climbed even higher. Words of God flew out of her mouth as she tumbled into oblivion again. One hand fought to grasp the bedsheets, and the other reached for Lynn, found her hair, and shoved her fingers through it, holding her there. This was the most spectacular feeling in the world.

When Lynn finally let her recover completely, she stroked her center one last time before she moved up and blanketed her with her body. Maggie was totally spent and felt comfort in the weight of Lynn's body on hers as she lay naked with her in bed. Lynn had obviously wanted to touch every part of her, and she'd done exactly that. Lynn had brought her to climax, sweetly, slowly, and methodically multiple times. At one point, she'd thought coming so hard might kill her, but she'd die happy.

The sun had begun to set when Maggie woke to the amazing scent of something baking. She crawled from beneath the sheet, pulled a T-shirt over her head, and padded into the kitchen. The sight of Lynn in her kitchen, dressed in her robe as she took something from the oven, was surreal.

"Whatever you're baking smells divine."

Lynn slid the pan onto the stove top before she spun around, snaked her arms around Maggie's waist, and kissed her. "Pound cake."

"You found all the ingredients for that luscious cake in the sparse pickings of this kitchen?" She raised her eyebrows and pointed to the cabinet.

Lynn nodded. "I did."

"You're very resourceful." She pulled the tie on Lynn's robe loose, slid her hands inside, and grabbed her ass.

Lynn nodded again. "I am."

"That deserves a reward." She pressed Lynn against the counter and kissed her, ready to love her all over again. Everything she'd dreamed of for the past four years had come true. "Bring the cake. I have more plans for you." She spun and headed back to the bedroom.

❖

"The next time I saw you, you looked so pitiful." Maggie slid a chunk of pound cake into her mouth, eating her second piece. "You were so sick, but you were still beautiful." The memory made Maggie's pulse jump. "Once I got past the cold sore on your lip."

"I did *not* have a cold sore."

"Yes. You did," she said with a chuckle and swept her finger across Lynn's top lip. "Right here."

"Oh, God. You must have really been smitten."

"I was. Completely, hopelessly captivated with a married woman."

She stroked Maggie's cheek with her thumb. "If I had only known then what I found out a few months later."

Maggie pulled her eyebrows together. "What happened a few months later?"

"The night of your graduation when Beth and Carrie went out." She shifted slightly. "Carrie went home with some friends, and Beth went home with an old college girlfriend."

"Are you fucking kidding me?" She bolted up in bed. "What an ass," Maggie said with a growl and fell back onto the bed. "So many years—wasted."

"It doesn't matter now. Everything happened for the better. Her infidelity pushed me into doing what I should've done months before. The reconciliation was a farce. I should've never tried to make it work when Beth didn't try to change." Lynn rolled over, draping herself across Maggie. "I should've given you a chance instead."

"Hindsight, huh?" Maggie smiled, remembering their bittersweet kiss. "For what it's worth, I hope you haven't been lonely, but I'm really glad you didn't find anyone else."

"I couldn't. No one made me feel the way I do when I'm with you, and I didn't really know how I felt until you were gone. By then I thought it was too late." She laid her head on Maggie's soft chest and closed her eyes.

"Not too late at all." She hated that they'd both suffered without each other for so many years, but now she was happy and content. The thought of making love to Lynn every night and waking up in her arms every morning sent a thrill through Maggie. She'd waited a long time for this and didn't intend to let her go.

Lynn had never felt comfortable and secure like this with anyone before. It felt so good for Maggie to hold and love her. She took her time and seemed to savor every minute. She felt absolutely free when she was with Maggie, with no rules and no insecurities to bind her. Maggie seemed to love her for the woman she was, not who she thought she should be. Over the past few years, Lynn had tried to convince herself that sex wasn't important, but what she'd just shared with Maggie had proved her wrong. Sex with just anyone wasn't important, but Maggie wasn't just anyone, and nothing was more important than their intimate connection this very moment. Nothing else seemed to matter. Being loved by Maggie had become the centerfold in her life. She'd done exactly what she'd sworn she wouldn't—entangled herself with a woman who would dedicate her life to medicine. She didn't know if she would ever be able to escape from the intricate mess she'd been engulfed in. She was in big trouble.

It wasn't light out yet when Lynn got up, went into the bathroom, closed the door, and flipped on the light. She looked in the mirror at herself, stunned at her reflection. Pinked cheeks, tousled hair. She actually looked happy—no, satisfied was what she saw. She ran her hand across her stomach and smiled. Her body had been spent in every possible way last night. She hadn't looked like this after sex in too long. Hell, she hadn't had sex in too long.

She heard the door click open and watched Maggie creep into the bathroom behind her and slide her arms around her waist. "You're beautiful, you know that?"

Heat rose in her cheeks. "No, you're the beautiful one. I'm just an out-of-shape woman who needs more exercise." Her body didn't compare to Maggie's, who was a runner and exercised daily. Lynn wasn't a runner, never went to the gym, and rarely made time for anything athletic besides softball. She'd become a workaholic since her divorce, always afraid that any kind of social activity might lead to the complication of romance. Now, standing here with Maggie's arms around her, she wondered why she'd thought of it as an unwanted chore. It must have been the company she'd kept. All those worries seemed to have faded last night. Maggie had changed everything.

She felt the softness of Maggie's lips on her shoulder as she peeked over it at her, taking in her reflection. "Not at all. I love your body. You're perfect just the way you are."

She could see in Maggie's eyes, the way she looked at her, that she meant every word. Lynn wasn't accustomed to being cherished, and it felt wonderful. She turned slowly in Maggie's arms and kissed her, and every nerve ending came to life again. She tingled with excitement, and when she slipped her hand between Maggie's legs and felt the wetness, she couldn't contain the moan that came from her mouth.

"You really want me just the way I am?"

"Don't you know that by now?"

"Apparently, I'm a visual learner."

"Come back to bed, and I'll take you through it again." Maggie tugged her back to the bed and kissed her.

❖

The weight of Maggie pressed against her was a comfort she couldn't describe. She didn't want to move, but if she didn't get some coffee, her head would be yelling at her soon. She'd never learned to live without caffeine and had needed more of it as she'd grown older.

Maggie held her tighter as she tried to move away. "Don't go. I like you right here."

"Just going to make some coffee. I'll be right back."

"It's in the fridge on the door." Maggie released her. "Hurry back."

She kissed Maggie on the forehead. "I will."

She took Maggie's robe from the bottom of the bed. Wrapping it around herself, she tied the belt before she pressed the collar to her nose. It smelled of lemon and sage, just like Maggie. She took in a deep breath and let the tingle zip through her as she watched Maggie sleep, so peaceful and serene. This was really happening. Having Maggie intimately as she had many times through the night was a dream she'd never thought would come true.

The coffee was on and brewing, and Lynn rummaged through the refrigerator to find something else to eat. They'd burned a lot of calories last night, but she wasn't really interested in eating again until her stomach let her know with a loud growl while she was making the coffee. She didn't find anything substantial in the refrigerator, so she cut them a couple more slices of pound cake and wrapped them in a paper towel. Pound cake was good any time.

She'd poured two mugs of coffee, tucked the cake slices under her arm, and headed to the bedroom when the door across the living room swung open. *Shit.* Maggie had told her Stacy wasn't coming home last night. Rather than hurrying to the bedroom, she froze like an animal stilling from its prey, which was weird. After all, she wasn't a squirrel who could flatten out so no one would see her.

To her surprise, Stacy wasn't emerging from the bedroom. It was Russell. Bare-chested and dressed only in running shorts, he smiled and said, "Good morning," like it was completely natural for them to run into each other as he continued past her to the kitchen.

She waited for a moment, hoping the other shoe wouldn't drop, and then it did.

"So, Mags finally made the move." Russell's deep voice swept around the corner from the kitchen. "I'm proud of her. I didn't think she would."

She closed her eyes for a moment before she took in a deep breath and went back into the kitchen. Russell was leaning against the counter drinking coffee as though expecting her.

She narrowed her eyes. "This goes nowhere. You understand?"

A grin took over his face as he looked at her over his coffee cup. "Of course not. I don't want any more work than I need at the hospital, and you can make that happen."

"I can." She would never play that card, but it was good that he knew she could.

He pointed to what was left of the pound cake. "You make this?"

She nodded. "I did."

"Smells great." Russell smiled, and poured another cup of coffee. "I've got your back," he said as he picked up the remaining cake and hustled across the living room to Stacy's bedroom.

The door to Maggie's bedroom pulled open, and Maggie rushed out. "Was that Russell I heard?"

She nodded. "I honestly would've never put those two together."

"I'm so sorry. They never come here."

"It's okay. I handled it. We had a short chat in the kitchen."

"You know he's in there telling Stacy right now. I bet she's totally freaking out." Maggie nudged her into the bedroom. "Come on. She'll be out here in a minute, and I don't want to deal with her this morning."

"So your friends must know something."

Maggie didn't respond as she crawled into bed and took a drink of coffee.

"Russell said as much." She patted Maggie's leg. "Don't worry. I'm not mad."

"I didn't tell them. They figured it out. I guess I'm pretty transparent."

She brushed the hair from Maggie's face. "Yeah, you are. Always have been." Lynn settled in next to her, wrapped her arm around her, and held her close. "I always know where you stand." That was sometimes harder than not knowing. It had been in the past, anyway.

They spent the rest of the morning in each other's arms, talking and laughing, with never a lull or a moment searching for words, but a free-flowing discussion with nothing out of bounds. They seemed to never run out of topics, the type of conversation she'd never had with Beth. She didn't suppress the urge to kiss Maggie's soft, sweet lips every few minutes. She'd been saving lots of kisses for her.

It was close to noon when Maggie's stomach let out a growl, and she laughed loudly. "I guess we should eat something other than pound cake."

"I should go home."

"No. Let's go get breakfast," Maggie said quickly. "Please?"

The sad look on Maggie's face was exactly what Lynn was feeling inside. "Maggie, this has been..." Heat rushed her limbs and smoldered throughout her.

"I know." Maggie took Lynn's face in her hands and kissed her gently.

"I'm not sure what to do." She looked across the room and then at her hands so she wouldn't get lost in Maggie's beautiful blue eyes again. What had she done? She didn't want to leave her, ever. Now she would never be able to live without Maggie, who would be permanently embedded in her mind forever. Lynn had never not wanted to leave someone before now, and it terrified her. "I'm a complication you really don't need in your life right now."

"Can you stop telling me that? I'm a big girl and know exactly what I want and *need*." Maggie's fingers were warm as she touched her face and forced Lynn to look at her. "We don't have to make a road map, you know. How about we just go eat for now?"

Still in a daze, Lynn didn't say another word as she put on her jeans and T-shirt. She picked up her shoes, slid them on minus her socks, and they went to breakfast together like they'd been doing it for years.

CHAPTER NINETEEN

Every time Maggie caught a glimpse of Lynn, the butterflies in her stomach returned. They'd been together every night this week, and it was so surreal Maggie was afraid to leave Lynn each morning to go to work. She'd get up early at Lynn's apartment, go for a run, and then return to her place to shower and change. Lynn wanted to avoid any more unplanned encounters with Russell or Stacy. Maggie knew she wasn't quite settled with the whole idea of them being a couple in public, and Maggie didn't really care about what anyone else knew at this point, as long as they were together.

She hadn't seen Lynn much today, and when she had, she'd just glimpsed her down the hall and received a slight smile. She seemed to be avoiding her, and Maggie was beginning to worry that something had changed. She was probably being paranoid, but maybe Beth had gotten to her again.

Lynn came out of a patient room with the vitals kiosk, glanced up, and then entered the next room without even acknowledging her. That was it. This confusion would end now. Maggie sped down the hallway and planted herself outside the room Lynn had just entered, waiting for her.

Lynn seemed startled when she came out of the room and found her. "Oh. Hi." She spoke but didn't smile.

"What's going on with you? You've hardly acknowledged me all day." She crossed her arms as though preparing for a battle. "The last few days weren't all me, you know."

Lynn seemed to scan the hallway to see if anyone was watching before she left the kiosk by the door and took Maggie into the nearest empty room. "I know." She took Maggie's face in her hands and kissed her. "I don't regret any of that. *At all.* I just don't want to become the subject of hospital gossip. This place is an incubator for rumors."

Everything she'd been worried about vanished, and relief washed through her. Lynn wasn't having second thoughts. "I wasn't expecting Stacy to come home and definitely wasn't expecting Russell to be with her. I told you they usually go to his place."

"So, always my place from now on, and we cool it at work, okay?"

"I'll bring dinner tonight." She couldn't stop a huge grin. "Oh, and I thought maybe we'd go to the zoo Saturday, if you're up for it. They have a new baby chimpanzee."

"I think Carrie's coming to town this weekend."

"That's awesome. She can go with us."

Lynn rolled her lips in. "I don't think that's a good idea."

"What? Why not?"

She tilted her head. "She thinks we haven't interacted in years. Don't you think she might have questions about you being around suddenly? You know it won't be easy keeping it hidden from her."

That was true. Now that her life with Lynn was on track, Maggie found it ridiculously hard not to share the news with everyone around her. "We have to tell her sooner or later. She's an important part of both our lives. She should understand."

"Yes, she should, but I'm not ready to fight that battle if she's not."

She put her hand on her hip and tilted her head. "When *are* you going to be ready?"

Lynn took in a deep breath. "Let me feel her out. I need to see where she's at about me dating in the first place. You know I haven't done much of that at all since my divorce."

"Oh my God. She certainly doesn't expect you to never have sex again. Does she?" Carrie was an adult. She must have considered that Lynn had needs.

"I don't know what she expects about me dating or who I might become involved with, but I'm pretty positive it's not you. I certainly don't want to have to choose between the two of you."

Panic rushed through her, and a huge knot formed in her stomach when what Lynn said hit her. "And you'd choose her over me?"

Lynn took her into her arms. "Like I said, I don't want to have to choose."

Maggie stiffened. "Fine. Whatever." She shrugged out of her embrace. "Let me know when you're ready to go all in on this because I'm already drowning." She took off out the door quickly, not wanting her anger to turn to tears. She refused to grovel. She'd never intended to compete with Carrie for Lynn's attention. She'd just never thought her importance to Lynn would be in question. She'd thought they were way past the point of no return, but apparently Lynn could just let her go if Carrie didn't like the relationship.

She checked on a few patients recovering from surgery, the only thing that would get her mind off the blow that Lynn had just delivered.

She was making notes on a chart when she felt someone walk up to her and wait. She hoped it wasn't Beth, because she couldn't take being around her right now.

"Hey. What's up? You seem really focused," Stacy asked.

"Just doing post-op."

"Problems?" Stacy's voice rose with the question.

"One with a minor infection setting in, but the rest are good."

"I meant with you," Stacy said with a smile. "I saw you come out of the room, and then Lynn came out after you. You both seemed upset."

"You got that right."

"Want to tell me about it?"

"She doesn't want to tell Carrie about us because she thinks the whole thing will upset her."

"That's possible, right?"

"Yes. Completely. But she also said she'd choose Carrie over me."

Stacy's eyes went wide. "She actually said that?"

"No. Not in those exact words, but that was pretty much the gist of the conversation."

"So what are you gonna do?"

"I'm so upset right now, I should just call Carrie and tell her everything."

"You're not going to, right?"

"No. Of course not. Lynn would hate me if I did." Tears welling in her eyes as she reminded herself that she'd told Lynn she could set the pace.

"Jesus. I thought this was all about sex, but you're actually in love with her, aren't you?"

She nodded and blinked a few times to clear the moisture. "Have been for far too long."

"Why don't we go out tonight?" Stacy smiled. "It's been too long since we have. We can both use a break from what may or may not be happening in our love lives." She took out her phone, typed in a message to Russell, and held up the phone for Maggie to read it.

Need a rain check on tonight. I'm going out with Mags.

Maggie typed in a message to Lynn. *Change of plans for tonight. I'm going out with Stacy.*

She held it up for Stacy to read, and then they both hit the send button on each other's screens.

The bubbles appeared immediately on her screen, and Maggie waited for the text from Lynn to appear.

Stacy's phone buzzed. She smiled as she read Russell's response and then held up the phone for Maggie to read it.

Maybe I can find you. It'll be like a treasure hunt.

"Wow. What have you done to him?"

"It's amazing what a little food and great sex will do to someone." Stacy chuckled as she typed in a response. "I told him good luck."

"Look at you." She smiled widely. "And you thought he was out of your league." If it were only so easy in Maggie's world. Her romance with Lynn was riddled with obstacles. She wouldn't be so easily pleased.

It seemed like it had been forever when the response from Lynn finally appeared.

Okay. We probably both need a night to think.

Agreed.

She slid her phone into her pocket without showing Stacy, ignoring her urge to throw it across the hall. She was tired of overthinking everything when it came to Lynn and planned to go out and have a good time in spite of her.

"So we're both good?" Stacy asked.

She plastered on a smile. "Yep. We're good."

She hadn't read Lynn wrong. She wasn't nearly as secure about their budding romance as Maggie was, and that made her question Lynn's motivations for entering the whole thing. Maybe it was just about sex. She hated to think that, but she wasn't a mind reader, and Lynn had just made her feel massively unimportant.

❖

Maggie and Stacy had eaten dinner at a local pub and moved to the bar. Maggie was nursing her third drink by the time Russell found them there. There were only three places they could be, and he'd picked the most obvious last. Stacy had told him they planned to get as far away from the hospital as possible, so they wouldn't run into any of their colleagues. At least their scheme had worked for a few hours.

His expression when he'd spotted them from across the room resembled that of a child who'd just found his first hidden Easter egg. When Stacy had seen him coming toward her, she mirrored his happiness. Maggie just couldn't understand why she and Lynn had to have so many obstacles in their path. When it seemed she'd turned into the proverbial third wheel, she'd called an Uber and taken off.

Maggie put both hands on the panes surrounding the door and took a deep breath before she knocked. Coming to see Lynn this late was a bad idea, but a little alcohol made everything in the world seem possible. She glanced at her watch. It was twelve thirty, later than she'd thought. Lynn was probably in bed and most likely wouldn't be happy to see her standing at her door.

It took a few minutes for Lynn to answer, and when she opened the door, Maggie immediately said, "I want you to want me enough to choose me over everyone else."

"You're drunk," Lynn said, her voice low and singed with disappointment.

"Not drunk, but definitely a little intoxicated, which was warranted since my girlfriend told me how unimportant I am to her today." She moved around her and into the apartment.

Lynn ignored the statement as she let the door close behind her. "How did you get home?"

She didn't turn around, just held up her phone as she walked into the living room. "Uber." She spun around and put her hand on her hip. "I just left two of the happiest people in the world wondering why you and I can't be like that."

"We can. You just have to be patient."

"Stop treating me like I don't have a say in this."

"You don't right now." Lynn took in a deep breath and clasped Maggie's hand. "I wish it were different, but it isn't."

There it was, that feeling she couldn't get past since the first day they'd met. She was hopelessly in love with this woman but more frustrated now than she'd been before they'd slept together. "When something in my life happens, you're the first one I want to tell. Can you say the same?"

Lynn didn't answer.

She released Lynn's hand. "I didn't think so. Why isn't it me?"

"You're not being fair, Maggie. I think about you a lot, but it's not that simple. I'm essentially Carrie's mother, and whatever I do affects her."

She swung around and dropped onto the couch. "Technically, you're not even her real mother." When she looked at Lynn, her stunned look made it clear that Maggie had crossed the line.

"Don't ever say that to me again. Carrie is my daughter. Period." The anger in Lynn's eyes pierced her.

She launched off the couch and went to Lynn. "I'm sorry. That was out of line. I just want to be as important to you as Carrie is."

"It's a different kind of important." Lynn shook her head. "Something you won't comprehend until you have children."

"I'm never going to win this battle, am I?" It was clear that Carrie would always be Lynn's first concern.

"I don't understand why it has to be a battle. She's your friend. You should care about her too."

"I do care. I just don't want her to come between us."

"I told you, I'll work on that, but I have to consider her feelings."

That was a start, more than Maggie thought she'd get from Lynn tonight. She could handle that. She took Lynn's hand and tugged her toward the bedroom.

Lynn came to a complete stop before they entered the room. "No. Not like this."

"A little more than you can handle tonight?" She took Lynn's face in her hands and gave her a breathless kiss.

Lynn removed Maggie's hands from her face and said, "More than I *want* to handle tonight."

"Okay. I'll go." Maggie was disappointed but didn't say another word as she gave her one last look, then turned and walked out the door. If she'd stayed, the conversation in the morning would've entailed more reality than she needed at this point. She couldn't push Lynn into anything. *She* had to choose to put Maggie and their blossoming relationship over everything else.

CHAPTER TWENTY

Maggie raced to the coffee shop. She'd done her best to remain calm and finish her shift for the day when she'd received the call, but once she'd changed and was out the door, she'd launched into a full sprint. She hadn't expected this complication because she thought she'd made things clear to Brenda before she left for Baltimore. She wasn't returning to Boston. When Maggie had received her assignment on Match Day she'd been disappointed, but it had pushed her to make the break with Brenda. She ran through the memory in her head. She'd left an opening she shouldn't have.

Even though Maggie was a little tipsy by the time she got home, she headed into the kitchen, opened a bottle of merlot, and poured herself a glass. After they'd taken pictures with all their friends on the steps of the university, a bunch of them, including Carrie, had gone to the closest bar to celebrate. Maggie's celebration was laced with trepidation, her comfort zone about to be challenged in a colossal way. She hadn't considered that she might be given a residency in Baltimore, and she hadn't realized how much the thought of seeing Lynn again would affect her.

After a few drinks, she'd finally decided that everything happened for a reason, and working at Johns Hopkins would be fine. She'd locked away her feelings for Lynn long ago, and when she got to Baltimore, she'd keep them that way. The chances that she'd see Lynn were slim unless one of them actually made an effort to do so, which wasn't likely.

"Hey. How'd you make out?" Brenda came out of the bedroom

and into the kitchen. Maggie wondered if she'd just gotten home as well. Judging by her disheveled hair, she'd been taking a nap.

She took another glass from the cabinet, poured a drink for Brenda, and handed it to her. "Johns Hopkins." She clinked the glasses together.

Brenda's face twisted into a grimace. "Baltimore?" She took the glass but didn't drink.

Maggie stepped around her and went into the living room. "Yep. Not my first choice. But it's an awesome hospital."

"I told you I don't want to move," Brenda said as she followed her.

"We already talked about this, Brenda. I didn't have a choice, and it's not like I can't go." Maggie flopped onto the couch. "No one's asking you to move. It is what it is."

Brenda narrowed her eyes. "You don't want me there?"

Maggie closed her eyes and blew out a breath. "That's not what I said." She took a drink of wine. "You're welcome to come." She didn't dare put any stipulation on that offer, or she'd wind up in a huge psychological conversation about Brenda's needs again.

The couch cushion sank as Brenda sat next to her. "So, what are we gonna do?"

"I'm going to Baltimore. You can stay here in the apartment." Maggie shrugged. "Find a roommate to help you with the rent." She took a gulp of wine. "Maybe Terry can move in with you."

Brenda conveyed her shock as she narrowed her eyes. "She has nothing to do with this."

"Just stop." Maggie finished her wine and put her glass on the coffee table. She was still tipsy, and after the news she'd just received she didn't feel like tiptoeing around Brenda's feelings tonight. "I'm not an idiot. Whether anything's going on with her or not, you're clearly enamored with her." Every conversation they'd had about Brenda's job in the past few months had been all about Terry and how sweet and wonderful she was. "And honestly, I don't care. It's probably for the best." She stood. "I have to concentrate on becoming a doctor."

"So, just fuck me?"

Maggie blew out a heavy breath. "Listen. I gave you a choice, but I don't have one." She stood and circled the coffee table. "I'm tired and a little drunk. I don't want to do this tonight, so I'm going to bed." She walked into the bedroom, stripped off her clothes, and crawled into bed. The day had turned out nothing like she'd expected, and the best she could hope for tonight was that the alcohol would take her to sleep quickly.

Maggie didn't know why she'd gotten involved with Brenda in the first place. The woman had probably never been monogamous, having had more lovers in her past than she could count. She stared through the glass windows of the coffee shop as she crossed in front of them and spotted her at a table in the corner. She remembered exactly why she'd gotten involved with her—dark hair, blue eyes, beautiful smile. And Brenda had seduced her so perfectly. She rounded the corner of the building to the door and took a deep breath before she entered.

Brenda clearly saw her coming and was on her feet by the time Maggie reached the table. The hug she received was long and awkward.

"Hi," Brenda said, excitement spiking her voice.

"Hi." She slipped into the chair across from her.

"Wow. You look great." Brenda stared for a minute, then said, "I didn't realize how much I've missed you until you walked through the door."

A little uncomfortable with Brenda's comment, she shifted in her seat. "Why are you here? I thought we worked this out before I left."

"No. You worked it out."

"I'm not coming back to Boston, and there's no place for you here."

Brenda stiffened and raised her eyebrows. "Do you miss me at all?"

She let out a sigh. "It didn't work between us, and my life is here now. I have no interest in rekindling whatever we had."

"That's not fair."

"Fair? You're talking to me about fair? I was gone for all of five seconds, and you were seeing Terry."

"That was a mistake." She reached across the table and took Maggie's hand.

"Yet you're working side by side with her in the lab every day." Maggie knew how hard it was to be around someone you wanted and not be able to have her.

"I can't just quit my job."

"I'm not asking you to. She's there, you're there. Have at her." She slipped her hand away. "My job is here. I'm not going back to Boston." They both turned when the clerk shouted, "Ma'am, you forgot your coffee."

Maggie saw Lynn rushing to the door. "Fuck. I have to go." She bolted out of her chair and flew after her.

❖

Within fifteen minutes, Maggie was pounding on Lynn's door, but she wasn't there. She knew Maggie would come here first. Where would she go? She paced the hallway and then rushed to the elevator. *Pam's. She'd go there.* The button remained lit as she pressed it multiple times before the doors opened. She sprinted the few blocks to Pam's house, and when she got to the porch, she knocked on the door before she grabbed her knees and took a few breaths.

Pam opened the door and raised an eyebrow. "You've got some explaining to do," she said as she crossed her arms.

"Fuck me. I know. She's an old girlfriend. That's all." She thought Pam might send her away, but then she opened the door wider and let her inside. She led her through the large, traditionally decorated living room and out onto the back porch, where Lynn was sitting on the steps staring across the yard.

"I'm going for a drive. Call me if you need me," Pam said and then went back inside.

Maggie stood at the edge of the porch, bracing herself on the railing. "Why'd you take off like that?"

Lynn glanced up and stared. "Who was that woman?"

"A friend." She didn't want to go into the details of a relationship that was never going anywhere. She might have been callous, but what she'd had with Brenda had never been anything more than a pairing of convenience.

"She's more than a friend."

"Yes. I mean, she was."

"God, I am so stupid. I thought you and I were—" She shook her head. "I don't know what I thought, but you're involved with someone else in Boston."

"No." Back to the one-word answers again. "Absolutely not."

She sat on the steps next to Lynn. "I was done when I left Boston, but apparently she was still invested."

"Why didn't you tell me about her?"

"What the hell, Lynn. You *never* told me about your divorce. I had to move to another city to even attempt to get over you, and it *still* didn't work."

Lynn was silent for a minute. "You're right. I have no right to be upset." She got up and walked to the screen door, then swung back around. "But just for my own sanity, what the hell happened to you four years ago? The week after graduation."

"The week after we kissed?"

"Yes." Lynn's voice softened. "I turned around and you were gone. You totally ghosted me."

"I couldn't just hang around waiting for you to want me." She couldn't tell her that Carrie had made her leave, threatened to never speak to her again if she broke up her parents' marriage. That would've changed everything in their future, even now.

"It wasn't a question of want, Maggie. You didn't give me a chance to make a decision."

"You were trying to make it work with Beth. I thought it would be easier if I left."

"And within six months, I was divorced."

"I know. Four fucking years, Lynn. Why didn't you call me?" She paced the deck.

"I did, but your girlfriend answered." She clenched the railing and looked out onto the yard. "I refused to interrupt your life." She spun around to face her. "I know what it feels like to have obligations."

"She was my roommate at the time. That was it. Absolutely nothing else." She let out a short breath. "You didn't give me a whole lot of credit, did you?"

"I just knew that I'd hurt you and—"

"And you thought I'd hop in the sack with the first woman I met?"

"No." Lynn shook her head. "I'm not sure what I thought."

"If I'd known you were divorced, I would've been back here in a New York minute." She'd waited for that call every night in Boston.

Lynn turned to the yard, clearly trying to hide her emotions. "And now your girlfriend is here and wants you back. Are you in love with her?"

"Damn it, Lynn. You're just as blind now as you were then."
Maggie slipped her arms around her waist. "I was telling her good-bye,
again." She pressed her lips to Lynn's neck. "I'd already told her when
I left Boston."

Lynn twisted around. "You told her again?"

She nodded. "No way in hell am I going to lose you twice."
Maggie moved closer, brushing Lynn's lips with hers. The rest of the
world faded away again. "Come on." Maggie took her hand and opened
the door inside. "Let's go home."

❖

After they entered Lynn's apartment, Maggie turned around and
flipped the deadbolt. She pushed Lynn up against the wall and covered
her mouth with hers. "I'm not letting anyone get between us again."
Her breaths were labored as she slipped her hands under Lynn's shirt
and grazed the curve of her hips up to the swell of her breasts. "God,
you feel good." She pulled her shirt over her head and had her bra off
in seconds. She put her mouth on Lynn's again, and Lynn moaned as
she pinched her nipple between her fingers. She slid her other hand
under the waistband of Lynn's scrubs and between her legs, pressed her
palm to her center, and Lynn bucked into her. Desire sparked wildly
throughout her, and she couldn't get enough of Lynn. She kissed her
deeply as she pushed her fingers between Lynn's folds. "God, you're so
wet." Lynn shuddered and suddenly gripped her shoulders for balance.

"Every day, since you came back," Lynn said, her breaths labored.

She held Lynn firmly against the wall and felt her tense as she
shoved her fingers deeper, then dragged them out slowly, raking across
the perfect spot. Lynn jerked and her legs wavered, but Maggie waited
for more to come as she continued to stroke the flesh between her fingers
and thumb. Lynn's face changed, her tongue pressed to her teeth, her
darkened emerald eyes fixed on Maggie's. She didn't want anything
more than to be right here right now. When she heard Lynn cry out, she
increased her rhythm, and Lynn gripped her tighter and launched into
orgasm. She moved faster and harder until Lynn loosened her grip and
urged her to stop.

Maggie slowed but wasn't completely done, Lynn's hips jerking as the tremors still coursed through her each time Maggie slightly touched her. When the tremors subsided and she backed up and saw Lynn gazing at her, tears sprang from her eyes. She'd never wanted anything more than to love and be loved by Lynn. She kissed her gently. "I don't want to do that to anyone but you." It had only been a day since they'd been together, but she craved Lynn every minute they were apart. "And I don't want anyone else to touch you."

Tears welled in Lynn's eyes too. "Same," Lynn said as she wrapped her arms around her. As they stood there holding each other, all Maggie's fears were swept away.

Lynn lay in bed holding Maggie in her arms, the thought of losing her terrifying now. Yesterday, when she'd stopped at the coffee house to pick up a latte on her way home, she'd been in a great mood. Maggie had reentered her life, and she'd finally thought fate was on her side again. After she'd ordered her favorite treat and moved to the other end of the counter to wait for it, she'd turned to look at the cups for sale on the center display, as she often did. Then, from across the room, she'd heard Maggie's voice. She was talking to a woman Lynn didn't recognize, a beautiful, dark-haired woman, whom she now knew as Brenda. When she saw Brenda reach across the table and take Maggie's hand, heat had penetrated her neck instantly and she'd felt nauseated. She'd almost knocked over the display when she'd grabbed hold of it to steady herself.

She'd abandoned her coffee and rushed to the door. When the clerk yelled, she saw Maggie's head turn, and her heart had almost launched into a complete arrhythmia. No way would she confront Maggie in the coffee shop. Then as she flew by the front window, she saw Maggie bolt out of her seat and knew she was coming after her. She couldn't talk to her right then, not after seeing her holding hands with another woman.

Instead of going home, where she knew Maggie would hunt for her, she ran to Pam and Heather's house a few blocks away and banged on the door until Pam let her in. As soon as she got inside, tears flooded her eyes. She couldn't believe what she'd just seen. By the time Maggie showed up at Pam's house, she'd calmed down, and Pam had convinced her to listen if Maggie attempted to explain. She had, and Maggie had told Lynn her innermost feelings. She'd laid everything she'd felt on the table, starting with the moment she'd first seen her years ago.

Lynn had almost drifted off to sleep when she heard the door to her apartment push open and Carrie calling her name. *Fuck!* She shoved Maggie aside and vaulted out of bed, barely hearing the thud as Maggie rolled off the bed on the other side.

She looked across the bed to see Maggie's head emerging. She whispered, "Oh my God. I'm so sorry. Stay there. Carrie's here." Then she shouted, "Be right out," before she sped into the bathroom. There she quickly splashed water on her face and finger-combed her hair with her wet hands. She didn't wear a lot of makeup on her days off, but her cheeks were seriously flushed.

"Auntie. You in there?" Carrie's voice resonated through the bathroom door.

Fuck, she's in the bedroom. Her mind scrambled as she tried to figure out what to do. She tugged the towel from the rod and wrapped it around her, opening the door to find Carrie rounding the bed to pull the blanket over it. "Hey. Why don't you go make us some coffee, and I'll do that."

"Since you were at the cabin on my last visit, I thought I'd come today." She dropped the blanket and gave her a strange look. "Since when do you wear boyshorts?" She held them up between her hands. "Do these even fit you?"

She swiped the boyshorts out of her hand. "Yes, they fit, and no, if you'd called I would've already been up and dressed. It's my day off, and it's still early."

"It's ten a.m."

"I didn't sleep well and thought I'd give myself a few more hours."

"Oh, sorry. I got off early from my shift at four this morning and left right after." Carrie glanced around the room, clearly noticing the disarray. "I went by to see Maggie, but she's not home."

"I haven't seen her much." She guided Carrie to the door. "I'll get dressed and be out in a minute." As soon as Carrie was out the bedroom door, she rushed to the other side of the bed to beg Maggie's forgiveness but saw no sign of her. Had she slipped out of the room somehow while she was in the bathroom? Did Carrie see her? Panic rushed her as she dropped to her knees and peered under the bed. Then happiness captured her when she found the most beautiful light-blue eyes staring back at her. "I'm so sorry." Lynn leveled herself on the floor facing her and smiled. "Maybe I should keep you right here under my bed forever."

Maggie raised an eyebrow. "Although that sounds tempting, I might lose my job." She sighed. "We need to tell her."

Lynn nodded. "I know. But not today." She brushed Maggie's cheek with her thumb. "You need to stay here until I dress and get her out of here."

"Can I at least have a blanket?" Maggie pointed to the air-conditioning vent near the wall. "That cold air is a killer."

She pulled the blanket from the bed and pushed it to Maggie. "We'll be gone soon." She started to get up and gazed at Maggie again. The most beautiful sight in the world seemed to be her dirty little secret. She would have to do something about that soon. "Thank you."

Maggie nodded. "Now go."

By the time Lynn entered the kitchen, Carrie had already made a pot of coffee. The empty pizza box left on the counter from the night before had been broken down and stuffed in the trash, and the carton of eggs from the refrigerator sat next to the stove. Apparently, Carrie wanted breakfast, which wasn't unexpected, but no way were they staying there. On any given day she would've been thrilled to fix it for her, but the prospect irritated her this morning. In the past, Lynn had always been available when Carrie needed her, but going forward, she needed to set some boundaries. If Carrie had shown up an hour earlier, she would've had a huge surprise, and the morning would be going much differently. Lynn had been so wrapped up in Maggie that neither of them would've heard her come in.

"Hey, let's go out to breakfast. I feel like pancakes."

"You won't get any argument from me." Carrie opened the refrigerator door and slid the eggs back onto the shelf. "Are you seeing someone?"

"No." Lynn had hoped to dodge any questions this morning, but they were inevitable. Carrie had started hitting her with them before they'd even left the apartment.

"Two wineglasses were on the coffee table."

"I had a friend over last night." As usual, she and Maggie had moved from the couch to the bedroom quickly the night before, and she hadn't cleaned up anything.

"Who?"

"Pam."

"Why is your bedroom a catastrophe?"

"I clean on my day off, and that's today." But Carrie wouldn't buy that. Lynn usually kept her place spotless and always cleaned before anyone came over, even Pam. Recently she'd been expending her energy on another activity.

"Since when?"

"Since I'm an adult and can do what I want."

Carrie scrunched her eyebrows. "You're acting really strange."

"Well, you did just burst into my apartment and wake me from a sound sleep."

"I thought you were in the shower."

"I was, after you woke me." Fuck. She needed to get her story straight. "A little warning would've been nice." She let her irritation ring in her voice. Carrie should've at least texted to let her know she was coming.

When they reached the door, Lynn turned to Carrie and put up her hand. "That's enough questions. Let's just have a nice breakfast, okay?"

Carrie rolled her lips in. "Okay. I just don't know why you're being so secretive."

"I'm not. But I am entitled to a life of my own. Now stop."

Once they were seated at the pancake house, Carrie changed the subject.

"Scott asked me to marry him." She held out her finger, and a nice-sized diamond sparkled as she wiggled it.

"Oh, honey, that's wonderful." It was beautiful, probably close to a full carat. She'd been too irritated to see it before.

"We want to do it right away."

"Like right away when?"

"Like this coming spring."

"Oh, wow. That'll take some quick planning." She tried to calm the alarms going off in her head. Most people started planning at least a year out, and it was almost the end of August, which meant they were already a couple of months behind in planning. They'd have to move quickly to find a venue that wasn't already booked. "Do you want to do it here in Baltimore or in Boston?"

"Here. Can you believe Scott's parents live in Mount Washington? He grew up here too."

"Okay." Lynn repressed her anxiety. Carrie had no idea how much planning went into a wedding and expected Lynn to make it happen just like that. And Lynn would, as always. No matter how much time it took.

CHAPTER TWENTY-ONE

Still a little irritated from Carrie's surprise visit this morning, Maggie stood in her kitchen putting the last of the groceries in the refrigerator. Carrie was as unpredictable as a thunderstorm and just as destructive. She didn't have regard for anyone's time but her own. Showing up at Lynn's this morning unannounced wasn't out of character. Weeks ago, before she'd gotten together with Lynn, they'd planned another girls' weekend, and Carrie had canceled on her twice. They'd decided to hang out, binge-watch shows on Netflix, and eat like they had in college. She'd been looking forward to it and had rearranged her schedule, only to have her cancel.

As soon as she'd heard the front door close this morning, she'd crawled from under the bed and found her clothes on the chair in the corner of the room. Apparently, someone had picked them up, and she wasn't sure if it had been Lynn or Carrie. If it was Carrie, she would have questions when she arrived. Her phone dinged, and she read a text from Lynn.

Almost done with breakfast.
How long until you get here?
About twenty minutes.
Stall, please. I need a shower.
No, you don't. You're beautiful.
You're all over me.
I like that.

She responded with a smiley face, dropped her phone to the counter, and headed to the shower. She didn't want to give Carrie any indication that she'd been with anyone, especially Lynn, this morning until she'd tested the waters.

After she showered, Maggie picked up a few things and actually ran the vacuum. Cleaning helped her think, and she didn't know quite how to determine whether Carrie would be okay with her and Lynn as a couple. Hopefully that information would come this weekend, somehow.

The doorbell rang through the apartment, and Maggie vaulted off the couch to open the door. She'd had more than enough time to shower and clean her apartment a little.

"You're here," she squealed as she pulled Carrie into a hug. She had to make it look like she hadn't expected her.

Carrie looked around her into the apartment as though she might find someone else. "I came by earlier, and you didn't answer."

"Sorry. I didn't know you were coming. I volunteered to help out someone with a shift." The circles under her eyes from her activities with Lynn would make the story plausible.

"No worries. I had breakfast with Auntie." She moved aside and motioned to Lynn, who stood behind her.

Lynn moved forward and gave her a hug. "You'll have to come up for dinner sometime."

"Maybe tonight?" Carrie asked.

"Oh, no," Lynn said and backed up. "You two haven't seen each other in a few weeks and need to catch up."

"Come on. It'll be fun. Just like old times." Carrie put an arm around both of them.

Maggie reached across Carrie's back, grazed her hand across Lynn's ass, and had to contain her laugh when she jumped. "I'm sure Lynn has something better to do than hang out with us dorks."

"As a matter of fact, I do. Not that it's better, but I have plans with Pam."

"What the hell? Doesn't Pam ever hang out with her wife?"

"Heather's working, so Pam and I are going to see a movie she doesn't want to see."

"That's a weird relationship. I don't think you should be spending so much time with Pam. Is something going on between you two?" Carrie asked. Maggie apparently hadn't been the only one that the two of them had fooled.

"Absolutely not. Pam and Heather are blissfully happy in their marriage." Lynn nudged Carrie into the apartment. "Speaking of marriage, have you shown that engagement ring to Maggie?" She held Carrie's hand up in front of Maggie.

"Oh, my God. This is huge. Why didn't you call me?" The ring was gorgeous and sparkly, just the kind Carrie loved.

"I wanted to tell Auntie before anyone else."

Now Maggie understood the reason for the unannounced visit. "So when did he propose?"

"Last weekend. He took me to a bed-and-breakfast, and we spent the whole weekend celebrating." Carrie grinned. "It was so romantic."

"Great news, right?" Lynn said as she spun around and headed to the elevator.

"Hey, you did that on purpose. This conversation isn't over," Carrie shouted after her.

Lynn's hand flew up and shook in the air. "Yes, it is."

Evidently Lynn had used Pam as an excuse more than once. "What was that all about?" she asked after closing the door.

"We kind of had a mother-daughter talk, only reversed. She says she's not seeing anyone, but I don't believe her."

"Why not?"

"This morning when I went into her bedroom, the bed was a mess, and clothes were strewn everywhere."

"Maybe she's just gotten sloppy."

"No. This was rip-off-your-clothes messy."

Maggie tried not to smile. Sex between her and Lynn was always passionate, and clothes were an obstacle they took care of quickly. "Ooh, was someone there?"

"I don't think so, but I didn't check the closets." Carrie chuckled. "Maybe I should have."

Fuck. How was she going to derail this situation? "What would you have done if you'd found someone there?" She widened her eyes. "That would've been a whole lot of awkward."

"Totally, but don't you think it's weird that she's being so secretive?"

"I guess, but maybe she's not sure yet. I mean about the relationship or how you'll react."

"I'm fine with her finding someone else, as long as whoever it is makes her happy," Carrie said firmly, and the huge knot in Maggie's stomach loosened.

"You are?" Maybe there was a light at the end of the tunnel after all.

"Of course. Beth moved on, and I'm okay with that. I just have a feeling she's interested in Pam, and she's married. I hope not, but she's acting weird and way too happy."

"Maybe she's found some young intern to keep her happy."

"Or just to fuck." Carrie shook her head. "That wouldn't be any better. She'll just get her heart broken."

Pain exploded in Maggie's chest. That possibility hadn't occurred to her. Were they just fucking? No. It was much more than that, but Carrie would think otherwise, and finding out the intern was Maggie would make it a million times worse.

"Well, I hope not on both counts." She reached for the remote control on the coffee table. "What do you want to watch?" Now she knew the waters were thousands of meters deep, with a deadly undertow. At this point, surviving without extensive preparation would be impossible.

❖

Maggie was close to dozing when her phone vibrated in the front pocket of her hoodie. The text alert said it was from Sunflower, which she'd changed from Lynn soon after they'd started sleeping together to keep their communications hidden from anyone who might see her texts.

The sunflower had been Lynn's favorite flower ever since she'd visited Clear Meadow Farm in Hartford County as a child. According to Lynn, the countless rows of sunflowers blanketing the countryside in the fall were spectacular. When she'd described the sight of the massive number of yellow flowers to Maggie, the excitement in her voice and the expression on Lynn's face showed true happiness and beauty. From then on, no other word could describe the beauty of Lynn in Maggie's mind.

How's your night going?

I've eaten too much junk food and watched too much TV.

Why don't you two go out?

I'm too sleepy. Can I come crawl into bed with you?
Awkward threesome...no.
Never mind.

She'd followed the last text with an eye-roll emoji.

Maggie hadn't noticed that Carrie was watching her text until she said, "Who is Sunflower?"

She dropped the phone to her chest. "Just a friend."

Carrie swiped the phone from her and looked at the text. "Looks like more than just a friend to me."

She grabbed the phone back, deleted the text, and slid it into her hoodie pocket. Thankfully, she'd thought far enough ahead to delete some of their old texts, at least the ones that were identifiable, before Carrie came to visit. "It's the woman I told you about before. But this part, the romance, is new."

Carrie quirked an eyebrow up. "Why did you delete her text? And why haven't you told me more about her?"

"Because friends like you are *really* nosy." She tilted her head and grinned. "And I'm not sure it's going to work out."

Carrie drew her brows together. "Why?"

"She's got a kid."

"What's the problem with that? You love kids?"

"A teenage kid."

"Oh, gotcha. That could be tricky." Carrie glanced at the paused TV screen. "Look at you. An older woman, huh?"

"Kinda, but she was a young mother."

"How many years?"

"I'm not sure, eight or ten." It was actually twelve, but Maggie tried not to be exact. She didn't want Carrie counting the difference in years between her and Lynn.

"Hell. That's nothing," Carrie said with a laugh. "I thought with a name like Sunflower, you were talking fifteen or twenty. Were her parents some kind of bohemians?"

"They're both artists. Her mom paints and her dad makes pottery." This lie was getting huge. Soon she'd have to write down the details so she could remember them all.

"Do they sell anything?"

"They have a gallery in Taos, New Mexico."

Carrie's eyes widened. "Cool. I've always wanted to visit there. We should go sometime."

"Yeah. If it works out, we will."

Maggie hit the play button on the remote. "Ready to finish this?"

"I'm in. Popcorn sounds good right now. Do you have some?" Carrie asked.

"Of course." She got up and headed into the kitchen, opened the box of popcorn packets, and put one into the microwave before checking her phone, which she'd felt vibrate again. She had five missed messages from Lynn in quick succession, each sounding more urgent than the last.

Where'd you go?

Is everything all right?

You didn't tell her, did you?

?????

Do I need to come over?

She quickly typed in a response. *Everything's fine, but we're going to have to be careful.*

What happened?

Carrie swiped my phone and read our messages.

Oh, shit.

It's okay, Sunflower. You're just a bohemian daughter with a teenager of her own. Lol.

Well, thanks for letting me know. Lol.

I gotta go. Popping popcorn to stuff myself even more.

Okay. Have fun.

Maggie deleted the last few text messages before she turned off her phone and slid it back into her hoodie. She didn't want Carrie accidentally seeing something she shouldn't. That would totally make Lynn have doubts about them. After she poured the popcorn from the bag into a big bowl, she grabbed a couple of sodas from the refrigerator and went back into the living room. Even though it pained her not to communicate with Lynn, the rest of the evening would be in the dark, absolutely Sunflower free.

❖

Season two of the show they'd been watching was starting when Carrie paused the TV, sat forward, raised her arms, and stretched. "How about some pizza?"

Maggie cleared the sleepy fog she'd been in and took out her phone. "Pepperoni and black olives?" Maggie had eaten light on the popcorn because she knew Carrie too well and also what came next. The girl could eat through the side of a mountain made of ice cream and still be hungry. She turned on her phone, and the screen immediately lit up with a missed text from Lynn.

"Wow. This Sunflower girl is really after you."

"Seems that way." She cleared the message from the screen without reading it, opened her contacts, and searched for restaurants. She had every restaurant that delivered within a ten-block radius dialed into her phone for quick access and nights she was too lazy to cook. She also had a delivery application on her phone for the times she craved something farther away. She loved modern convenience. After she ordered the pizza, and while Carrie went to the bathroom, Maggie read the texts from Lynn.

I want to come down.

Hello...Are you there?

I miss you.

Maggie's heart thumped faster at the last message, and she responded. *Pizza will be here in 20, bring wine.*

On my way came through next, and suddenly Maggie was full of energy again.

Carrie flopped onto the couch and picked up the TV remote.

"Season two might have to wait until later. Lynn called. I told her we'd ordered pizza, and she's on her way down."

"Oh, okay." Carrie didn't seem upset, just surprised.

"Unless you think she'll want to watch with us."

The TV screen flickered as Carrie started clicking through the other show choices. "Nope. She doesn't like gore. We'll have to find something much lighter."

Hearing a soft knock on the door, Maggie bounced from the couch to let Lynn in. The smile she was met with was incredible, something she would never grow tired of, and she smelled fantastic. She closed the door slightly behind her, took Lynn into her arms, and kissed her. She wanted to push her out into the hall, kiss her long and hard, and do so much more, but that was too risky.

"You're making this really difficult."

"I know." Lynn kissed her one last time before pushing past her through the doorway. "I brought wine," she shouted to Carrie as she went into the living room.

"Awesome," Carrie said.

Maggie took the bottle from her, went into the kitchen, opened it, and poured a glass for each of them. She sat between Carrie and Lynn on the couch and picked up the remote. "So what do we want to watch?"

They'd just settled on a romantic-comedy movie when the pizza came. Maggie went to the door and tipped the delivery guy. When she took the pizza to the coffee table, Carrie immediately shifted to the middle of the couch where Maggie had been sitting, capturing the space between her and Lynn. It seemed to be a purposeful act, so it was clear Carrie hadn't let go of the discussion they'd had years ago in college. But even so, Maggie was grateful for the space. Sitting so close to Lynn without being able to touch her would make for a very long night. She would actively have to force herself not to reach for her.

CHAPTER TWENTY-TWO

Lynn lay in bed thinking about how much fun it had been to spend the evening with Carrie and Maggie. The thought of waking up to Maggie next to her in bed with Carrie asleep in the spare bedroom was a weird kind of dream she hoped would come true someday, but it was way too soon for that. She fluctuated between giddiness and terror. Telling Carrie wouldn't be easy. She pushed the thought from her head. Nevertheless, she missed Maggie's warmth and wished it was her reality right now. She picked up her phone and typed a message to Maggie.

I'm less than five minutes away. Why aren't you here?

Because I'm in bed with your daughter. She's a great snuggler.

She gets that from me.

Last night she said she wants to run with me this morning.

She'll be asleep for hours.

I'll try to sneak out, but be prepared for a run just in case.

Lynn rolled out of bed and changed into her running gear. She didn't want to seem like a slug if Carrie was going to run as well, but when the next text from Maggie said it would just be the two of them, she quickly abandoned her shoes. They could get their exercise this morning in a different way.

As soon as Lynn heard the first rap on the door, she looked out the peep hole and saw Maggie standing—no, she was more like bouncing—in the hallway in her running gear.

When she opened the door, Maggie rushed in and kissed her. "We have to stop meeting like this."

"Never. I like it." She kissed her urgently as she tugged at Maggie's clothes. She slid Maggie's running pants off, and, trailing her fingers back up her thighs, she pressed her mouth to her center, inhaling her scent through the silk material of her panties. She kissed her way up Maggie until their lips met again. She quivered when Maggie slipped her hand down her pants and slid a finger into her folds. With each stroke the wetness increased between her legs, and she was certain Maggie knew how much she wanted her.

"These have to come off." Maggie hooked each side with her fingers, pulling them down, before taking Lynn's hips and crushing them with hers. Maggie stepped out of her pants and reached to remove her shirt, but Lynn beat her to it, pulling it over her shoulders.

"Take me to bed," she uttered.

Maggie smiled and clasped her hand.

"Wait." Lynn gathered their clothes, refusing to get caught like that again.

Maggie smiled, kissed her again, and led her into the bedroom, where she immediately pushed her onto the bed and attempted to go back to where she'd left off, but Lynn wasn't giving up control this time. She'd let Maggie take charge many times, but not this morning. Maggie looked up at her in surprise when she flipped their positions.

The soft sweetness of the inside of Maggie's thigh filled Lynn's senses as she bathed it with her tongue and slowly worked her way up to her soft folds. She wanted to savor the taste of her skin, take her time, and bring Maggie to climax slowly and completely, but Maggie was already thrusting against her, clearly wanting more. She prodded the soft, sweet flesh of her opening with her tongue before sliding one finger, then another, inside.

Maggie lifted into her and said, "Oh my God. Yes. Right there."

Liquid gushed into her panties as Maggie writhed beneath her, pressing into her mouth. Wanting only to please, she held Maggie's hips firmly as she quickened her rhythm and gorged herself on the tangy taste of her. She'd become addicted to Maggie—her taste, her scent, the feel of her skin, everything about her. Maggie tensed, grabbed Lynn's head, and tugged her hair before she tightened her legs around her and launched into orgasm, Maggie's stomach bouncing as she swept her finger through her folds again.

"Stop," Maggie said with a chuckle.

"I like watching you bounce."

"Come here, so I can kiss you."

She crawled up next to her and did just that. The warmth that enveloped Lynn when she saw the happiness in Maggie's eyes overwhelmed her. Maggie was clearly in love with her, and Lynn felt the same.

Maggie glanced at her Apple Watch. "As much as it pains me to say this, I need to get back upstairs. I told Carrie I'd be back in thirty minutes. With doughnuts." She searched for her clothes.

Lynn picked up her phone, clicked a few buttons, and set it back on the nightstand. "I ordered coffee and a half dozen of Carrie's favorites. They'll be here in ten minutes." She patted the spot next to her. "Now come back to bed and keep me warm."

Maggie stopped and tilted her head. "You're dangerous, you know that?" she said, and slid back under the covers.

"I do and I like it." Being with Maggie was the most incredible feeling in the world. For once in her life, she was truly happy.

The doughnuts and coffee arrived on schedule. Lynn answered the door and tipped the delivery girl a few bucks before she went back into the bedroom, crawled into bed, and nudged Maggie, who had fallen back to sleep. "The doughnuts are here. You should go."

Maggie heaved out a breath. "Please don't make me." Maggie trailed her finger down Lynn's neck to the valley between her breasts.

"But Carrie might be awake by now and looking for you."

"Damn it. Can't you control your daughter better?"

She laughed loudly. "You know better than that. I can't control her any more than I can control you."

"You have complete control of me." Maggie looked at her with drowsy eyes, and her stomach dipped. She wanted to forget about Carrie for the next few hours, but that was impossible.

"Is that so?" she asked before kissing her softly.

"Uh-huh."

She let out a sigh. This situation tempted her, and any other time she'd take full advantage of it. "Then go. We'll continue this after Carrie leaves for Boston."

"On it." Maggie kissed her long and soft before she got out of bed and put on her clothes.

Lynn curled on her side as she watched. She still couldn't believe this beautiful young woman wanted to be with her every day and every night. Her life was so surreal right now she didn't know if anything could ruin it.

Maggie took Lynn's face in her hands and gave her another long, lingering kiss. "Don't move from this spot. I'm coming back later, and we're going to do this again."

For the past few weeks they'd been spending most nights and mornings in one apartment or the other exploring each other's bodies, a habit Lynn couldn't seem to break. Something had always been missing in her life, and Maggie seemed to fill every crevice of the void.

❖

Earlier, when Maggie had woken Carrie to go running, she'd opened one eye and simply said "No," then rolled over onto her side. After that, she'd immediately flopped to her back and said, "Bring doughnuts."

Maggie had rushed out the door and upstairs to Lynn's apartment, not expecting anything that had come next. Her knuckles had barely hit the door, when it swung open. She was ecstatic knowing that Lynn wanted her as much as she wanted Lynn, and that thought settled her fears of losing her once again. Carrie was a huge obstacle in their path to happiness, but Maggie hoped in some roundabout way she could convince Carrie that she loved her aunt and would never do anything to hurt either one of them. First, she would clue Carrie in on how wonderful her new relationship was. Lynn would remain Sunflower until Carrie's acceptance became clear. If she could tolerate a relationship between Maggie and an older woman, how could she not understand it if the older woman turned out to be Lynn?

It had taken Maggie forever to get Carrie moving today. They'd drunk coffee and eaten doughnuts on the couch while they continued binge-watching shows and were still watching TV when Stacy came home and suggested they go out to dinner and hit the usual bar after.

She'd hoped her new relationship with Lynn didn't become the topic of conversation tonight. It usually did, even though she tried to avoid it as much as possible. Several other interns were at the bar, but only Stacy and Russell knew Maggie's secret. They were very supportive, in between their sarcastic jabs that she was cougar bait and had a curfew. She couldn't help that she was attracted to smart, older women. They possessed a finesse and maturity she'd never found in anyone her age. She craved emotional maturity in a relationship—always had. The meaningless drama she found in younger women didn't exist. Plus, Maggie admired people like Lynn who had done well for themselves in the midst of adversity.

"So when are you moving?" Russell asked.

The jabbing had started sooner than she'd expected, but she was prepared. "What? I'm not moving. Stacy's my favorite girl. She handles all my needs."

Stacy winked. "And vice versa."

"Not nearly as well as your lovely lady," Russell said as he raised an eyebrow. "You don't hit your own bed much."

"Ever think that's because you two make too much noise?" The smile that came across Russell's face made her realize that was the wrong thing to say. *Damn it.*

He tilted his head and raised his glass to Maggie. "I think we're pretty even in that category."

"Can we talk about something else?" Just what she needed tonight—her half-lit friends spilling all kinds of information to Carrie.

Carrie put up a hand and said, "Hold on. Aside from your wild sex life, I want to hear what your friends think about your love interest."

Stacy raised an eyebrow and leaned closer to Carrie. "Many others have attempted the ice queen but have gotten nowhere." Her voice was low and covert, as though she were plotting a coup to overthrow the woman sitting on the iron throne.

She shot Stacy a look of warning. "She's not an ice queen. She just doesn't fraternize with the riffraff." She pointed to each of them.

"And you've risen above that title, while the rest of us are still struggling to climb the side of the castle," Stacy said, irritating as fuck. She'd thought she at least had an ally in her. Stacy didn't mean any harm, but alcohol always made her mouthier.

"Seems Mags here is the special one. Either that or they have a past." Russell bounced his eyebrows at her. "You went to college in Baltimore, right?"

"Okay, that's enough." The table rattled as she shot up from her chair. They were definitely trying to sabotage all her efforts to keep her relationship with Lynn from Carrie. "We're out of here." The confusion on Carrie's face was clear when Maggie took her hand and tugged her out of her seat and to the door.

Carrie stopped and jerked Maggie around to face her. "Why are you so sensitive?" Maggie was silent. "You're really hung up on this woman."

She blew out a breath and nodded. "You're right. I'm totally in love with her, but that doesn't change the circumstances or the obstacles between us." She moved toward the door, and her arm stung as Carrie yanked her back.

"So she has a kid. Get to know him or her?" Carrie said, as she squeezed her hand.

"Her," she said into the air as she stared across the room. She couldn't look at Carrie, or she'd crumble and spill everything.

Carrie moved in front of her and made Maggie look at her. "You're awesome. What's not to love about you?"

"It's not about me. It's about getting between her and her mother."

"That's not a big deal if she likes you."

"You really think so?"

"Yeah. I mean if Auntie started seeing someone, I'd be okay with it as long as I liked her."

"Would you? Even if she was a lot younger?"

Carrie's eyebrows pulled together. "Are you—"

"Dance with me, Mags. Stacy won't get out of her chair." Russell didn't wait for an answer as he dragged her onto the dance floor and left Carrie standing at the edge. She immediately went to the bar, ordered another couple of drinks, then walked over to the table and sat with Stacy. Maggie couldn't wait for the song to end. Stacy was drunk, and who knows what she was telling Carrie.

"You need to shut it," she shouted at Russell as they danced, and he leaned in closer to hear. "Carrie is Lynn's daughter."

He twisted his head and stared at their table. "Oh, shit. I had no idea."

"Well, you do now. She doesn't know, and she can't." She slapped him on the shoulder to stop him from staring. "Not until I know how's she going to take it."

"Why don't you just tell her?" He shrugged.

"Lynn doesn't want me to say anything until she's ready." Maggie really wished she could, but Lynn would never forgive her if she did.

"Gotcha. I wouldn't do anything she didn't want either." Russell had worked with Lynn enough to know how tough she could be if you crossed her.

"You want another drink?" Russell asked as the song faded.

"Nope. I'm done for the night," she said, and rushed back to the table as Russell strolled to the bar.

Carrie and Stacy were deep in conversation when she got back to the table. "You ready?" she asked. Neither of them paid any attention to her as she stood at the table, so she gripped each of their chairs and squatted between them. If she sat down, they'd be there for at least another hour.

"Your friend, Stacy, here is the best."

"Oh?" A chill went through her, thinking Stacy had let out the information.

"She won't tell me a thing about Sunflower other than she's smart and sweet and you two really click."

Maggie sat and relaxed in her chair as she realized she was safe for now. Stacy had clammed up, and Maggie knew she'd almost blown it. She was thankful Russell had dragged her away, because Maggie had been just about to spill her guts to Carrie about Lynn. If she'd told Carrie, it would've been a colossal mistake.

Maggie's stomach bounced when she heard the knock on the door, and she rushed to answer it. Carrie had texted Lynn earlier and asked her to go to breakfast with them. She yanked the door open and then slipped into the hall and kissed her.

"Well, good morning to you too," Lynn said with a huge smile. "Miss me?"

She nodded and kissed her again. "I love your daughter, but I can't wait for her to go home."

The door swung open and Carrie said, "Are we ready?"

"Yep," Maggie said, hoping the heat in her cheeks didn't show.

"How was your night? Did you girls go out?" Lynn asked.

"We did," Carrie said as they walked to the elevator. "Maggie's friends are awesome. We hung out and drank for a while, and I got some inside info on her new love interest." She swung around to Maggie. "Ooh, I forgot to ask you. Have you seen anyone new roaming around the building? I think Auntie has a new thing going too."

Maggie's neck tingled as the elevator doors opened to the lobby. She leaned forward and sliced Lynn a sideways glance. "Seriously?" Happiness rolled through her. Had she told Carrie about them? "Who?" Lynn's mouth dropped open, like she'd just been blindsided on *Survivor* and voted off the island in the final tribal council. Her eyes widened, and Maggie knew she hadn't told Carrie anything. She was fishing.

Lynn sped out of the elevator into the lobby and out the door ahead of them onto the sidewalk, so Maggie probed Carrie for more information.

"How do you know she's seeing someone?" Maggie asked Carrie as they failed to keep pace with Lynn.

"I found boyshorts under her bed, and she was really evasive when I asked her about them."

So that's where they ended up. "Are you sure they're not hers?"

They weren't. Maggie had searched for quickly removed clothing many times in recent days, both hers and Lynn's.

"She may not wear a lot of makeup, but Auntie's a pure femme in the undergarment category." Carrie flattened her lips and raised an eyebrow. "She would never wear boyshorts."

"No. I guess not." It was true. Maggie couldn't imagine Lynn wearing anything the slightest bit butch. She was all woman, and Maggie loved her femininity.

They were all silent until they were seated at the restaurant with menus in their hands. Maggie and Carrie sat on one side of the booth, Lynn on the other.

Lynn looked up from her menu briefly. "Why is my love life so important to you all of a sudden?"

"I don't know. Maybe because I don't want you to be alone for the rest of your life? Or because I want you to be happy? Is it wrong for me to want that?"

Although Maggie was encouraged to hear Carrie's explanation, she was thrilled to see the waitress approach. Lynn wasn't at all ready for this conversation. "You ladies ready to order?"

Carrie glanced at the waitress, then at the menu, then back at the waitress. "I need a minute."

"I'm ready," Maggie said, not wanting her to leave and let Carrie continue her interrogation. "Scrambled eggs, bacon, and a short stack of pancakes." She handed the waitress the menu. "Oh, and coffee." She glanced across the table at Lynn and widened her eyes. "Lots of coffee."

"Me too on the coffee, and I'll have the spinach and mushroom omelet," Lynn said.

"Orange juice for me, but I'll have the same as her." Carrie pointed at Maggie.

"Thanks, ladies. I'll be right back with your coffee and juice." The waitress picked up the rest of the menus, left them in silence, and immediately returned with their drinks.

Carrie laced her fingers together on the table in front of her and stared at Lynn. "You haven't answered my question."

Lynn took a sip of her coffee. "Okay, fine. I'm seeing someone." The cup rattled against the table as she set it down.

"I knew it." Carrie's eyes widened. "What's her name? Is she cute? Where'd you meet her?"

Maggie stiffened as she anticipated Lynn's next words and readied herself for Carrie's reaction.

"Her name doesn't matter," she said as she glanced at Maggie and then back at Carrie. "She's beautiful, I met her at the hospital, and it's very new."

Conflicting emotions flew though Maggie. She'd wanted Lynn to tell Carrie so badly, yet in an odd way she was relieved that she hadn't. It seemed neither one of them was completely ready. What exactly did that mean?

"Is she a nurse?"

"A doctor." Lynn's voice wasn't as strong as Maggie had hoped it would be.

Carrie sat quietly for a moment, seeming to gather her thoughts. "Are you sure you want to get involved with another doctor?"

Maggie didn't mistake the worried look on Carrie's face as she stared at Lynn, and that was only the first problem. Lynn seemed to be planning to give partial details and possibly come up with some kind of story to pacify Carrie, which would only complicate their relationship more.

"Am I sure? No. Do I like her enough to see if it works? Yes."

Maggie took in a breath and settled her nerves. This was far from the end of their secrets, though it wasn't a make-or-break moment. It was only the beginning.

"Wow. You really like her."

Lynn nodded. "I do. So just let me see where it goes for now."

Maggie's cheeks warmed as Lynn made subtle eye contact and then quickly went back to Carrie.

"Okay." Carrie blew out a breath. "But I want to meet her as soon as you're sure."

"Count me in on that," Maggie said, trying not to make it obvious that she already knew Lynn's secret.

"Deal," Lynn said and took a drink of coffee.

Maggie was relieved to see the waitress bringing their food, her timing perfect once again. As Carrie's curiosity progressed, Maggie wondered if she'd connected her and Lynn's stories. Lynn hadn't indicated that she was seeing someone younger, or Carrie would've already figured it out. Hopefully, Carrie was satisfied for the time being. Lynn had just dug herself into a whole lot of untruth, and the walls would collapse on her soon.

CHAPTER TWENTY-THREE

A glove spilled onto the floor as Maggie yanked another from the wall dispenser. She tried to catch her breath as she tugged the pair over her fingers and immediately went to work assessing the young girl, who looked to be about twelve. It was near the end of her shift, but once she'd received the page from the ER for the consult, she'd shot down the stairs as fast as she could.

"What happened here?"

"Boating accident. Boat going too fast, hit the wake of another, and plowed right into theirs, splitting it in half." The ER doctor spoke so fast, Maggie almost couldn't make out the words. "She's complaining of dizziness and abdominal pain."

Maggie put light pressure on her abdomen in several areas and found the upper left quadrant to be tender. Suddenly Beth stood behind her waiting for her assessment. "Possible ruptured spleen." She pulled the girl's eyelids up and looked into her eyes. "Did she hit her head?"

"From what the witnesses said, they all hit the water hard." She glimpsed Andi standing outside the curtain as she spoke. She must have caught the call.

"Check her CT scans for a head, chest, and abdominal," Beth said, then walked to the next bay.

"Got it." She looked at the CT results and determined the girl had a ruptured spleen. She needed to take her up to surgery, where Beth would meet her in the OR.

"Wait." The girl grabbed her hand on the railing. "My brother. Where's my brother?"

As Beth pushed the curtain back in the next bay, Maggie overheard Andi tell Beth, "Thrown from the boat as well, became unconscious after they pulled him from the water, head laceration, and possible spinal injury."

She glanced over and saw him strapped to a backboard and collared to keep his neck immobile. It looked like Beth was examining his head injury. "Dr. Monroe is checking on him. She'll take good care of him."

When she turned around she ran right into Lynn, almost knocking her over. "Are the parents here?" she asked.

Lynn shook her head and whispered, "They didn't make it."

Maggie's stomach bottomed out, but she had to ignore her reaction as she raced back to the girl. These two children had a long road ahead of them. Life without parents would be horrible. "Can you call plastics if Beth hasn't already? The boy has a pretty bad laceration on his forehead."

"Sure." Lynn grabbed the other side of the gurney to push along with her to the elevator and then held eye contact while they waited.

Maggie knew what she was thinking. "I'm fine. I need to get her up to surgery."

Lynn nodded as the elevator door opened and she rolled the gurney inside. Lynn kept eye contact as the doors closed with her on the other side. When the doors opened again she rushed her patient straight into the operating room.

Beth arrived only a few minutes after Maggie. "Looks like your lucky day. You get to remove another spleen."

Her stomach churned. It was difficult to think of this little girl's misfortune as her luck. "How's the boy?"

"He has a broken leg. Other than that, he's okay. Ortho will set it."

"And the head?"

"I left it to plastics to suture. Seems someone had already called them."

She'd decided to have them called so he'd have less of a scar. The boy wouldn't need something in the mirror to remind him of the day he lost his parents.

❖

When the surgery was finished, Maggie removed her surgical gown and mask, then leaned against the wall outside the OR. She'd let the adrenaline rush carry her through the trauma and the surgery, and now she had to keep her mind off what was going to happen when the children learned about the loss of their parents. She'd couldn't bear to even think of that now. Who would they call? Did they have grandparents, aunts, or uncles? The thought of other siblings rushed her thoughts. What if they had younger brothers or sisters? Whether it was the exhaustion or the accident, the loss hit her like nothing she'd ever experienced. Her mother hadn't been the best parent in the world, but at least she'd had her after her father died. She had no idea what she would've done if she'd lost them both and how these children would survive without theirs.

The stairwell door clanged loudly as she threw it open and took the stairs by twos. She had to get out of there now. She rushed to the locker room, gathered her things without changing out of her scrubs, and headed home before she turned into a sobbing idiot. She couldn't let anyone at the hospital see her like this.

The run home was a blur. She saw only the streetlights as she dodged everything on the sidewalk. Lynn was waiting outside her apartment when Maggie bolted out of the elevator and down the hallway.

She tried her best to slide the key into the lock but couldn't make it happen. She pressed her head against the door. "They went out for a fun day at the lake, and some asshole changed their life forever."

"I know." Lynn rubbed her back gently.

She let out a huge sob as she turned, fell into Lynn, and grabbed hold as all her strength left her. Lynn held her close while she cried until she could finally catch her breath.

Lynn took the key from her and unlocked the door before she wrapped her arm around her and led her inside. She moved on autopilot to the bedroom, stripped her clothes off, and crawled into bed. She couldn't get the horrible thoughts out of her head, and then the memories of the day she received the news of her father's death hit her. Her whole life had changed in that instant. A drunk driver had killed her idol and her mentor, and she'd had to pick up the pieces when her mother fell apart. She hadn't had time to grieve then, and now everything rushed back full force. As she sobbed into her pillow, she felt Lynn slide in behind her and caress her arm softly.

"Talk to me," Lynn said.

"When my dad died, I was all alone with no one to help me. My mother was a complete zombie."

"I know, honey. I'm sure these kids have family to help them."

"You think?" She certainly hoped they didn't have to go through the same shit she had.

Lynn nodded. "We won't know for sure until tomorrow, but I plan to think positively, and you should too."

She sucked in a ragged breath. "I'll try." Maggie twisted to face her, and when Lynn kissed her forehead, she wrapped her arm around her waist, pulled her closer, and buried her head in Lynn's shoulder. No matter how it turned out, everything would be all right as long as Lynn was with her.

❖

Lynn went to check on the children, whom they'd placed in the same room to lessen their stress. She stopped just outside the door and listened while Maggie finished reading them a story. This morning, she'd gone directly to the bookstore and picked up a number of coloring books and pens, as well as some storybooks for each of them. *Captain Underpants* for Chase, teen magazines for Tiffany, and *The Hunger Games* boxed set to read to them both, a happy medium that they seemed good with. Maggie had told Lynn before that reading had always provided an escape for her when she was a child.

They were both keeping a close eye on the children, who were doing better than anticipated. Still somewhat medicated and in recovery mode from their injuries, they hadn't been hit by the reality of the situation yet. Although the staff had no way to lessen the impact of them losing their parents, they wanted to make the children as comfortable as possible during their hospital stay.

Maggie glanced up and raised a finger to Lynn, signaling she'd be out in a minute. Lynn let the door close and rested a shoulder against the wall while she waited just outside. Maggie wouldn't take the news about the children's guardian well.

Maggie came out and leaned against the wall facing her. "Were they able to contact the grandparents?"

She shook her head. "No grandparents or aunts and uncles."

Maggie pushed off the wall. "Then who's going to take care of them?"

"They have an older sister—"

"Where is she? Why wasn't she with them?"

"She's been away at college in Boston."

Maggie put her hand to her forehead and paced the floor. "Oh my God. Her life will be ruined. Has anyone talked to her?" Maggie stopped pacing and stared at her. Lynn felt the tears well in her own eyes. "You told her?"

She swiped the moisture from her eyes and tried to gain the courage to speak. She hated everything that had happened to this family. "I told her about her brother and sister over the phone, but not about her parents. That needs to be done face-to-face." Maggie swept her into her arms and held her there until she regained her composure. She knew people would see them, but Lynn didn't care. She'd found an ID badge in the father's wallet and contacted his place of work. Once she'd been connected to the right person in human resources, they'd transferred her to his supervisor, and he'd filled her in on the lack of extended family and given her the contact information for the older sister, Ariel, in Boston. After a number of unanswered calls to the girl's cell phone, Lynn had finally located her through the college, and Ariel was scheduled to arrive today sometime.

Thankfully, she'd gone to college close to her home and not halfway across the country. Boston was only a five-hour trip, so she'd be here soon. It was common for kids to want to go to college just far enough away to experience their freedom, but also close enough to drive home. Lynn ached for her, for what she would learn when she arrived. She couldn't imagine how it would've been for Carrie or how she would've handled it even without any siblings to care for.

When Lynn got news that Ariel had arrived and was in the family waiting room, she rushed straight there. She rounded the corner to the room designated on the fifth floor where the children were being cared for and came to a complete halt. Between the grief counselor, the chaplain, and the social worker, every seat in the room was occupied. Her stomach dropped when she found Maggie holding an inconsolable young lady. *Ariel.*

How had Maggie gotten there first? It was difficult to tell anyone they'd lost a family member, but being with someone from what seemed to be such a close-knit family was gut-wrenching. Lynn had wanted to spare Maggie such pain, but Maggie was taking charge on this one.

After Maggie got Ariel somewhat settled down, Lynn approached. "Do you have a minute?" she asked.

"Sure." Maggie patted Ariel on the leg and said, "I'll be right back."

"Are you okay?"

"I've got this." Maggie glanced back over her shoulder. "She'll be all right. She just needs time to absorb everything."

She shook her head. "You can't be her counselor, Maggie."

"I know, but she needs my support at this moment."

"Are you sure that's wise?"

Maggie nodded. "I'm fine, and she will be too once she sees her brother and sister."

"Is she prepared to see them without losing it? She hasn't even had time to grieve for her parents."

"It's better for her not to." She stared straight ahead as though reliving something in her head. "If she does, she won't be able to do anything for Chase or Tiffany, and they'll all be screwed."

Something between sorrow and pity filled Lynn. Maggie hadn't taken time to mourn the loss of her father right away and had lost any opportunity to do that when her mother stopped getting out of bed every day. Maggie hadn't confided in anyone. She couldn't. If she'd let anyone know what was going on, they would've removed her from her mother's care, and neither one of them might have ever recovered. As it was, Maggie's mom had come out of her depression with the help of medication and a good counselor, but Maggie had still never fully dealt with losing her father.

CHAPTER TWENTY-FOUR

How many different choices?" Lynn rubbed her forehead. "Okay. I'll be there as soon as I can." She punched the off button on the phone and dropped it onto the counter. "I don't remember having to make so many decisions when I got married." She pulled her sweatshirt on. "I have to go. Carrie's already in town and is meeting with the caterer in an hour. I can't help her over the phone."

"What?" Maggie said as she towel-dried her hair. "I thought you weren't supposed to meet her until later. Did she come in last night?"

"I guess so. They must've stayed at Scott's parents' house."

"Just wait a few minutes until I dry my hair, and I'll go with you."

"No. I really should—" Maggie's hands slipped around her waist, and at that moment it was the most comforting thing she could've ever done for her.

"They won't be there for an hour." She rested her chin on Lynn's shoulder. "Besides, you need to calm down before you get into that car. I don't want you taking out any fences or possibly ending up in a ditch on the way there."

"God, you know me so well." She rested her head against Maggie's.

"Come on. I'll fix you a cup of coffee. By the time you finish it, I'll be done, and we can go." She released her waist and took her hand, leading her into the kitchen.

❖

"I don't know if I made the right choices, but I'm glad that's over," Lynn said as she came through the door. They'd been out making wedding choices since early that morning. First the caterer, then the bridal shop to get a dress fitting, next the card shop for the invitations, and the last and the best part of the day, which was tasting wedding-cake samples. She didn't know how they were going to accomplish everything with their crazy schedules and lack of time. It felt like they'd crammed everything into one day as it was, and they still had so much more to do.

"I'm sure everything's going to be perfect," Maggie said, following her inside.

Carrie was right behind them. "I'm starving. Are we going to eat out or order in?" Her phone rang, she answered it, and then she paced as she listened. "Okay. I'll see you soon, then." She hit the end button on her phone and tossed it into her purse. "Change of plans. That was Scott. I need to run over to his folks' house for a bit. He has a few aunts that have come into town and want me to meet them."

"More aunts? I thought you were going to get to hang out with me and relax tonight."

"Sorry, Auntie. He has a huge family, and knowing them, we'll be there late," she said as she rushed into the spare bedroom and emerged with a small bag. "We'll probably stay there tonight. So I'll see you both tomorrow to work on the other arrangements." Carrie gave her a quick hug and left.

Lynn was a little disappointed but understood that Carrie had to get to know Scott's family. Even though she hadn't been able to spend any time with Scott, she still had time before the wedding.

"What a day," Maggie said as she flopped down in the corner of the couch. "If I'd known it'd take that long, I would've let you two go ahead without me this morning."

Lynn could see the mischief in her eyes as she widened them. "No, you wouldn't have." Lynn picked up Maggie's legs, swung them onto the leather cushion, and sat down on the edge of the couch near her waist. "I don't know what I'd have done without you these past few days."

"You would've managed." Maggie reached for a pillow at the end of the couch, coming within inches of Lynn's face. "What?"

"I think I'm going to kiss you now."

"Think?" Maggie cocked an eyebrow and tilted her head.

"I am going to—"

Maggie pounced, her lips on Lynn's before she could finish. She fell back to the couch, pulling Lynn on top of her. "I know it's only been a day, but I've missed you." Maggie's words came out in a breathless whisper between kisses.

"I've missed you too." Lynn moaned as Maggie's hands moved up the length of her and then into the strands of hair draping her shoulders. It was amazing how she'd gotten used to the subtle touches Maggie gave her when they were together and how much she craved them when she was stressed, like today. "Thank you for helping me."

"It was my pleasure." Maggie kissed her again gently. "I'm really glad Scott has lots of aunts."

A jolt of pain shot through her as she shifted closer. "Ow."

"That's a new one," Maggie said as pulled her brows together. "What hurts?"

"Just a kink in my neck." She sat up and rubbed the tendon between her neck and shoulder.

"Let me help you with that." Maggie scooted behind Lynn, moved her hair to the side, and massaged her shoulder.

Maggie pressed her lips to the spot where her shoulder blades met, and the jolt that coursed through her blocked out all the pain. "That feels wonderful."

"I need a dress. Apparently we're going out to dinner," Carrie said.

When Lynn heard her voice, she shot to her feet. She'd been so wrapped up in the sensations Maggie produced in her that she hadn't heard her come in.

Carrie stopped for a moment and assessed them. "Are you okay?"

"I'm fine. Maggie was just helping me work this kink out of my neck." She kneaded her shoulder as she crossed the room and flopped into the recliner.

Carrie hesitated, and Lynn thought she might say something more, but then she hurried into the bedroom and came back out carrying a dress. "See you tomorrow." She gave them one last stare and walked out the door.

Lynn wiped away the sudden perspiration that had beaded her forehead. She was going to have to tell her soon or change the lock on the door.

❖

Lynn had actually sent Maggie home last night. Yesterday, when Carrie had come back to get her dress, had been a really close call, and she couldn't chance her walking in on them again. In fact, Carrie had shown up ridiculously early this morning. Lynn suspected she might have been trying to catch her with someone, because Carrie pushed open the bedroom door without knocking.

She usually loved for Carrie to visit, but between her recent questions about who she was seeing and dealing with all the wedding arrangements this time, her visits had been more stressful than fun. Hiding her relationship with Maggie was becoming more difficult with each visit. When Carrie had arrived at Lynn's door before she'd left town last time, Lynn hadn't expected more questions, and she hoped she'd pacified her with the minimal amount of information she provided.

"I'm so glad you decided to get married at Clear Meadow Farm. It's absolutely beautiful in the fall, and I love the sunflower fields," Lynn shouted from the bathroom. "Hey. Where'd you go?" She came out of the bathroom and found Carrie sitting on the side of her bed holding up a T-shirt and staring at it.

Carrie flipped the shirt around so Lynn could see the Boston University logo. "You're sleeping with Maggie." It wasn't a question.

Heat rose on her neck. "What? No." She snatched the shirt away. "She must have left it here yesterday."

"She wasn't wearing it yesterday."

"Where did you find it?"

"Under the bed with these." She held up a pair of black boyshorts between her fingertips.

Fuck. "Those are mine." She tried to take them from Carrie's hand, but she pulled them away.

"No, they're not. You'd never wear these." Carrie held them from edge to edge. "They're not even your size." She tossed them onto the bed and shook her head as the pieces seemed to come together in her head. "You're Sunflower."

Lynn took in a breath and nodded.

"How long?"

"A few weeks."

"I should've known she'd do this. She's always had a thing for you."

"What?"

"Ever since we were in college. Don't you think I know she wasn't coming over to see me? She always spent more time with you." Her eyes widened. "Were you two fucking then?"

"Watch your language," Lynn said. She refused to let Carrie turn what she had with Maggie into something cheap and dirty.

"Were you? Is that why you and Beth split? Because of Maggie?" Carrie bulleted her with questions.

"Absolutely not. Beth was never home. It was like being single, except I had to cook and do laundry for her."

"So you *weren't* fucking Maggie then."

"No. I *wasn't* fucking her." Even if she had been, she would never reduce what they had to just fucking.

"But you knew how she felt about you."

Lynn nodded. "She told me. That's why she distanced herself during your last year of college. I was still trying to make it work with Beth."

"I told her to stay the fuck away from you."

"You did what?"

"I saw what was going on. I'm not blind. She was like a lovesick puppy helping you in the kitchen and in the yard, and following you all the time. It was disgusting." Carrie rolled her eyes. "I told her if she wanted to be my friend, she had to stay away from you."

It all made sense now, especially that night she'd found Maggie drunk on the porch in the rain. Even though Lynn had squashed whatever was happening between them, Maggie hadn't *chosen* to stop coming around. She'd left because of Carrie. "Are you planning to give her the same ultimatum now?"

"I might." She rushed through the apartment to the front door.

"Stop right there, young lady. I'm a grown woman and can make my own decisions about who I see."

"She's the reason you never came to Boston. Come to think of it, you never wanted to see her the whole time we were in med school." Her eyes went wide. "You felt something for her too. You were seeing her then."

"No. No. Never. Believe me, I tried to make it work with Beth, but it was always a one-sided effort."

"I don't believe you."

"Ask Maggie. She'll tell you."

"I'm going to do just that." Carrie swung around and put up a hand as she got into the elevator. "You stay here."

The back of Lynn's neck stung as she watched the doors close. Then she ran back to her apartment and searched for her phone. She looked in the kitchen, then the bedroom. *Think, Lynn. Where did you leave it?* She rushed to the couch in the living room and yanked off the cushions. It fell to the floor, and she immediately put in Maggie's number. It rang three times and then went to voice mail. *Shit.* She dropped down onto the couch. All she could do now was wait.

❖

When Maggie opened the door, she was totally surprised to see Carrie standing in the hallway and even more surprised to see her scowl. "Hey. I thought you and Lynn would be on your way to Clear Meadow Farm by now."

Carrie pushed past her into the apartment, spun around, and threw the T-shirt and boyshorts at her. "You're fucking my aunt?"

"Wow. You sure know how to make something sound cheap."

"Don't even." Carrie came at her hot. "You've been after her for years."

She balled her fist around the clothing in her hand and stood her ground. "You know what? You're right. I begged Lynn to love me back then, and it just about killed me when she said no."

"You just couldn't leave her alone, could you?"

"Honestly, I asked her point-blank when I found out she was single, and she told me no again, asked me to back off. So I did." Her face heated as anger bubbled inside. "But you can't stop something that's meant to be."

"If you choose to continue with this ridiculousness, we will no longer be friends."

"I made that mistake once before and lost four years with her because of you. I'm not letting her go again."

Lynn rushed into the apartment. "Both of you stop. Right now. I could hear you from the elevator." She stood between them. "No one makes decisions for me, except me." She took Carrie's arm and pulled her to the door. "Let's go."

"Lynn. Wait," Maggie called after her.

Lynn turned back, put a hand up, and said, "Not now. I can't." She turned away quickly and pulled the door shut behind her.

Maggie's logic had been flawed. Of course Carrie would be okay with Maggie dating an older woman, but she wasn't aware that older woman was her aunt. How stupid could she be? How could she throw that in Carrie's face after lying to her about everything? She had no idea how she was going to make this right. She spent the rest of the evening pacing the apartment and then finally ended up curled into a ball in bed. It was past ten p.m. and she hadn't heard from Lynn or Carrie. She'd forced herself not to text or call either of them, but her resolve was weakening. They needed time to work things out between them. Hopefully Lynn could convince Carrie that her feelings for Lynn were genuine and that she'd never intended to hurt her.

She jumped when her phone chimed. A text from Lynn.

She's gone home.

I'll be right up.

No. I have an early shift. I need to rest.

Maggie hit the button to call her. She refused to have this discussion via text. It was too important. The phone rang a few times before Lynn answered, not a good sign.

"Did you talk to her? Explain we haven't done anything wrong?"

"I did."

"Sooo—"

"She doesn't care. According to her, we've both betrayed her trust. We lied about the whole thing."

"So, she's upset that we lied, or she's upset about the relationship?"

"Both."

"You know she'll come around."

"She didn't the last time," Lynn said, sounding deflated and weary. "You spent four years away, and she didn't once tell you it was okay, did she?"

"I want to see you." She went to the door, held the knob. "We need to talk about this."

"Not tonight. I need to think."

"What does that mean?" Her voice cracked, vulnerability seeping out. Was Lynn really considering breaking up with her?

"Honestly, I don't know."

"So you're just going to stop seeing me because of Carrie?" She paced the living room. "That's crazy."

"I need to go." Lynn's voice wavered, and Maggie knew she was on the verge of tears. "Please don't come up. I need some time to sort this out."

"Okay," she said, and the line went dead.

She couldn't deny the pain slashing through her heart as she sank to the couch. She'd just found out how insignificant she was to Lynn and might have lost the only woman she'd ever really loved.

CHAPTER TWENTY-FIVE

Maggie's stomach jumped when she spotted Lynn at the nurses' station. It had been two days since they'd spoken, and she hadn't seen Lynn at all since she'd asked her for space. Maybe she should turn around and walk the other way, but her heart wouldn't let her. Her feet, almost on autopilot, took her to the spot right next to Lynn, where she waited as Lynn finished charting a patient's vitals. She couldn't avoid Lynn at work. They were both very involved with Tiffany and Chase, and Maggie didn't intend to abandon them because she was uncomfortable.

When Lynn looked up, her eyes were dull, circles surrounding them as though she hadn't slept. The sight cut through her, but at least she was feeling the pain too.

"Hi," Lynn said softly.

"Hi. Are you okay?"

"No." She shrugged. "I can't see you until Carrie comes around to the idea. No matter how long it takes."

Her neck burned, and she almost couldn't catch her breath. "And if she doesn't?" A lump formed in her throat, and she fought to hold the tears threatening to spill from her eyes.

"Then I don't know."

That wasn't a sufficient answer. She couldn't just wait in the background while her best friend dictated her future. The fact that Lynn was going to let Carrie call the shots made her wonder if she was wrong about their whole connection. For her to just let her go without a fight didn't make sense and was incredibly hurtful.

"How are the Roberts kids today?" Lynn asked.

So, this was the way she was going to play it from now on, strictly business. Maggie took in a deep breath and shoved all her emotions back into the cage they'd begun crawling from. "Being released soon," she said, hearing the waver in her own voice. She'd always been good at concealing her emotions when she had to, but this time it was so much harder.

"Oh. That's good. Who's taking them?"

"I don't know. Social services hasn't cleared them to go with Ariel yet. I don't think they're convinced she's prepared to care for the children."

"Maybe she's not. She's barely twenty-one and living away at college. In another state." Lynn spoke with such conviction, maybe she was right.

She shook the thought from her head. "I've talked to her. She'll be okay."

"She's not you, Maggie. She may not be able to handle it. Don't you remember how difficult it was for you?"

"It wasn't that hard."

"It was. You ended up at my house in tears."

"That was because of my mother, not because my dad died."

"It all goes together. Don't you see that? Think about what you had to do when your dad died."

"This has nothing to do with that."

"It has everything to do with that. You had to step into the world of adulthood immediately. You didn't have an opportunity to be a teenager, to go through adolescence normally. She'll have to give all that up too. Do you want that for her?"

"She's not an adolescent. She's twenty-one, much older than I was when I lost my dad. She can handle it."

"She's still in her formative years. What if she can't? You just don't stop raising kids when they turn eighteen. Your expectations for Ariel are just as high as your mother's were for you. You need to realize the differences between you and Ariel. She's already on her path, and it's going to be interrupted, put on hold at the very least."

"Don't bring my mother into this." This was not the day for this discussion.

"You're more like her than you'd like to think. That demanding streak in you—"

"I'm nothing like my mother." She stiffened. Even thinking she could be anything like the woman was ridiculous.

"She had no idea how hard it was for you. She just sent you out on your own. Now you're going to do the same thing to Ariel, only she has a sister and brother to care for as well. She'll be even more scarred than you."

"Oh. So now I'm scarred as well as demanding?"

"Jesus, Maggie. I didn't mean it like that." She took her by the arms and held her. "We always say we aren't going to be the same as the ones who hurt us, but the pattern has to be broken."

Maggie pushed out of her grasp. "No. You don't get to do that anymore. I'm not a child, and I won't be in that kind of relationship with you. There are things you *can't* do, and there are things I *won't* do."

"You're just like Beth. You have no idea what it takes to be a good parent."

She was tired of being compared to someone who didn't have a shred of compassion. She bit her bottom lip, trying to hold in her anger, but it spilled out anyway. "I'm nothing at all like Beth, and the fact that you can't see that makes me wonder if we ever even had a shot. If I'd just stayed in Boston…" She took in a breath, trying to keep her voice steady. "My heart would still be mine, and life would so much easier now." At least her life would be hers and hers alone, without Lynn to make her doubt all her choices.

"You don't mean that." Tears gathered in the corners of Lynn's eyes. The statement had clearly cut deep. Lynn didn't say another word. She just swiped away the tears, spun around, and took off down the hallway. Maggie wanted to run after her, take her into her arms, and tell her she didn't mean any of it. But she couldn't hold her anger back any longer. It had been festering for days and was now front and center in everything she did. She'd needed to release it.

She stood just outside Chase's room and took in a deep breath. These kids would not see the turmoil in her life. It was now or never. She plastered on a smile and pushed open the door. "Hey, guys. How are we doing today?"

Tiffany didn't look up, just kept her eyes on the computer sitting on her lap, but Chase smiled widely. Ariel glanced up from the magazine she'd been reading but remained seated in the corner chair.

"I can wiggle my toes more," he said as he did exactly that.

"That's awesome." She touched his big toe. "This little piggy went to market, this little piggy stayed home…"

Chase quickly joined her. "This little piggy had roast beef, this little piggy had none. This little piggy went wee, wee, wee, all the way home." They both laughed when they finished.

She glanced over at Tiffany, who had looked up from the laptop and was smiling. It usually took her a minute, but she always seemed to join in the fun. "What are you playing today, Princess Tiff?" Maggie had used the nickname since Tiffany had first come out of anesthesia after surgery, and she seemed to like it.

"No game today." She glanced at Chase's leg. "The internet says he's going to need physical therapy for a while." Tiffany seemed very smart and was very inquisitive.

"That's true. Probably outpatient a few times a week."

"So, we can go home?"

"I think we may be able to spring you both tomorrow."

"Will you come see us?"

"Of course. I'll put you on my schedule." She never got involved with patients. It was best to let them go when they left the hospital. But these children were different and had earned a small place in her heart, so in this case she'd make an exception.

"They really like you," Ariel said. "They're never that happy to see me."

"You just have to be interested in what they have to say."

"You talk to them like my mom and dad did." Tears began to well in her eyes. "I don't know if I can fill that role."

"Hey. Why don't we get out of here?" She held out her hand and Ariel took it. "I'm borrowing your sister for a little while. Don't cause any trouble while we're gone."

"We will," Tiffany said as they left the room.

She stopped by the nurses' station and grabbed a couple of sodas before she led Ariel to the family waiting room, where they sat in the corner.

She handed Ariel one of the sodas, then opened hers and took a drink as she relaxed into her chair.

"Child Services hasn't signed off on you taking your brother and sister yet. So, they'll probably be placed in foster care until that issue is resolved."

"What? They can't do that, can they?"

"They can and they will, but hopefully only for a couple of days."

"Will they stay together?"

"I don't know. They always try to keep siblings together, but it depends on who's available to care for them."

Ariel stared across the room. "My parents would never forgive me if I let that happen."

She took Ariel's hand. "Listen. I know this is hard."

"You don't. You have no idea."

"Actually, I do. I didn't lose both my parents, but I did lose my dad." She stared into Ariel's eyes, not losing contact. "It hit my mom so hard that she was a wreck for a long time after that."

"So you and your brothers and sisters were placed in foster care?"

"No. I didn't have any brothers and sisters, and I didn't go into foster care, but I had to take care of my mother." She took in a deep breath. "It won't be easy, but they'll be okay until you get custody. I'll be here to help you." She reached into her pocket and took out her phone. "What's your phone number?"

Ariel rattled off her number as Maggie typed it into the "To" area of the text. She typed in her name and her address and sent the text.

"You can call me anytime you need to."

The phone chimed from Ariel's pocket, and she smiled.

"Do you have kids?"

"Not yet, but someday."

"You'll make a good mom."

"I hope so," she said with a smile, warming at the comment. But the warmth vanished when she thought about the argument she'd just had with Lynn.

❖

Lynn had seen Maggie leading Ariel from the hospital room and had followed them to the family room down the hall. She'd stood just outside the open door and listened as they talked. A mixture of admiration and trepidation washed over her as Maggie calmed Ariel.

Everything she'd said would put Ariel on the right path to caring for her brother and sister, except the part where Maggie would be there to help. Maggie couldn't guarantee she would be involved in Ariel's life and shouldn't promise, especially with her schedule at the hospital. There was a line between doctor and patient for a reason, even with children. Each day in pediatrics Lynn fought the battle to stay detached. It wasn't easy, but she forced herself to leave the after-hospital issues to social services.

The Maggie standing in front of her earlier was so much different than the Maggie she'd held in her arms a few nights before. The raw emotion she'd seen was gone, replaced with some sort of skewed logic. It was possibly the only way Maggie could deal with the set of circumstances, considering the similarities between Ariel's and her own adolescent situation.

The other big game-changer had been Carrie's discovery of their relationship and her own lack of certainty in dealing with it. She'd made a horrible mistake by not talking to Maggie after Carrie left to explain her concerns and make her understand. She'd tried to call Maggie several times, but each time her phone had gone directly to voice mail. Lynn didn't know if she could walk this tightrope much longer. Her heart was being torn in two different directions. She did love Maggie and couldn't imagine a future without her, but she couldn't go back on everything she'd promised Carrie in the past either.

At the end of her shift, after circling the hospital outside several times, Lynn found herself sitting in Heather's office located in her private practice in the medical building adjacent to the hospital. Heather had one more patient to see and then would be done for the day, and Pam would be there shortly to pick her up.

The door clicked open and brought Lynn out of her thoughts. Pam walked in and sat in the chair next to her and said, "Hey. What are you doing here?"

"Carrie found out about Maggie, and I don't know what to do." Normally she would've started with something simple, but she couldn't muster small talk right now. She hadn't told Pam about Carrie's reaction to her discovery of her relationship with Maggie, or how she'd discovered it.

"I take it she was upset?"

She nodded. "I've never seen her like that or heard her use the word 'fuck' so much." She went through how it had all played out and tried to keep her emotions calm.

"Hmm." Pam seemed thoughtful. "What do you think that's about?"

"Apparently, she knew Maggie had a crush on me before."

Pam's eyebrows went up. "When she was younger?"

She nodded. "When they were in college. Maggie spent a lot of time at our house. She practically lived there."

Pam's face relaxed as she took in the information. "So she thinks you and Maggie were involved while you were married to Beth."

"Yes."

Pam tilted her head and asked, "Were you?"

A chill ran through her as memories floated through her mind. "We weren't. I swear. I put a stop to that as soon as I knew what was happening."

"And she doesn't believe you," Pam said.

The breath she took in caught in her throat as she thought about Carrie's ultimatum. "She told Maggie to stay away from me or they would no longer be friends." Hearing that demand had ripped at Lynn's heart. How could she possibly do that to Maggie again? Yet Carrie had done exactly that, and Lynn had stolen the choice from Maggie and made it herself. She could never let anyone or anything ruin her relationship with her daughter. Could she?

"Okay." Pam seemed to be putting the pieces together in her head. "You always wondered why Maggie disappeared so quickly and never kept in touch."

"I did." When Maggie had reappeared in Baltimore, Lynn had told Pam about Maggie's ghosting her after going to Boston for medical school. "Now Carrie has given us both the same ultimatum, and she's not backing down."

"You want me to talk to her?"

"I don't know if that will help. Since her mother left, she's always had insecurity issues where I'm concerned." She rubbed the fabric of her scrubs on her legs. "And Beth's continued absence didn't make things any better. I'm the only stable person in her life." Carrie had been so closed off when she'd first come into Lynn's life. It took her an enormously long time to adjust, and when Carrie had finally realized

Lynn wasn't going anywhere, she'd opened up completely. Her raw vulnerability was heartbreaking, and Lynn would never break the bond they'd forged.

"The only stable person besides Maggie."

She nodded. "Yeah, besides Maggie." No matter what had happened between them, she was grateful that Maggie had always been there for Carrie.

"And how's Maggie taking it?"

"I haven't handled that very well. I kind of put Carrie first." Her stomach rolled as she thought about the confrontation.

"But you do love Maggie."

She swiped at the tear that had escaped her eye. "So much I can't imagine my life without her."

"Okay then. You've explained all this to Carrie, right?"

"Yes, but she's not accepting any of it."

"You should talk to Maggie. You can't have a relationship with her and live in a silo. It impacts both of you, and she needs to be part of this. Let her help."

"I don't want to lose Carrie."

"I doubt she'll cut either of you out of her life. She's playing you both like a child, using your feelings against each other."

The door opened, and Heather came into the room. "Well, this is nice. Two of my favorite people." She kissed Pam and then looked at Lynn and said, "Where's your other half?" She took a double take. "What's wrong?" she asked, the concern in her voice clear.

"Maggie's wrapped up with the Roberts kids," Pam said, knowing she didn't want to go into the whole story again and that she would fill Heather in on the personal details later. "They're being released tomorrow, and Lynn's worried she's become too involved with them."

"If she continues down this path and promises these children things she can't do, it won't end well for any of them." Maggie's distress had made more sense after Lynn learned of the similarity between the children's situation and Maggie's.

"I'll check and see if I can help out." Heather jotted a note on the pad sitting on her desktop. "Are they seeing a counselor yet?"

"No. Not yet. Maggie hasn't pushed that."

Heather frowned. "I'll make a few calls and get something set up."

Tears burned her cheeks. "You two are so awesome. I don't know what I'd do without you." And she really didn't. Since her divorce from Beth and returning to work, Pam and Heather had become her family.

"We gotcha," Pam said as she patted her leg.

"Maggie is going to be a wonderful mother someday. This just isn't the right time." Lynn had seen Maggie's dedication and her change of views on the parent-child relationship. If she decided to have more children, Maggie would be the only person she'd consider raising them with.

❖

The parking lot was full when Maggie arrived at Andi's apartment, and as she stood in front of her door, she wondered if she was doing the right thing. Andi had told her she had a spare bedroom, and after discussing it with Rita to avoid any more jealousy issues, Andi had told her she was welcome to stay as long as she wanted. Going home was depressing, and she couldn't bear running into Lynn right now. She needed time and space to gather her thoughts, to concentrate on being a doctor, or she was going to screw up everything she'd worked so hard for.

She forged ahead and knocked. It wasn't long before the door swung open and Andi swept her into a hug. "Hey. I'm glad you decided to come." She moved aside and waved her in.

"Thanks for letting me stay," she said as she entered.

"Of course." Andi took her bag and carried it into the bedroom. "How are the kids?" Andi asked as she came out again. She knew Maggie had made a connection with them from the start, and she'd been keeping up on their progress as well.

"They're good. Should be able to go home in a couple of days."

"With the older sister?"

Maggie nodded. "Ariel."

"How's she dealing with all this?"

"She's okay. She's staying at her parents' home here in Baltimore until social services finishes their review. Chase still needs physical therapy, so he and Tiffany will stay at the hospital until Ariel's approved. That's the best place to care for them until that happens."

"What about foster care?"

"Finding someone who can handle Chase's needs might be tough. Besides, Ariel wants them with her."

"I thought I heard someone say Ariel goes to college out of state."

"Boston University. I made some calls to my old academic counselor, and she arranged for her to continue her studies online until she gets through this semester. Then they'll reassess."

"How about you? How are you doing?"

"I've been a thousand times better, but I'll survive." Maybe that was true or maybe not.

"You want to talk about it?"

"Lynn doesn't want me as much as I want her. I'm not sure what more there is to say."

"Let her work it out. Kids can complicate even the most perfect relationships. Even when both their parents are involved."

"That's what I'm finding out." She rubbed her head. "What I don't get is that Carrie is my best friend. I've never done anything to make her think I'd hurt her or Lynn in any way. Why is it so difficult for her to get that?"

"She just had different expectations, and sometimes those are hard to adjust. Have you talked to her?"

"She won't answer my calls, and I've sent a few texts. No response."

"Lay low and let her get used to the idea."

"Easier said than done."

"Isn't it worth waiting it out?"

"Absolutely." Maggie had mastered patience at work, but not in her personal life. She hoped Andi was right and Carrie would rethink her position, but having known her for some time, Maggie wasn't counting on it.

CHAPTER TWENTY-SIX

Still temporarily living in Andi's spare bedroom, Maggie hadn't spoken to Lynn outside of work in more than a week. Ariel had been approved by social services to care for Tiffany and Chase and had taken them to their family home. That left Maggie and Lynn with nothing to discuss since they were still at an impasse regarding Carrie. Functioning in a numbing, zombie-like state, Maggie was resigned to bury her feelings just as she had in the past and focus on her work to get through it all.

After showering and crawling into bed, she drifted off to sleep with the same dream as always floating through her head, one that included lying next to Lynn and feeling content because it would happen every day for the rest of her life. After having enjoyed that reality briefly, it was now a vivid fantasy she was having trouble getting past. Waking up alone and wishing things were different only made her more miserable. She reached for her phone, found the meditation application, and started the sounds of light rain to calm her thoughts. Before she could return it to the nightstand, the phone rang. Stacy's name popped up on the screen, and she hit the green button to answer.

"Hey, Stace. What's up?" she asked as she pulled the sheet over her shoulder.

"Where are you?" Stacy's voice was low but urgent.

"At Andi's." Stacy had been spending most of her nights at Russell's lately and was unaware Maggie had been staying at Andi's place to avoid running into Lynn.

"You need to come home, *right now*," Stacy said, still in a whisper. She figured Stacy must have gone out tonight and had enough alcohol to conduct party-counselor office hours. Stacy gave lots of advice when she was drunk.

"Listen, I'm tired. I don't want to talk about my fucked-up life right now. I'll be home in a few days."

"No. You need to come now." Stacy's voice was firm. "Your patients are here."

"What? Who?"

"Tiffany and Chase."

"Alone?"

"The sister is here too. She brought them. So get your ass home."

"On my way." Her mind swirled as she pulled on her yoga pants and stuffed the rest of the belongings she'd brought with her into her bag. On her way out, she stopped in the kitchen and wrote a note to Andi, then snuck out silently and hurried down the stairs to her car.

When Maggie rushed through the door of the apartment, the look of pure terror on Ariel's face alarmed her. "Are the kids okay?" she asked as she sped across the room and dropped her bag to the floor.

"The kids are fine," Stacy said very calmly, not losing eye contact with Maggie. "I've settled the younger kids in my room watching a movie, for the time being." She was sitting on the couch with Ariel, holding her hand.

"But Ariel needs some help. Why don't you come sit down?" She patted the spot on the couch next to her and then looked back at Ariel. "Go ahead. It's okay. Tell her."

"I can't take care of them. It's too much." Ariel's eyes were red and swollen as though she'd been crying.

"But in your texts, you said everything was good." She couldn't hide the irritation in her voice. Ariel should've never taken them if she couldn't handle the responsibility.

"I lied because I didn't want to disappoint you...or my parents. I thought I could do it, but school is too hard."

Thoughts sprang into Maggie's mind of how she'd had to scramble to find money, create unique ways to handle the finances, and quickly learn to forge her mother's signature. School had never been at the forefront of her mind, but then again she was in high school, not college. "Do you need food? Money? What? All you have to do is ask me," she said, her voice rising as irritation rang through again.

"Chase isn't sleeping at night, and he wants my attention all the time. I can't concentrate on my schoolwork at all. Every time he hears a noise, or even if the TV is too loud, he freaks out." She bolted up and paced across the room. "I can't even drive on the highway without him freaking out. He fucking grabbed the steering wheel the other day, and we almost hit someone head-on."

Maggie followed Ariel across the room. "Irritability or outbursts of anger, difficulty concentrating, hypervigilance, and exaggerated startle response are all normal facets of PTSD," she said as she rubbed Ariel's back, not sure quite how to handle the situation. Sure, she'd calmed many hysterical family members, but never for something like this. Counselors were always available at the hospital to refer patients to.

"Caring for him is too hard. I've never been the best big sister, and I'm just not ready for any of this." Tears sprang from her eyes, and Ariel fell into her arms. "Not full-time anyway."

"Sure you can. It's just new. You'll get used to it." She didn't know who she was trying to convince, herself or Ariel.

"They don't listen to me at all, and they hate me for bossing them around. I can't even remember to put money in their lunch accounts, let alone *make* them lunches to take to school." She was sobbing so hard, she could barely get the words out. "And getting Chase to physical therapy takes a lot of time, so I'm falling really behind in my homework."

The vulnerability and fear she saw in Ariel was a wake-up call, and she suddenly realized what Lynn meant when she said parenting didn't stop at eighteen. Just because she was forced to be an adult so early in life didn't mean it was the right thing for her, and it wouldn't be for Ariel either. She wanted to take Ariel's pain and fear, lock it in a box, and throw away the key. She had only one choice now.

"Okay, then I'll help you." She glanced over at Stacy, who had widened her eyes in a silent what-the-fuck-are-you-doing question. "You can stay here with me until we figure it out." She glanced back at Stacy. "You can stay with Russell for a while, can't you?"

"I can, but—"

"Then it's settled. We'll do this together." She put her arm around Ariel's shoulder and squeezed. "I'll rearrange my schedule, and you can all stay with me for the next few days." Maggie didn't intend to contact the social worker until she got them all calmed down because they would remove the children from their sister's custody immediately. Maggie planned to do everything in her power to make sure they remained together, or at least connected in some way.

"Come on. We'll put you and Tiffany in my room. I'll take the couch for now and keep an eye on Chase."

Once she'd gotten the two girls settled into her bedroom, she grabbed some sheets and a blanket from the hall closet and dropped them on the end of the couch.

Stacy was in the living room waiting when she came back out. "Are you really serious about this?"

"They have nowhere to go. I'm not letting those kids be forced into foster care with complete strangers. Not after what they've been through."

"*You* were a complete stranger a couple of weeks ago."

"But I'm not now. I'm all they have."

"You can't do this alone and still work all your hours at the hospital," Stacy said, and she was probably right. "Are you going to call someone to help you?"

Stacy meant Lynn, and that had been her immediate instinct since they'd both been so involved in the children's care after the accident. She picked up her phone and hit the button and called Heather instead. She hadn't asked her for help, but Heather had set up the grief counseling and assisted with the funeral arrangements when she'd found out none had been made. She didn't know where she'd be right now if Heather hadn't taken charge. She certainly couldn't go to Lynn with anything, because Lynn had already lost enough faith in her.

She sat in the chair next to Chase, who had finally fallen asleep in Stacy's bed. The innocence in his face was clear, and the thought of him dealing with such a tragedy so early in life made her gut twist. She'd just dozed off when he shot straight up and stared into space like a zombie. An earsplitting scream quickly followed his look of pure terror. She bolted out of the chair to the bed, gathered him in her arms, and held him as he shook. She'd never felt so helpless as she did at that moment. A horrible accident had torn his parents from him, and she couldn't do anything to make his pain and fear go away.

❖

Heather had been gracious enough to meet with Maggie the next morning, and she'd advised her of how big a commitment caring for the children would be, just as Stacy had the night before. Heather hadn't been against it. She'd simply pointed out all the obstacles it posed for her in the future. She'd also said she'd support Maggie in whatever she decided to do.

Heather had consulted an attorney, a friend of hers, to figure out the logistics of the fostering path if Maggie chose to pursue it. Ariel had custody of the kids, so giving Maggie any type of parental rights would be difficult unless Ariel relinquished them. Medical care, school issues, and finances would all have to be shared with Ariel.

While Ariel seemed all in on receiving Maggie's help, she was hesitant to change anything legally, which Heather viewed as a wise move. After all, none of them knew each other that well outside of the patient care Maggie had provided for the kids in the hospital. Plus, since Maggie wasn't a relative, she would have to go through the standard process to become a foster parent or guardian for the children. So for now, they would live at her place but remain in Ariel's custody until they made a decision.

She'd avoided Lynn's calls for the past few days, but when Lynn had sent the last text apologizing and begged her to meet her, she'd agreed to visit Lynn's apartment tonight to talk. She didn't know what Lynn had to say, and she had so much on her plate right now she was honestly too tired and indifferent to care. Ariel had essentially given up responsibility, and the children had become much more of a handful than Maggie had anticipated.

The door swung open immediately after she knocked, as though Lynn was waiting just on the other side. Her belly dipped at the sight of Lynn dressed in a flowered summer dress and flip-flops. The subtle liner outlining her eyes made her emerald-green eyes pop, and her smile was wide and beautiful.

"Come in." She moved to the side so Maggie could enter. "I'm glad you're here."

"Sure." She glanced back at her. "I won't stay long. It looks like you might have plans." She swore to herself she was going to play nice but couldn't seem to do it.

"No. No plans. I mean, other than talking to you," Lynn said with a tentative smile.

A jolt zapped through Maggie, knowing the dress and the makeup were meant for her and no one else. "I don't have a lot of time. I need to get back to the kids."

"The Roberts kids?"

She nodded. "Ariel was having a hard time, so they've been staying with me for the past few days."

Lynn's eyebrows pulled together. "What are your plans with them?"

Debating if she should confide in Lynn, she turned and walked farther into the apartment but didn't sit. "I'm thinking about fostering them."

"Maggie." The concern in Lynn's voice was clear. "Fostering those children will change your life completely. Your goals of becoming the doctor you've prepared to be will be pushed so far out of reach. I've lived this scenario, and I know exactly how it can affect your life."

"Did you regret raising Carrie? 'Cause it certainly sounds like you gave up a lot for her." She hadn't expected support from Lynn, but she hadn't expected such opposition either.

"No." She shook her head. "I never regretted putting my career on the back burner to raise Carrie, but I know the dedication it takes."

"And you don't think I have the dedication to care for these kids?"

Lynn took in a deep breath and shook her head. "No more drunken nights out with your friends."

Maggie narrowed her eyes. "You know that's not an issue for me."

"Do I?" She raised an eyebrow. "Not too long ago you were getting IV-hydrated at the hospital."

"That was because of you." She pointed a finger at Lynn. "If you'd been truthful with me from the beginning, it would've never happened."

"Don't count on these children being truthful with you all the time, because kids hide things, and they get into trouble, intentional or not. Parents can't slip up. You can't drink or disappear on them."

The jab indicated that Lynn was upset that Maggie hadn't responded to her calls or texts until today. "You don't get to tell me what I can and cannot do."

"No. That will be up to social services to monitor." Lynn rolled her lips in. "You want to be a doctor, Maggie. You have ever since you were a kid. You can't become one and raise kids successfully all on your own. Look at the mess you're in now."

"Is that what you're calling them? A mess?"

"I didn't mean it that way." She let out a sigh. "Not them. The situation. Chase is going to need someone who can take him through this full-time, and you can't do that. Plus, you'd be taking on not just Chase and Tiffany, but Ariel as well. You essentially have three children to care for, because Ariel is nowhere near not needing a mother. Can you fill that role for all of them? Alone?"

Maggie held back her tears and swallowed the lump in her throat. She wanted all of it, but she'd fully expected to have it with Lynn someday, and that wasn't going to happen. She had to let go of that dream of her fairy-tale life. "You know what? You're right. If you think that little of me, you and I will never work. I'm not a child. I've pretty much been on my own since I was eighteen. I'm not Beth either, but you keep comparing me to her, and I can't be with someone who doesn't believe in me." Her phone chimed, and a text from Ariel popped up, asking if she had any catsup. She brushed past Lynn and went to the door.

"Is it the kids?"

"No. I have to go," she lied and rushed out the door. Was it true, what Lynn had said? Did she have no clue about the commitment it took to raise kids? Her mother hadn't been much of a parent, but Maggie wanted to be so much more than her mother ever was. Even so, she'd turned out okay, hadn't she?

She took out her phone and texted Ariel, telling her the location of the catsup and that she'd be home later, to call if she needed her. After that, she went straight to Heather's office. What if Lynn was right? What if she was doing the worst thing for all of them?

Heather relaxed into her chair. "You're a very strong woman, that's not in question here, but let me ask you something," she said, and waited for Maggie to look at her. "How old were you when your father died?"

"I'd just turned sixteen." Her stomach twisted as the memory flashed in her head. She'd been at a friend's house spending the night after they'd had a fantastic day at the lake with her and her family. She felt so guilty for even remembering the fun, like her father's death was some sort of interruption. From then on her life had become about her mother.

"Would you have taken a different path if you hadn't had to care for your mother?"

"I'd still be a doctor, if that's what you're asking. Probably a better one. I didn't have as much time to prepare." Her choices had disappeared, and her days had changed from ones of freedom and fun to including more responsibility than she'd ever imagined. "Oh, my God," she whispered as she bolted out of her chair. "I've done the same thing to Ariel, haven't I?"

Heather pressed her lips together. "It's okay, honey." She stood, crossed the room, and took her into her arms.

Everything she'd said to Ariel flashed through her head as she sobbed into Heather's shoulder. "It kills me that I can't do anything to help then. Raising children shouldn't be so hard."

"It can be ridiculously hard at times, but it can also be wonderful at others. You'll be a great mentor to Ariel, but Tiffany and Chase need support that neither Ariel nor you can provide right now." Heather released her, lifted her chin with her fingers, and stared into her eyes. "Do you agree?"

She nodded. "But I don't want them to be separated."

"I don't want that either." Heather took in a deep breath. "Maybe Pam and I can help. We've been trying to have a baby for so long, but life hasn't given us that gift. Maybe this is where we're needed more."

"You'd do that?"

"Well, I have to talk to Pam first." She smiled and nodded. "But, yes, I think she'll agree."

"Oh my God, that would be so wonderful." She hugged Heather hard. "Then Ariel could go back to school and still see Tiffany and Chase on breaks."

"We'll have to get a bigger house, but I think we can handle it."

"You and Pam will be much better parents than I would be." She wiped the tears from her eyes. "She'll be okay. They'll all be okay."

Maggie felt like a monstrous weight had been lifted from her shoulders, and she could envision a brightness in the future for the children. If only she could see that same brightness in hers.

CHAPTER TWENTY-SEVEN

The kids had seemed happy earlier this morning when Maggie had dropped them off at school. Heather and Pam had engaged an attorney to assist them in gaining custody of Tiffany and Chase, and it didn't appear to be an issue as long as Ariel was willing. In the meantime, Ariel had returned to college in Boston, and Tiffany and Chase were still living with Maggie. The past week had been an adjustment for them all. They hadn't had to change school districts, which was fortunate, but late arrivals, switched lunches, and unexpected meltdowns were just a few of the obstacles they'd had to overcome. Somehow, this morning had been uneventful, and they'd gotten it all right.

Now she sat in the coffee shop across from the hospital waiting for Carrie to arrive. The text message Maggie had received from her had been unexpected, the invitation to still be her maid of honor in her wedding even more of a surprise. Carrie had always been unpredictable, and Maggie had learned that surviving their friendship meant rolling with her moods. Although this controversy had created a huge wedge between them, it wasn't the first time she'd been on the outs with Carrie.

Maggie had been sure she wanted to be included when Carrie first asked her to be part of her wedding party, but that was before she and Lynn had become involved. Just like her, Scott was a guy who knew who and what he wanted for his future, so that made him okay in her book. It would be a shame if Carrie couldn't get past Maggie's feelings for Lynn and let them both be happy. They still hadn't resolved the argument she'd had with Lynn when Carrie discovered their relationship, but even with the anger Carrie had felt, Maggie hoped they might still be a family.

Air whooshed past her as Carrie rushed in and took the seat across from her. "Are you still mad at me?"

She raised her eyebrows. "You're not being serious, are you?"

Carrie frowned like a seven-year-old that had just been scolded. "You are."

"You blew up my whole life. Lynn won't even talk to me."

"I can't help you with that." Carrie threaded her fingers together and clasped her hands.

"So you're sticking with your ultimatum?" She shook her head. "I thought maybe you'd grown up since college."

Carrie narrowed her eyes. "Lynn and Beth would probably still be together if it wasn't for you."

"No. You can't put that on me." She leaned forward. "I did everything you asked. I stayed away from Lynn the whole time I was in Boston. I didn't contact her once, and when I came back to Baltimore, I did my best to avoid her." Her stomach knotted as she remembered the first time she'd revealed her feelings to Lynn.

"Seems you completely failed at that."

"It's a hospital, Carrie. I was never going to be able to avoid her entirely." She didn't want to tell her the whole story, how she couldn't stay away and how Lynn had asked her to stay away too, but then relented. A jolt shot through her as she thought about the moment she'd seen her again. They couldn't avoid their attraction.

"It doesn't really matter now anyway." She shrugged and took in a breath. "Beth is going to take the admin job she was offered, and she'll be able to cut back her hours to spend more time with Lynn. Life will be better for them."

"They're getting back together?" The back of her neck heated as crazy thoughts spilled in her brain. Was that true? Had she totally missed some interaction between them? Chosen to blindly ignore it? She took in a breath and gathered her thoughts. No. She hadn't missed anything. No way would Lynn go back to Beth, whether or not Maggie was involved. Carrie was holding out for something that was never going to happen.

"Possibly. Beth is willing," Carrie said, her voice lilting with optimism.

"Beth has never been good for Lynn. She never paid a bit of attention to her, and she was miserable because of it. Who raised you,

Carrie? Not Beth. Think about it. Every time you fell, who picked you up? Lynn. Every big event in your life, who was there? Lynn. Have you ever seen her as happy with Beth as she's been for the past four years without her?"

"That's not true. They were happy." Carrie seemed thoughtful.

"You don't see it because Lynn never let you. She kept all the bad from you."

Carrie looked away, staring out the window. "So you're just going to abandon me for the wedding?"

"I'm going to abandon *you*?" She shook her head as she realized Carrie's avoidance ran deeper than she could ever reach. "You're a real piece of work. You know that?" She launched out of her chair. "You're my best friend, and I love you like a sister, but you are so fucking selfish."

Carrie's eyes went wide, as though she'd never heard that accusation before, but Maggie knew better. "Do you want Lynn to be alone for the rest of her life? Because that's where you're pushing her. Beth hasn't changed at all. She's manipulating you the same way she manipulated Lynn all those years." She held her forehead as she paced in front of the table and then sat again. "Do you ever remember her being there for either of you when things got tough, or even when things were good? I don't. You complained about it all the time." Little pieces of her heart had been torn away each time Carrie told her about another instance of Beth's neglect.

Carrie shook her head. "That's not true. She always supported us and paid for everything."

"Oh, and money solves everything, right?" She leaned across the table and narrowed her eyes. "If you met someone richer and cuter than Scott, would you marry him instead because he could pay for everything you need?"

"Of course not. I love Scott."

"Whether you like it or not, I love Lynn, and she's happy with me." She stood, reached into her pocket, pulled out some folded bills, peeled off a few, and dropped them on the table. "Grow up, Carrie. She's not going back to Beth."

She took off to the door, and when she got outside and down the sidewalk, she stopped and reached out to the building for balance. She had intended to go straight to Lynn and pour out everything in her heart, tell her she couldn't live without her, but that wouldn't make a bit of difference until Lynn felt that way too. Besides, she had lives at home to worry about. It was the first time since her father died that she'd had any doubts about whether she could really do something. She'd tried her best, but caring for the kids had been too much for her, both physically and emotionally, which had her seriously questioning her parenting abilities. Maybe Lynn was right and she wasn't cut out to be a parent. Would her work with children at the hospital be enough to make her happy? She shook the thoughts from her head. She didn't have time for doubts right now.

❖

It was going to be another busy weekend with Carrie in town planning her wedding, but it would be just her and Carrie this time, and Lynn was missing Maggie more than she cared to admit. It had been a miserable week since they'd argued, and she longed to have her to talk to, to hold, to be held by. On more than one occasion she'd wanted to run downstairs and apologize, tell Maggie she'd made a mistake, that she loved her with all her heart, and she'd help her with Tiffany and Chase. She just needed time to get Carrie through the wedding. Then Carrie would be back in Boston and everything would be okay. Wouldn't it?

She cracked a couple of eggs and beat them before pouring them into the heated pan on the stovetop. "You'd better hurry. The eggs will be done in a few minutes," she shouted into the living room.

Carrie began typing into her phone as she came into the kitchen. "I thought I might invite Beth to come along. She can keep you company while I'm in the dressing room."

"No. You will not." She snatched the phone from Carrie's hands and slid it into her back pocket. Even thinking Beth would come was a delusion Carrie never seemed to recognize. "I don't want or need Beth's company today, at the wedding, or any other time. I certainly hope you haven't bought into her whole story of wanting to get back together with me, because that's not going to happen."

Carrie's look of surprise wasn't unexpected. "Would that be so bad?"

"Yes. It would be miserable. I cannot go back to that one-sided relationship. She's a narcissist at her best, and I've already spent too many years in a lonely world catering to her needs." She'd tried to shield Carrie from that side of Beth, but it had become more difficult as Carrie grew older. Beth had missed so many school events, prom, and almost all her graduations because her career came first. Somehow, in the last few years, Carrie had either forgotten or chosen to ignore those absences.

"You were happy once, right? Why can't you get to that place again?" Carrie's voice rose with the question.

She stopped stirring the scrambled eggs and dropped the spatula on the counter. "Listen to me, Carrie. I'm not getting back together with Beth, and if that's why you're objecting to Maggie being in my life, then you'd better rethink my future and your involvement in it."

"Funny. Maggie said the same thing."

"You talked to Maggie?" she asked, her hand shaking as she reached for the spatula to stir the eggs.

Carrie nodded. "I don't know if she's still going to be my maid of honor, and I'm not sure I want her to be."

The pan rattled as she pushed it to the back burner. "You need to stop being so selfish. She's done nothing but support you in everything you do, including this whirlwind of a wedding." Her lip quivered as she spoke. She could barely keep it together, sure she'd alienated Maggie for good the last time they'd spoken. "Do you know she's been taking care of three children all on her own because their parents died?" She had no idea how Maggie was handling such a load and hated herself for criticizing her.

"I saw, but that won't last. She's never committed to anyone. I'm still pissed that she took advantage of our friendship to get to you."

"That's absolutely not true. I started the whole thing and then let it happen. I'd be lying if I didn't admit I was excited to see Maggie again. She brings me a happiness I never had with Beth. I knew how you'd feel about it, yet I still got involved with her. So you need to stop blaming her for my feelings and for something I did." Lynn was surprised at herself. She'd never really yelled at Carrie for anything. "Beth was a horrible wife, and if I hadn't met Maggie back then, I would've never known any other kind of love was possible for me."

Carrie seemed startled at her response as she rolled her lips in and attempted to gather her words. "What if she breaks your heart?"

"Well, you know what? I'm thirty-eight years old. I don't need you to protect me. I think I've done a pretty damn good job of taking care of myself for the past four years."

Carrie's expression was blank. "Auntie, you really love her, don't you?"

Tears sprang from her eyes and she wiped them away. "Does that really matter to you?"

"I'm sorry. I didn't know how you felt. I thought this was just a fling and she was going to hurt you." Carrie embraced her and held her close. "And now that's exactly what *I've* done. I need to fix this."

"You can't. I'm afraid I've burned that bridge from end to end."

"If she loves you as much as I think she does, she'll let me grovel."

Lynn had no words. All she could do was squeeze Carrie as hard as she could and hope she was right.

CHAPTER TWENTY-EIGHT

Maggie hadn't expected to see two cars in the driveway when she pulled up to the cabin. Pam and Heather must have driven solo because one of them had to handle an emergency. If Heather had let her know, she would've been glad to pick up either of them. She glanced at Tiffany sitting next to her and then at Chase, sprawled out in the back seat. Not that she had the room, but they would have managed somehow.

Tiffany's eyes widened when she saw the golf cart parked in front as they pulled in. "Can I drive that?"

"Do you have a license?"

"No, but you can teach me," Tiffany said excitedly.

"We'll see." Maggie chuckled.

She helped Chase out of the car and handed him his crutches before she retrieved the bags from the trunk. "Hey, Tiff. You going to help me with these?"

Tiffany was already checking out the golf cart. "I'll get it in a minute."

From previous experience, Maggie knew that a minute in Tiffany-time meant at least ten in actual time. She slung her backpack over her shoulder and grasped a bag with each hand, then walked the pathway to the front of the cabin. By the time she got there, the door was open, and Chase was already inside. She wasn't expecting to see Carrie when she entered.

Maggie darted her gaze between Heather and Pam. "What's she doing here?"

Neither one of them answered as they ushered Chase to the door. "Come on. Let's ride down to the pond. There are fish and frogs and—"

"Snakes?" Chase asked.

"I'm sure there are some of those too," Heather said.

"Can we catch them?"

"No," Pam and Heather said in unison as they went out the door, closing it behind them.

"I need to talk to you," Carrie said, coming closer.

She turned and went to the door. "I'm really not up for this battle again, Carrie."

"I'm sorry," Carrie blurted, her voice rising as vulnerability tinged it.

Hand on the doorknob, she stopped but didn't turn around. She hadn't expected any of this from Carrie.

"I was embarrassed, and I freaked out when I found out that my best friend and my mom were sleeping together. You can't blame me for that. I know she's really my aunt, but she's the only mom I've ever had, and I didn't want her to get hurt."

She spun around. "I would *never* hurt Lynn."

Tears welled in Carrie's eyes. "I know that now. I think I always knew you two would be together, but I was pissed that you both lied to me."

"You always knew?"

"You never dated anyone." Carrie shrugged. "Not until Brenda in med school, and that wasn't permanent." Carrie grabbed the counter behind her for balance, looked at the floor, and moved her foot back and forth across the wood floor in front of her. "I'm not stupid, you know. It was so obvious. You always wanted to come home with me but spent all of your time with Auntie. I think I was even a little jealous back then." She glanced back at Maggie. "Not in a romantic way."

"So you've changed your mind now? Are you okay with me seeing Lynn, or is this just a smokescreen to get me back into the wedding?"

"No." Carrie shook her head. "No smokescreen. I know I've been selfish. I was worried that two of the most important people in my life might hate each other if things don't work out." She took in a deep breath. "It just took me a while to settle into the idea, plus a few choice words from Lynn. I can't stand seeing her so sad and knowing I'm the cause of it. After I thought about it, I realized that she's crazy happy when you're around. Always has been."

"That goes both ways, you know. I've never felt for anyone what I feel for her. She's the love of my life."

Lynn appeared from one of the bedrooms. "You've never said that to me." She moved past Carrie to Maggie and reached for her hand. "You should've told me."

"And made this even harder for you?" She caressed Lynn's cheek with her thumb. She'd missed the softness of her skin. "No. It had to be your choice," she whispered, brushing a stray strand of hair from Lynn's eyes. "I need to know this is what you want. That I'm who you want."

Lynn took her in her arms and held her. It felt so good to have Lynn close again. Her anger of the past few days washed away. "You're everything I want. I love you too."

Lynn glanced over her shoulder at Carrie, and Maggie took Lynn's face in her hand and returned her gaze to her. "Get the hell out of here, Carrie. Lynn and I need to talk." She spoke without breaking eye contact with Lynn. She heard the door open and close again before she kissed Lynn with everything she had.

They spent the next several minutes in each other's arms, enjoying the softness of each other, holding each other, sharing tears between tender kisses. Maggie had thought she'd never get to hold Lynn like this again, and she didn't want to ever let her go. She wanted to spend the rest of her days showing her just how much she loved her.

Lynn sucked in a ragged breath as she broke away. "I'm so sorry about everything. I know I handled it badly. I just didn't know what to do."

"Horribly," she said as she trailed tiny kisses to her ear and then to her neck.

"I needed to think and make Carrie see how much I love you," Lynn said in a breathless whisper.

She trailed back to Lynn's neck. "I'm glad you succeeded."

"Me too." Lynn caught her mouth and kissed her softly.

"I'm never letting you go again." Every emotion Maggie had felt over the past few days exploded inside her as she kissed Lynn long and deep. Their tongues mingled like they were meant to live together forever, bodies touching, firing each one of her senses.

Lynn broke away breathlessly. "We better stop. The people at the pond might be back at any minute."

"Lock the door and send them away." She kissed her again softly. "The kids will be glad to see you."

"They will?"

She smiled as she stared into Lynn's tearful eyes. "Yeah. They ask about you all the time."

"Pam and Heather told me their plan to foster them."

"They'll be awesome parents."

Lynn nodded. "They will." She swiped away a tear that slipped over the rim of her eyelid and slid down her cheek. "You would've been as well."

She shook her head. "Not right now, I wouldn't. You were right. They need more care than I can give."

"Someday then?"

Every part of Maggie warmed as she took in a deep breath and nodded, tears streaming down her face. "Someday." Raising children with Lynn was a dream she'd never thought would happen, and that she was even considering it gave her even more hope for their future.

EPILOGUE

Maggie had planned the drive to Clear Meadow Farms so they would arrive in late afternoon to catch the blanket of vibrant yellow sunflowers against the orange and red hues of the sunset. The owners had recommended the timing, and the sight was absolutely magical.

It was their last visit to the farm before the wedding. Lynn had convinced Carrie to postpone it until the fall when the sunflowers were in full bloom, and Maggie was glad she had. Lynn hadn't been exaggerating when she'd described their beauty. There seemed to be infinite rows of perfectly bloomed sunflowers, their bright, happy, yellow-orange faces preening in the sunshine. They perfectly represented the transition from the hot, lazy days of summer to the crisp, cool weather of fall.

It hadn't been easy to keep Lynn from leaving earlier in the day. She'd been eager to get there and wrap up the last of the wedding details. Maggie had suggested Lynn wear something other than jeans, so they could go out to dinner somewhere nearby when they were finished, but Lynn had given her nothing but opposition. It was close to an hour's drive each way, and Lynn knew the farm closed at dusk regularly. When Maggie had dressed in white capri pants, a royal-blue V-neck tunic, and leather sandals, Lynn had relented and decided to wear a powder-blue flower-patterned sundress and sandals that went along with Maggie's outfit.

When they arrived and before they were to meet with the caterer, Maggie had ushered her away from the main venue and into the fields, where they basked in the glory of yellow and orange.

"Aren't they beautiful?" Lynn said, sounding giddy.

She gazed at Lynn standing in front of the flowers that surpassed her head by at least a foot. "They pale in comparison to the sight standing in front of me." She took Lynn in her arms and kissed her, making the moment perfect.

"I could wander out here with you forever, but we should get back." Lynn gazed at the gorgeous sunset. It would be dark soon, and Maggie didn't have much time. "I'm sure Carrie and Scott are waiting for us."

She took Lynn's hand and walked with her through the fields to the main building. Her heart thudded as she thought about what she'd planned for the evening, hoping it all came together smoothly.

"Looks like they're preparing for a special party," Lynn said as they emerged from the field and headed to the main building. "I didn't know they offered anything other than wedding events." She glanced through the plate-glass windows and saw that a long table had been set just inside, looking out onto the fields. Sunflowers adorned every foot of the table in tiny vases on the middle runner, and white plates and wineglasses were placed at each setting. "They're going to have a beautiful view for dinner."

Lynn turned and looked at Maggie, then back to the sunflower field, where people were coming toward her. She shielded her eyes from the sun with her hand. "Is that Tiffany and Chase?" Heather and Pam followed them as they came out of the rows of flowers and moved closer. "What in the world are they doing here?" She rushed toward them.

"Hey. I didn't know you all were coming here today." She glanced at each of them, assessing their appearance. "You're all dressed up. Are you going to the private party?"

Maggie glanced around the field and saw everyone she'd invited as they approached them. Carrie and Scott, Heather and Pam, as well as Ariel, Tiffany, and Chase were all here—everyone in her life she considered family. Last year at this time, she'd never expected to be here with Lynn in this space and time, yet here she was. The whole scene was surreal.

Pam shook her head. "I'm so sorry, Maggie. The kids wanted to see the sunflowers."

Lynn pulled her eyebrows together and glanced at Pam and then Maggie, her expression unreadable.

Maggie laughed. "It's okay, Pam. They're hard to hold back." Warmth spread through her as she decided to do this right here in front of all the people she loved. She reached down and picked a small sunflower from one of the smaller plants by the building.

"Oh no. Don't do that. They don't like for you to pick them," Lynn said, seeming not to have a clue what was happening.

Maggie smiled as she held the beautiful flower out to Lynn. "It's okay. I got a special dispensation," she said as she took the ring from her pocket and then dropped to one knee.

Maggie opened the box, and as the diamond glistened in the sunlight, Lynn covered her mouth, and tears sprang from her eyes.

"Life has never been better than it has been with you, and I want to go on spending each and every moment of every day together for the rest of our lives. Will you marry me?"

Lynn took her face in her hands and kissed her.

"Is that a yes?"

"Of course it's a yes."

She bolted up, kissed Lynn again, and swung her around as everyone clapped. She'd just made her the happiest woman in the world.

About the Author

Dena Blake grew up in a small town just north of San Francisco where she learned to play softball, ride motorcycles, and grow vegetables. She eventually moved with her family to the Southwest, where she began creating vivid characters in her mind and bringing them to life on paper.

Dena currently lives in the Southwest with her partner and is constantly amazed at what she learns from her two children. She is a would-be chef, tech nerd, and occasional auto mechanic who has a weakness for dark chocolate and a good cup of coffee.

Books Available From Bold Strokes Books

Femme Tales by Anne Shade. Six women find themselves in their own real-life fairy tales when true love finds them in the most unexpected ways. (978-1-63555-657-5)

Jellicle Girl by Stevie Mikayne. One dark summer night, Beth and Jackie go out to the canoe dock. Two years later, Beth is still carrying the weight of what happened to Jackie. (978-1-63555-691-9)

My Date with a Wendigo by Genevieve McCluer. Elizabeth Rosseau finds her long-lost love and the secret community of fiends she's now a part of. (978-1-63555-679-7)

On the Run by Charlotte Greene. Even when they're cute blondes, it's stupid to pick up hitchhikers, especially when they've just broken out of prison, but doing so is about to change Gwen's life forever. (978-1-63555-682-7)

Perfect Timing by Dena Blake. The choice between love and family has never been so difficult, and Lynn's and Maggie's different visions of the future may end their romance before it's begun. (978-1-63555-466-3)

The Mail Order Bride by R. Kent. When a mail order bride is thrust on Austin, he must choose between the bride he never wanted or the dream he lives for. (978-1-63555-678-0)

Through Love's Eyes by C.A. Popovich. When fate reunites Brittany Yardin and Amy Jansons, can they move beyond the pain of their past to find love? (978-1-63555-629-2)

To the Moon and Back by Melissa Brayden. Film actress Carly Daniel thinks that stage work is boring and unexciting, but when she accepts a lead role in a new play, stage manager Lauren Prescott tests both her heart and her ability to share the limelight. (978-1-63555-618-6)

Tokyo Love by Diana Jean. When Kathleen Schmitt is given the opportunity to be on the cutting edge of AI technology, she never thought a failed robotic love companion would bring her closer to her neighbor, Yuriko Velucci, and finding love in unexpected places. (978-1-63555-681-0)

Brooklyn Summer by Maggie Cummings. When opposites attract, can a summer of passion and adventure lead to a lifetime of love? (978-1-63555-578-3)

City Kitty and Country Mouse by Alyssa Linn Palmer. Pulled in two different directions, can a city kitty and a country mouse fall in love and make it work? (978-1-63555-553-0)

Elimination by Jackie D. When a dangerous homegrown terrorist seeks refuge with the Russian mafia, the team will be put to the ultimate test. (978-1-63555-570-7)

In the Shadow of Darkness by Nicole Stiling. Angeline Vallencourt is a reluctant vampire who must decide what she wants more—obscurity, revenge, or the woman who makes her feel alive. (978-1-63555-624-7)

On Second Thought by C. Spencer. Madisen is falling hard for Rae. Even single life and co-parenting are beginning to click. At least, that is, until her ex-wife begins to have second thoughts. (978-1-63555-415-1)

Out of Practice by Carsen Taite. When attorney Abby Keane discovers the wedding blogger tormenting her client is the woman she had a passionate, anonymous vacation fling with, sparks and subpoenas fly. Legal Affairs: one law firm, three best friends, three chances to fall in love. (978-1-63555-359-8)

Providence by Leigh Hays. With every click of the shutter, photographer Rebekiah Kearns finds it harder and harder to keep Lindsey Blackwell in focus without getting too close. (978-1-63555-620-9)

Taking a Shot at Love by KC Richardson. When academic and athletic worlds collide, will English professor Celeste Bouchard and basketball coach Lisa Tobias ignore their attraction to achieve their professional goals? (978-1-63555-549-3)

Flight to the Horizon by Julie Tizard. Airline captain Kerri Sullivan and flight attendant Janine Case struggle to survive an emergency water landing and overcome dark secrets to give love a chance to fly. (978-1-63555-331-4)

In Helen's Hands by Nanisi Barrett D'Arnuk. As her mistress, Helen pushes Mickey to her sensual limits, delivering the pleasure only a BDSM lifestyle can provide her. (978-1-63555-639-1)

Jamis Bachman, Ghost Hunter by Jen Jensen. In Sage Creek, Utah, a poltergeist stirs to life and past secrets emerge. (978-1-63555-605-6)

Moon Shadow by Suzie Clarke. Add betrayal, season with survival, then serve revenge smokin' hot with a sharp knife. (978-1-63555-584-4)

Spellbound by Jean Copeland and Jackie D. When the supernatural worlds of good and evil face off, love might be what saves them all. (978-1-63555-564-6)

Temptation by Kris Bryant. Can experienced nanny Cassie Miller deny her growing attraction and keep her relationship with her boss professional? Or will they sidestep propriety and give in to temptation? (978-1-63555-508-0)

The Inheritance by Ali Vali. Family ties bring Tucker Delacroix and Willow Vernon together, but they could also tear them, and any chance they have at love, apart. (978-1-63555-303-1)

Thief of the Heart by MJ Williamz. Kit Hanson makes a living seducing rich women in casinos and relieving them of the expensive jewelry most won't even miss. But her streak ends when she meets beautiful FBI agent Savannah Brown. (978-1-63555-572-1)

Face Off by PJ Trebelhorn. Hockey player Savannah Wells rarely spends more than a night with any one woman, but when photographer Madison Scott buys the house next door, she's forced to rethink what she expects out of life. (978-1-63555-480-9)

Hot Ice by Aurora Rey, Elle Spencer, and Erin Zak. Can falling in love melt the hearts of the iciest ice queens? Join Aurora Rey, Elle Spencer, and Erin Zak to find out! A contemporary romance novella collection. (978-1-63555-513-4)